HOT SHOT

Books by Fern Michaels:

Deep Harbor
Fate & Fortune
Sweet Vengeance
Holly and Ivy
Fancy Dancer
No Safe Secret
Wishes for Christmas
About Face
Perfect Match
A Family Affair
Forget Me Not
The Blossom Sisters
Balancing Act
Tuesday's Child
Betrayal
Southern Comfort
To Taste the Wine
Sins of the Flesh
Sins of Omission
Return to Sender
Mr. and Miss Anonymous
Up Close and Personal
Fool Me Once
Picture Perfect
The Future Scrolls
Kentucky Sunrise
Kentucky Heat
Kentucky Rich
Plain Jane
Charming Lily
What You Wish For
The Guest List
Listen to Your Heart
Celebration
Yesterday
Finders Keepers
Annie's Rainbow

Sara's Song
Vegas Sunrise
Vegas Heat
Vegas Rich
Whitefire
Wish List
Dear Emily
Christmas at Timberwoods

The Sisterhood Novels:

Safe and Sound
Need to Know
Crash and Burn
Point Blank
In Plain Sight
Eyes Only
Kiss and Tell
Blindsided
Gotcha!
Home Free
Déjà Vu
Cross Roads
Game Over
Deadly Deals
Vanishing Act
Razor Sharp
Under the Radar
Final Justice
Collateral Damage
Fast Track
Hokus Pokus
Hide and Seek
Free Fall
Lethal Justice
Sweet Revenge

Books by Fern Michaels (Continued):

The Jury
Vendetta
Payback
Weekend Warriors

The Men of the Sisterhood
Novels:

Hot Shot
Truth or Dare
High Stakes
Fast and Loose
Double Down

The Godmothers Series:

Getaway (E-Novella
    Exclusive)
Spirited Away (E-Novella
    Exclusive)
Hideaway (E-Novella
    Exclusive)
Classified
Breaking News
Deadline
Late Edition
Exclusive
The Scoop

E-Book Exclusives:

Desperate Measures
Seasons of Her Life
To Have and To Hold

Serendipity
Captive Innocence
Captive Embraces
Captive Passions
Captive Secrets
Captive Splendors
Cinders to Satin
For All Their Lives
Texas Heat
Texas Rich
Texas Fury
Texas Sunrise

Anthologies:

*Coming Home for
Christmas*
A Season to Celebrate
Mistletoe Magic
Winter Wishes
The Most Wonderful Time
When the Snow Falls
Secret Santa
A Winter Wonderland
I'll Be Home for Christmas
Making Spirits Bright
Holiday Magic
Snow Angels
Silver Bells
Comfort and Joy
Sugar and Spice
Let it Snow
A Gift of Joy
Five Golden Rings
Deck the Halls
Jingle All the Way

FERN MICHAELS

HOT SHOT

KENSINGTON PUBLISHING CORP.
http://www.kensingtonbooks.com

KENSINGTON BOOKS are published by

Kensington Publishing Corp.
119 West 40th Street
New York, NY 10018

All Kensington titles, imprints and distributed lines are available at special quantity discounts for bulk purchases for sales promotion, premiums, fund-raising, educational or institutional use.

Special book excerpts or customized printings can also be created to fit specific needs. For details, write or phone the office of the Kensington Special Sales Manager: Kensington Publishing Corp., 119 West 40th Street, New York, NY 10018. Attn. Special Sales Department. Phone: 1-800-221-2647.

Kensington and the K logo Reg. U.S. Pat. & TM Off.

Library of Congress Card Catalogue Number: 2018912559

ISBN-13: 978-1-4967-1453-4
ISBN-10: 1-4967-1453-9
First Kensington Hardcover Edition: June 2019

10 9 8 7 6 5 4 3 2 1

Printed in the United States of America

I'd like to dedicate this book to a very special lady—the real Frances Gossett and her beloved companion, Sawdust, both featured as characters in this book. I hope you enjoy the book, Frances.

Fern

Prologue

Cosmo Cricket turned the key in the lock, hoping his father hadn't put on the deadbolt, and entered the house he'd grown up in. He winced, wrinkling his nose as every ugly scent in the world enveloped him. He called out, "Pop! It's me, Cosmo. Where are you?"

"Where do you think I am? I'm right where I was the last time you came uninvited to my house. What do you want this time? How'd you get in here, anyway?" came the snarling reply.

Cosmo sucked in a deep breath, then wished he hadn't as he headed to what his late mother had called the family room, where his father basically lived. Cosmo had always loved the room because his mother had made sure it was a *real* family room. Everything was homemade, warm, and cozy. *Was* being the operative word, he reminded himself.

"You know what, Pop, I've had enough of your attitude. You need to give up this 'oh poor me' crap. I get that you don't want me coming here, but you promised to answer the phone when I call, which is three times a day. I'm here because you didn't answer the phone. And let me tell you something else. If you'd had that damn deadbolt on, I would have kicked the door in. Mom's been gone for almost two years. She's not coming back. You're still here, and I don't want to lose you, too. Now, having said that, I'm here to make some changes, whether you like it or not. From here on in, it's my way since your way didn't work. Look at you! You should be ashamed of yourself. Mom has to be spinning in her grave at what you've become."

Without another word, the giant who was Cosmo Cricket trundled on feet as big as canoes into the family room, where he picked up his frail, scrawny father, who used to be as big as Cosmo, and headed for the bathroom. He turned on the shower and pushed his father, clothes, shoes, and all under the hot, streaming spray. "Take off your clothes and use soap. If you don't, I'll come in there and soap you up myself. Do not forget to wash your hair. Three times will be good. I'm going to lean up against the door, and you are not getting out until I decide you smell like a flower. Do you hear me?" he roared.

"Half the state of Nevada can hear you. The other half has to be totally deaf," Henry Cricket roared in return. Cosmo grinned to himself. What he just heard was music to his ears, the most emotion he'd heard from his father since his mother's passing.

"I'm taking you out of here, so think about that as you soap up. I'm going to have this house fumigated and rent it out."

"Like hell you are! This is my house, not yours. You don't have any say where I am concerned." To make his point, Henry Cricket pushed his weight against the shower door to no avail.

"You should have thought about that before you signed over your power of attorney to me. Remember you did that when you told me you were going to die? So, yes, I can do what I just said."

"I hate smart-ass lawyers. Your mother and I must have lost our minds when we sent you to law school. Oh, right, you're the head of the Nevada Gaming Control Board these days! Well, la-di-da and all that. How could I forget something so important?" Henry roared so loud that, as a result, Cosmo stuck his fingers in his ears. When he decided it was safe to remove them, his arm shot upward as he pumped it in the air. He continued to grin in pure joy. The old man was actually talking, communicating. They were arguing, which was even better. Progress. Real progress.

"Okay, I'm ready to come out. Move away from the door."

"No, no, no! Soap up a couple more times. You smelled like three-day-old roadkill. I mean it, Dad. Stop dicking around and do what I tell you."

Twenty minutes later, the old man had calmed down enough to say, "Okay, you win. I'm shriveled up to nothing. I smell like gardenias. You happy now?"

"Yep!" Cosmo reached for a towel that he knew had last been washed when his mother was still alive. It smelled musty. Out of respect for his father, he turned his back so the older man could dry off and wrap himself in the towel, giving Cosmo time to find a set of clean clothes. "We need to do some clothes shopping," he muttered.

"I heard that! I don't need any new clothes."

"Yeah, Dad, you do. You haven't washed anything since Mom died. When you walk out of here, you are going with the clothes on your back."

"Where are you taking me, Cossy?" his father demanded.

His old nickname from when he was a little boy punched Cosmo in the chest. "To a great place. A place that needs you. You have great organizational skills, and you are going to be running the place. Mom would approve. And just for the record, Dad, Mom would be pissed to the teeth to know how you've spent these past two years. And you know it!"

"I needed to mourn. Your mother was the love of my

life. I'm nothing without her. You saw that for yourself. I'm sorry if you feel like I let you down, Cossy," the old man whined.

"You are one wily, crafty son of a gun, you know that! You're trying to sweet-talk me, and I'm not buying it. You are going with me, and you are *not* coming back here. I have big plans for you. And the first thing is a shopping trip, after which we're going to stop at a florist, buy them out, go to the cemetery, and have a talk with Mom before I take you to your new digs."

"What are my other options?"

In spite of himself, Cosmo laughed out loud. "You don't have any options. When was the last time you ate a good meal?"

The old man shrugged. "At my age, food isn't all that important. If you were so worried about my meal planning, why didn't you bring me food? Aha, see, I got you there." He cackled.

"I did bring you food, but you wouldn't let me in. You had the deadbolts on all the doors. I left the food outside the door. Don't go trying to throw this back on me. You screwed up royally, Dad, not me. Mom would definitely not approve. Most definitely not."

"And you're a smart-ass too," the old man said, finally giving in. "Cossy?"

"Yeah."

"Did you really mean it when you said I wasn't going to be coming back here ever again? Or were you just funning with me?"

"I'll bring you back anytime you want, but not to stay. This place—and Pop, I love it as much as you do—it's the past. Neither one of us can function here. Like I said, Mom wouldn't want us to do that. This big old house, with all its warts, is now just a memory for us. I need you to tell me you understand before we walk out that door."

The old man took his time responding. Cosmo was about ready to put his fist through the wall just as his father responded. "I understand, Cossy. I really do."

"Okay, then. Let's do what we have to do and hit up Longhorns for the biggest rib eye they can conjure up. You think you can handle a pitcher of beer with that rib eye?"

"Do dogs have fleas?" Henry Cricket said, laughing. The sound brought pure joy to his son's heart.

Chapter 1

Ten years later

It was a room.

But it wasn't just any room. This room had no windows. Aside from a closet built into the wall and a small lavatory off to the side, it was just a square box of a room.

What made this particular room different was the single hospital bed and the machines that beeped and pinged constantly along with the sound of a wheezing ventilator.

And, of course, the second difference was the VIP patient hooked up to the ventilator and the machines that beeped and pinged every second of the day.

The third difference, if you were counting, was the woman dressed in a blue paper gown who sat at the side of the hospital bed holding the patient's hand. She'd barely moved, eaten, or slept in the ninety-six hours she'd been in the box of a room.

Her eyelids drooped in weariness, but she forced herself to stay awake as she mumbled words she couldn't even understand. Somewhere, a long time ago, she'd read that if you held the hand of a patient who was in a coma and spoke to him, he could hear you in the dark hole he was in. Because she wanted to believe that was true, it was exactly what she'd been doing since she arrived. She was hoarse from talking about the very first picnic they'd gone on, but she forced herself to keep speaking, leaning in closer to the patient so he could hear when her voice threatened to give out, believing the patient could still hear her whispered words. How many times had she recounted the picnic—a hundred, a thousand, more? She didn't know. They were familiar words, and they came easily to her parched throat because it had been such a happy time in their lives. But when the words wouldn't come anymore, she switched to their son, whose goal it was to become an Olympic swimmer.

The room was quiet as a tomb except for the beeping of the ventilator. For some reason, she was able to block those sounds from her mind and concentrate on her own voice and the otherwise absolute quiet that surrounded her and the patient in the bed.

Suddenly, her head jerked upright. What was that noise? Something different. Something . . . some noise . . . was invading the tomblike quiet. She stood up on wobbly legs, the paper gown making its own strange noise, and walked to the door. She looked around, panic and terror on her beautiful face. What was that sound? She reached out for something to hold her upright. Somehow she managed to get to the door and open it. She squinted in the bright overhead lighting, wondering if she was seeing a hallucination.

She thought she shouted "Jack!" but it came out in a bare whisper as her weary gaze took in Jack and the rest of the guys all standing outside her husband's door. She said his name again, and this time her voice was full of pain as she saw Harry Wong move to be closer to Jack Emery so they could both catch her when she toppled into their arms.

"Lizzie!" the gang said in unison, their voices holding as much pain as her own.

The men of BOLO, which stood for Be on the Look Out, had come immediately upon hearing the news. They had formed the group after years of working together, undertaking dangerous missions on behalf of those incapable of helping themselves. The group of friends never hesitated to help someone in need, and that went double when one of their own was in need. And they most definitely counted Lizzie as part of their surrogate family.

Jack scooped her up into his arms, Harry at his side just as an ugly, fussy little man with a stethoscope around his neck and too much facial hair tried to shoulder the boys out of the way.

"You people need to leave right now! How did you *even* get up here? Don't make me call security! You need to leave *right now*. This floor is off-limits to visitors."

That was exactly the wrong thing to say to Harry Wong. Before he pivoted on the ball of one foot, he made sure Jack's hold on Lizzie was secure before he reached for the ugly, fussy little man's nose and tweaked it. "We walked up here. On our two feet. We came to see the patient in that room. Think carefully before you answer if there is any part of that you don't understand." The ugly little man dropped to his knees as he tried to figure out what had just happened to him.

"I can stand, Jack, put me down," Lizzie Fox said hoarsely. She turned as she struggled to focus on the ugly little man, who was still on his knees, sputtering and mumbling. "These people are my and my husband's friends. That means they are family. They have every right to be here."

Fergus Duffy stepped forward, and announced, "I represent Countess Anna de Silva. She is a fifty-one percent owner of this private clinic. I can call her and have her speak with you if you like."

Out of nowhere, a tall string bean of a man, wearing a white coat with a stethoscope in the pocket, a pearl-white

Stetson, and cowboy boots stepped through the gaggle of people. "That won't be necessary, will it, Dr. Brackman?" There was a ring of steel in the string bean's voice that did not go unnoticed by the others.

"I'm the doctor in charge of Mr. Cricket. Do I need to remind you he is my patient? You are overstepping your bounds, Dr. Wylie," the ugly little man barked.

"The only reason you are the patient's doctor of record is because I was half a world away and wasn't here when the patient was admitted. By all rights, Dr. Simon Simmons is Mr. Cricket's doctor of record since he is the one who performed Mr. Cricket's surgery. We're going to correct that as soon as we make sense out of what's going on here. Lizzie, you need to go home and get some rest. You aren't doing yourself or your husband any favors by staying here twenty-four hours a day. You need at least twelve hours of sleep, a good hot meal, and a steaming shower. Then and only then can you come back. I promise you I will stay with your husband until you return," Dr. Wylie said gently.

"My money is on the string bean, Lizzie," Jack whispered. "Let's take you home so you can follow the doctor's orders, and we'll bring you back when you're ready. The others will stay here if Dr. Wylie says it is okay. You good with that, Lizzie?" Lizzie's head bobbed up and down as her legs finally gave out. Harry scooped her up and slung her over his shoulder in a fireman's carry. Lizzie was finally out for the count.

Jack looked around and shrugged. "Works for me." He stuck out his hand, and Dr. Wylie grasped it. "We need to get Lizzie home. The guys will introduce themselves to you and will do whatever you want them to do. With the exception of leaving, that is."

"So you guys are Annie's posse?" the string bean asked, a grin stretching across his face. "When she hired me, she also taught me how to shoot craps the same day. She told me all about you guys. It took only ten minutes for her to hire me, and then we spent the rest of the day getting to know each other. She's one hell of a lady."

Jack laughed. "It figures. No grass grows under Annie's feet. Next time you see her, ask her to teach you how to pick a lock or crack a safe. Take good care of our buddy in there."

"I will. You take good care of my patient's wife, you hear. I meant it when I said I won't let her come back here until she's stable. She's exhausted."

Jack gathered his group and spoke quietly. "We need to know what the hell is going on here. I want details, and I mean details. Once we get Lizzie settled, we'll either come back or call, so be prepared to give me answers." That said, Jack turned on his heel and raced after Harry, who was already at the elevator and about to step in.

"Just out of curiosity, how are we going to get Lizzie home? Do you have her car keys? And where the hell is her car? Jack, what the hell happened back there?" Harry demanded.

"I have her purse right here. The car has a keyless gizmo. We'll find it, don't worry. As to what happened, I'd say some kind of turf war between the doctors. Annie told me about this place five years ago when it was being built. The casino owners all got together and decided to build a state-of-the-art clinic. She said the trauma center here is better than the one they have for the president. Top-notch doctors. The best of the best. This place cost millions, high millions. Annie agreed to help finance it only as long as she had the controlling interest. It's private in the sense that the owners and their families get first dibs, but they take outside patients. They also have a free clinic, something Annie insisted on. That guy Brackman, she said something about him, but right now I can't remember what it was. It was nothing positive, though."

"Okay, we're in the parking lot. Which one is Lizzie's car?" Harry asked.

Jack pressed the fob in his hand and waited for a sound that would tell him which car was Lizzie's. A silver Mercedes sedan chirped to life. He led the way.

It took both Harry and Jack to get Lizzie settled on the backseat and buckle her in. She didn't resist or even move. "I think that's good enough. One seat belt should do it. Lizzie lives only about eight miles from here. You driving, or you want me to drive?" Harry shrugged. "Okay, then I'll drive. Just punch in the GPS and hit Home and we're good to go." Harry did as instructed.

"I don't want to talk about this right now, Harry, because it's scaring me shitless. So let's talk about something else. You should probably get in touch with your guys and tell them what's going on. We promised to show them Vegas. I liked those guys a lot. You really have a great bunch of friends. Did I tell you that Annie arranged for suites for all of them at Babylon? For all of us, actually. Hell of a perk, wouldn't you say, plus all the chits for free food and drinks." Jack was babbling, more to have something to say so he wouldn't have to think about Cosmo Cricket and Lizzie and what the future might hold for the two of them.

"Yeah, yeah, yeah. I'll do that, but Jack, what the hell happened to Cricket? I need to know."

"I don't know, Harry. I heard it on the TV this morning when I was shaving. They didn't mention a name, but from what they said, I knew it had to be him. He got shot in the head, back, and shoulder. They said some VIP at the Gaming Control Board. Now you know as much as I know. We left right away. You were with me, and we had the radio on, and nothing else was said on the drive here from Reno.

I guess that ditty about 'what happens in Vegas stays in Vegas' is true."

"It doesn't make sense," Harry grumbled. "Cosmo Cricket is no schmuck. How would he allow himself to be in a position where he could get shot; plus, Lizzie told us a while back he has security when he's out and about."

"I don't know, Harry. When Lizzie wakes up is when we'll find out. It could be something as simple as he was in the wrong place at the wrong time. Okay, we're here. How do you want to get her out and into the house?"

"I'll carry her. You go ahead and open the door. What are you going to do if there's an alarm?"

Jack grinned. "The code is Little Jack's birthday, so I know it. Okay, let's do it," Jack said as he sprinted to the front door of a low, sprawling, gorgeous Mediterranean-style house. He unlocked the door and immediately hit the code for the alarm system, right next to the front door. The armed red light turned green the minute he pressed in the code. Jack let out a sigh of relief, glad that Lizzie hadn't changed the numbers.

"Do you know where the bedroom is?" Harry asked as he marched into the house, carrying Lizzie like a baby.

"Actually, Harry, I know that, too; it's down the hall, and the master suite is at the end. I used to play hide-and-seek with LJ when he was little, and he'd always hide in his mother's closet. Yep, here it is."

Harry gently lowered Lizzie to the bed.

"Whoa! Whoa! We have to turn the bed down first, take off her clothes, and get her under the covers. How do you expect her to get twelve hours of sleep on top of the bed?"

Harry turned to leave. "Have at it, Jack. There is no way in hell I am taking off Lizzie Fox's clothes."

"No, no, no, it doesn't work that way, Harry. We gotta do it. Now come on and help me."

"*NO!*"

"C'mon," Jack wheedled. "We can close our eyes and do it. I won't tell Yoko, and you agree not to tell Nikki. Deal?"

"When Lizzie wakes up and wants to know who undressed her, what are you going to tell her?" Harry demanded.

"The unvarnished truth. We did it together and kept our eyes closed."

"I hate you, Jack," Harry seethed, as Jack rolled Lizzie over so he could pull down the covers.

"Yeah, yeah, and I love you too. Okay, on the count of three, you work her skirt and . . . any anything else. I'll do the . . . top. I think we should leave the . . . the fancy stuff on her. We're just taking off the top layer. Okay?"

Four hands fumbled and fluttered as both men squeezed their eyes shut, their breathing ragged and raspy as they stripped Lizzie of her outer garments.

"Done! We did it! Good job, Harry! Look at me, I'm shaking. You look kind of funny, Harry. Are you okay? See, see, you're shaking too."

"I'm going to kill you, but first I am going to make you suffer, you . . . you . . ."

"Shhh," Jack said. "Lizzie is mumbling something. Listen."

"What's she saying?" Harry asked, forgetting for the moment that he was going to kill Jack.

"Sounds like she's saying something about chicken soup. Noodles. That must mean she wants chicken soup with noodles when she wakes up. Chicken soup always makes things better. Do you know how to make chicken soup, Harry, because I sure don't," Jack fretted, his face twisted in panic.

Harry clenched his teeth and stared at Jack. "I know how to make tea."

"Yeah, yeah, I get that, Harry. I can grill, that's it. Maybe we should call Charles and ask him how to make it. We don't want Lizzie to be disappointed when she wakes up, and there's no chicken soup. Do we?"

Harry gave Jack his evil eye and refused to comment.

"I have an idea. We could go to some Chinese restaurant and get some of that soup they put wontons in. Throw in some veggies and voilà, chicken soup. Do you think that would pass muster?"

"What about the noodles?" Harry asked, intrigued at the lengths Jack was willing to go for Lizzie. Not that he himself wouldn't, it was just that he didn't know how to cook. Nor did he want to learn. Making tea was taxing enough.

"Ah, now that might pose a problem," Jack said thoughtfully. "Maybe when you go to the Dip Sing, you can ask them to make you some noodles." Seeing the murderous look on Harry's face, Jack hastened to add, "Or I can go. It's just out on the main drag, I saw the sign when I turned off to come down Lizzie's street. I think we should get that out of the way first in case Lizzie wakes up sooner rather than later."

The murderous look on Harry's face turned even more dangerous. Jack quickly scooped up the car fob and beat feet to the door, calling over his shoulder for Harry to get in touch with Charles to find out what the hell was going on.

Harry's foot shot out, knocking over a chair the minute the front door closed behind Jack. "Chicken soup, my ass," he muttered as he turned on the television set on the kitchen counter. A commercial for repairing broken windshields set his teeth on edge. He hated television. He looked around the state-of-the-art kitchen, comparing it to the kitchen in his apartment over the dojo. Yoko would love this kitchen even though she said she loved their cramped apartment with its outdated kitchen. Women were known to lie. At least according to Jack, who said he knew everything there was to know about women. Harry didn't believe it for a minute. Men, and that included Jack, were dumb as dirt when it came to women.

Harry rummaged in his pocket for a handful of the seeds and sprouts that he nibbled on constantly and pulled out a little pouch with his special brand of tea. He put water on to boil and waited until he saw the bubbles before he dropped the mixture into the little pot he found in one of the cabinets under the counter. He stirred it, waited for all the bits and pieces to sink to the bottom, then let it steep for five minutes before pouring it into a cup.

Harry turned down the volume on the TV and pulled out his cell phone. He punched in the number 3 and waited for Charles to pick up. He explained about Lizzie and Jack's going for the soup before he asked if Charles had any information on Cosmo Cricket's condition. He listened for a solid ten minutes, his eyes widening from time to time at what he was hearing. He was so caught up in what Charles was saying that he had let his tea cool to the point where he grimaced when he took a sip.

The moment Charles wound down, Harry said he would explain everything to Jack on his return, and the moment Lizzie was good to go, they would head for Babylon and meet up. "How are my boys doing?"

"Ted and Espinosa are showing them around Vegas. Ted's going to incorporate their impressions in the article he's writing for the *Post*. They love playing the slot machines and spending their winnings from the trials."

"Did Abner arrive yet?"

"Yes, but I haven't seen him yet." Abner was always the last to arrive because he couldn't fly due to eardrum problems and drove wherever he needed to go. "Young Dennis has volunteered to stay here with Fergus and me until Dr. Wylie has time to sit down with us for a long talk."

Harry broke the connection and stared at the gleaming

Sub-Zero refrigerator. Even from where he was sitting, he could see his reflection. He leaned back in his chair and closed his eyes. He needed to think.

He was still in thinking mode when Jack returned with a huge container of soup and a second one he assumed held noodles from the Chinese restaurant. Jack rummaged for anything in the cabinets that resembled a soup pot and poured the contents from the containers into it.

"That's enough soup for an army. Who's going to eat all that?"

"I had to order three quarts for them to make me the noodles. Lizzie said noodles. I didn't want to disappoint her. Smells like chicken soup to me. All we need to do is toss in some carrots, celery, parsley, and maybe an onion. That's what they told me to do. Want some?"

"Maybe later. What did you do with the wontons?"

"See, that was the problem. I tried to cut a deal with them—keeping the wontons in exchange for the noodles. No deal. They made out, that's the bottom line. What did you find out from Charles?"

Harry repeated his conversation with Charles. "Then I called back, but nothing. It just rang and rang and didn't even go to voice mail. I had some questions after I thought about what I had been told. I called twice more, and it went to voice mail again. I called back, and Charles said he would get back to me because he couldn't talk just then. So far, nothing more than what I've already told you. Now that you have the chicken soup thing going on, do you want to go back to the clinic? I just looked in on Lizzie, and she's good for many more hours of sleep."

"It's getting late. I say we stay here. Charles will call when he has something concrete to tell us. Let's go into the family room and chill out. This whole thing is making me crazy."

"This is a fabulous room, isn't it, Harry?" Jack said,

looking around at the beautiful room, with its vaulted ceilings, tasteful artwork by local artists hanging on the walls, the highly polished floors, and the comfortable but worn furniture that adorned the room. It was definitely a room that a family lived in on a daily basis. It was clear to both men that the room was divided and yet worked as a whole at the same time. One section screamed it was Lizzie's space, and another section left no doubt it was Cosmo's area, because all of the furniture was oversized and custom-built. The third section belonged to Little Jack and held all the stuff the kid had collected in his happy little life. And then there was the family section, with one huge—as in *huge*—chair with matching ottoman that was obviously Cosmo's and a deep comfortable recliner both men knew was Lizzie's. The last chair was a scaled-down version of Cosmo's chair, but not so small that it wouldn't hold an adult. Kids didn't stay little for long. The family unit. This unit was where Jack and Harry headed, with Jack taking Lizzie's chair and Harry Little Jack's.

"Now what?" Harry asked, knowing full well Jack was going to turn on the huge television, which took up the entire wall in front of them.

Jack shrugged. "I'm not much in the mood for TV. If you want to watch it, it's okay with me. I can tune it out. I need to think, Harry. We both need to think."

Harry settled himself into the depths of his chair. He looked over at Jack and was about to ask a question when Jack said, "I don't know, Harry. It's at the top of my worry list."

"What the hell, Jack. How do you know what I was going to ask you?"

"Because I know you as well as I know myself, and I'm wondering the same thing. You were going to ask me what Lizzie will do if things go south for Cosmo. If ever there were two people meant to grow old together, it's Lizzie and Cosmo. Yeah, she's tough, but that's the career part of her. That's the part the world sees, not what the girls and we guys see. She's first a mother and wife or maybe wife and mother. I'm not sure which takes precedence. Knowing Lizzie, I guess it would be equal. You want me to guess, is that what you're asking, Harry?"

"Well . . . yeah, I guess. I mean, we all know the backstory about how you saved her life that night in the snow. Will she go that route?"

Jack closed his eyes and tried not to think about that long-ago night. "Lizzie is a different person today than she was back then. She has a son now. That will help. But to get back to the question you didn't ask, I don't know.

"While I was waiting for the people at Dip Sing, I googled Dr. Joe Wylie. Man, that guy is one impressive dude. Leave it up to Annie to hire the best of the best. He's the top neurosurgeon in the country. He's second in the world. Brain surgery scares the living shit out of me. Spinal cord surgery scares me just as much. Cosmo had both surgeries done by someone other than Wylie. I googled Simon Simmons, and he's good, but he's no Wylie. He studied under Wylie, however. Not sure where that little toad Brackman who tried to kick us out fits into all of this. Say something, Harry."

"Oh, so now you want me to say what you're thinking," Harry groused. "You want me to say Cosmo could end up in a vegetative state or paralyzed. There, I said it. You happy now?"

"No. But at least it's out in the open. That's what Lizzie was dealing with these last four days. It's all she had to think about when she sat there, refusing to leave. All we can do now is think positive, pray, and hope to God Wylie will get Cosmo through this."

Harry's phone vibrated in his pocket. He fished it out. "It's Charles."

Never one to say five words when two or three would do, Harry said, "Talk to me."

Jack watched in horror as the color left Harry's face and

his hands started to shake so badly that he almost dropped the phone. "I'll tell Jack," Harry said, in a voice Jack had never heard before.

Jack's heart kicked up a beat as he waited for whatever Harry was going to say. Finally, he barked, "What?"

"They just took Cosmo back into surgery. Wylie is the surgeon. Something went wrong, but Charles doesn't know what it is. He said nurses and doctors all came running, and they were told to leave. They're all in the chapel right now."

"Oh shit!"

"Oh shit is right," Harry said.

"How do we play this?" Jack asked. "Do we wake Lizzie up and head back to the hospital? Or do we let her sleep and get some strength back so she can . . . so she can deal with whatever happens?"

Instead of answering Jack's question, Harry said, "You know what I wish right now? I wish that damn dog Cooper was here. I really do. Things always worked out the right way when he was with us. Does that make sense, Jack?"

"As much as anything I could come up with."

Harry's voice was fretful and strange. "So we're going to let Lizzie sleep, eat, then we tell her."

"Hell no! Well, you had part of it right. We let her sleep and eat, then we go back to the clinic, where a doctor will tell her what she needs to know. Unless you want us to end up dead right here when we tell her."

"I see your point," Harry said. "Let's go eat some of that soup."

"You know, Harry, that's a great idea. I guess we're going to skip the veggies, or we put them in and let them cook while we eat it as it is. Lizzie is going to need the veggies. I got a ton of noodles. I know how you love noodles.

I like noodles, but not so much that I crave them. Lizzie must like them a lot. Noodles! Who knew?"

"Jack, you're ranting. Will you just shut the hell up already?"

Jack clamped his lips tight as he stomped his way to the kitchen.

Harry slumped down into the captain's chair with the bright red cushions and closed his eyes while Jack heated up the chicken soup. Then his eyes snapped open almost immediately. He looked at Jack, his voice full of panic when he said, "Holy crap, we forgot about the boy! How could we have forgotten him? Where is he, Jack?"

"Easy, Harry, easy. Little Jack is at sleepaway camp. It's a swim camp; LJ is into swimming. It's July, school is out, and kids go to camp. You told me yourself that Lily is at camp."

"How do you know that?" Harry asked, not sure if he believed Jack or not.

"Because he sent me a text the first week asking for advice."

Suspicion rang in Harry's voice. "What kind of advice. Why would he ask you and not his parents?"

Jack grinned. "Because he thinks I know everything. I have no idea where he got that idea, but it's in his head. But to answer your question, it was girl advice he was looking for."

Harry groaned. "The kid is ten years old! What kind of girl advice does a ten-year-old need?"

"Seems a girl named Emily, same age as LJ, is his competition on the swim team he was assigned to. It would appear, according to LJ, that she is better and faster than he is, and it's rubbing him the wrong way. She seems to be a little more mature than LJ and knew which buttons to push, because she told him the reason he was so slow in the water was he had *fat knees*. LJ was wounded to the quick over that. Plus, she's cute; she has curly hair and big blue eyes and dimples. Here's the thing, though—her front teeth protrude a little, and she has an overbite. He's smitten and jealous at the same time. End of story."

"No, it isn't," Harry sputtered. "What did you tell him? I know you told him something. Fat knees! What?"

"Well . . . I might have said *something*. What you need to understand is this, Harry. Women, girls of all ages, they stick together, and it's a sure bet that the female counselors are telling her how to get to LJ, and because male counselors are all macho and crap like that, they aren't really equipped to counsel kids like LJ. So, I just . . . you know, helped out my godson. The kid's goal in life is to go to the Olympics and outdo Phelps. Cosmo is even having an Olympic-size pool built out back for him to train, and when he gets back from camp, he's going to have his own personal trainer. True or false, I don't know. LJ told me that, so who knows. It might be wishful thinking on his part. He is good, though—swims like a fish. How's the soup? Are there enough noodles?"

"It's okay. Not great but passable. Yoko's is better. I don't think Lizzie will complain."

"We should have heard something by now," Jack said fretfully.

"It's three o'clock in the morning, Jack. Surgeries take hours, and then the patient is in recovery. Call Charles if it will make you feel better."

Jack had his phone in hand when he looked past Harry to see Lizzie standing in the doorway dressed in what he thought was Cosmo's bathrobe, her silver hair soaking wet, her face shiny and scrubbed. "Is there news?"

"Um . . . no, guess not. No one is answering their phones. It's late. How about some chicken soup? With noodles. You need to eat something."

"You made chicken soup! That was so sweet of you,

Jack. Sure, I'll have some with lots of noodles. You can talk to me while I eat. Then I want to go back to the hospital. I don't care if it is the middle of the night."

"Sure, sure, whatever you want, Lizzie. Eat up," Jack said, putting in front of her a bowl of soup that was loaded with skinny noodles. He crossed his fingers that Lizzie wouldn't mention the lack of vegetables in the soup.

"This is good. Kind of tastes like Dip Sing's soup, but they put wontons in it."

"No kidding!" Jack said, feigning surprise. "Harry and I will take that as a compliment."

Harry winked at Jack as he handed him his empty bowl.

Time froze when Jack's phone, which was lying in the middle of the table, chirped to life.

Lizzie stopped eating. "Someone should answer that."

"Yeah, someone should." Jack reached for the phone.

Chapter 2

Elizabeth Fox Cricket, lawyer extraordinaire.

Lizzie Fox, or as she was often referred to in legal circles, the Silver Fox.

Lizzie Fox, a legend in her own time.

Lizzie Fox, White House counsel to two-term president Martine Connor.

Lizzie Fox, nominated for a seat on the Supreme Court, but every lawyer's and judge's dream was not her dream. She said thanks but no thanks. She explained she had a husband to care for, a son to raise, and more cases to try.

Prosecutors lived in fear of going up against her, often caving in before they even got to present their case because no one won against Lizzie Fox.

Judges loved Lizzie Fox, and it was rumored that they often waggled and finagled among themselves to sit on any case she was trying. True or false, no one was sure.

The sun had just crept over the horizon when all those thoughts rushed through Jack Emery's mind as he watched the friend he was in awe of dressed in what he knew was Cosmo's robe, her glorious wet mane of silver hair piled high on her head in a scrunchy. She was freshly showered, but she still looked tired and beaten. He ladled out a second helping of soup and noodles into a bowl. Harry poured coffee into a mug that had a casino chip and a dollar sign on it and handed it over to Jack, who set it down next to Lizzie's soup bowl. Both Jack and Harry watched Lizzie as she greedily tore into her meal.

"Just keep eating, Lizzie. Harry and I will talk and then you can tell us what you know and how we got to this point in time. In case you are wondering what we're doing here or how we got here so fast, we were all up in Reno for the martial arts trials. Harry was a judge, and he also participated in one event. We heard on the radio yesterday morning that some big VIP here in Vegas got gunned down outside an apartment complex he owned. They didn't mention a name, but we all came to the same conclusion, so we packed up and drove down here with five of Harry's friends from the trials. They're visiting from China. They were planning on coming with us anyway, so we just left a day early. Everyone is here, even Abner, but he was the last one in. He has Cyrus with him. That's about all we know. You need to tell us what you know, as we're all pretty much in the dark."

"I googled the clinic; its trauma unit is top notch. Cosmo couldn't be in a better place," Harry said.

Lizzie stopped eating for a moment and looked at the two men sitting across from her. "Yes, it is the best. I just wish it were Cowboy who had operated on Cosmo. Simon is good, don't get me wrong, but I would have preferred to have Cowboy perform the surgery."

"By Cowboy I assume you are referring to the string bean Dr. Wylie," Jack said. "Why do you call him Cowboy?"

Lizzie smiled wanly as she went back to the mound of noodles in her soup. "That's what Cosmo calls him. They're great friends. He's six-foot-eight, did you know that? He eats nonstop. I think he has the same kind of metabolism that Maggie Spritzer has. The guy is so in demand, he could charge anything he wanted for his expertise in the operating room. Here's the kicker, though—most of the surgeries he performs are freebies. He even pays his own airfare when he travels out of the country to perform his one-of-a-kind surgeries. He's not into money or the trappings that go with it. His only goal in life is to save lives. You saw how he was dressed. That's Joe making a statement. Take it or leave it. That was some really good soup, Jack. Call the hospital, Harry, please, to see if there's any change."

"Lizzie, it's just coming up to seven in the morning. You know how busy hospitals and clinics are this early in the morning. I called right before you came down," Jack outright fibbed. "No one answered. Get dressed and we'll head on out. But before you do that, you have to tell us what happened. Everything, Lizzie, don't leave anything out, even if you think it's not important. We'll be the judge of that. We're all here now, so it's personal with us."

Lizzie sighed. "Honestly, Jack, I don't really know. I'm not sure anyone really knows. It happened late in the afternoon . . . I guess it's five days ago by now . . . I've sort of lost track of time. Fiveish. I got a call from the clinic saying my husband had just been brought in and that he had been shot multiple times. I was home. Little Jack is away at camp, so I was cooking dinner, you know, foods Cosmo and I like that Little Jack won't eat. It was supposed to be a special dinner for just the two of us. I had the kitchen TV on but wasn't paying attention to it. I keep it on more for sound than anything else. With LJ gone," she said, "the house is just way too quiet.

"The phone rang, and a male voice told me that Cosmo was being rushed into surgery. I was so stupid, Jack. I just stood there and went about cleaning up the kitchen, putting everything away, turning off the stove. It was as if I heard what the voice said but I didn't believe it. I actually poured myself a cup of coffee, sat down, and drank it.

Who does something that stupid after a phone call like that? Me! Me! I did that. It wasn't until I finished the cup of coffee that I came to my senses. It hit me full force. I was out of here in a nanosecond, driving like a bat out of hell. I don't think it took me ten minutes to get there, park, and go up to the waiting area. No one would tell me anything. Even when I raised all kinds of holy hell, they still wouldn't tell me anything other than that if I didn't calm down, they would make me go down to the first floor. I could tell they meant it, so I had no choice but to settle down. I was a basket case. Me! Do you believe that?

"It was two o'clock in the morning when Simon Simmons, the surgeon, came out to talk to me. Cosmo was in recovery and would be moved to the intensive care unit. I know Simon, he's a great guy, and Cowboy says he's almost as good a surgeon as he is. He was making a joke, of course. Simon didn't sugarcoat it. He said it was touch-and-go. Five gunshot wounds—one to the head, one to the shoulder, two to the back near his spinal cord, and one that creased his neck and took off part of his ear. Cosmo is a big guy, as you well know, and has lots of flesh on him. Simon said all that worked in his favor with the back bullets. The shoulder was in and out and not a real problem. The ear shot . . . well, anyone can live missing part of an ear. It's the head wound that was crucial. They put him in a medically induced coma. That's it."

"Was it a hit on Cosmo himself? I thought he traveled with security. Was he at the wrong place at the wrong time? Do you know, Lizzie? Did you talk to the police?"

"I don't know the answers to any of those questions. The police did come to the clinic. I spoke to them briefly, only to tell them I knew nothing. No one in authority has contacted me, not even the casino owners, which I find strange. Then again, maybe they tried but the clinic staff kept them away from me. I'm going to get dressed now, okay?" Harry and Jack nodded as they shooed Lizzie out of the kitchen. Jack cleaned up as Harry sat down and went into a trance.

Twenty minutes later, Lizzie reappeared. Jack and Harry gaped at her, their jaws dropping. It was a long time since they had seen Lizzie dressed in anything but court attire. Here she was wearing a very worn sweat suit with running shoes. Her long silvery hair was pulled back into a ponytail. Her face was freshly scrubbed and devoid of all makeup. There was no jewelry to be seen other than her gold wedding band.

This is the real Lizzie Fox, Jack thought. He looked over at Harry, who appeared to be thinking the same thing.

"Hey, guys, I have a question. Who put me to bed? Who undressed me?" Lizzie asked in a voice neither had ever heard before. Jack winced.

Harry stepped up to the plate so fast, Jack got dizzy. "Now, who do you think did that since we're the only ones here? I give you my word we closed our eyes when we . . . um . . . got you ready for bed."

"Oh, okay. Thanks."

And that was the end of that.

The trio piled into the car—Harry driving, Jack in the passenger seat, and Lizzie in the backseat by herself. The short drive to the clinic was made in virtual silence. The moment Harry pulled into the parking lot, Lizzie had the door open and was sprinting toward the main door, even before Harry could park the car.

"Can we use your car?" Jack bellowed out the open window. Too far away to respond, Lizzie just waved her hand. "Guess that means yes. I don't see any point in our going in. We would have heard from someone if we were needed. Let's head back to Babylon so we can shower and change. Then I want to go to the police station to get a copy of the police report, unless one of the guys has already done that. And you want to check on your guys, too, don't you?"

"Yeah, I do. Sounds like a plan. Why haven't we heard from anyone? Something must be going on," Harry grumbled.

"No news is good news, Harry. I'm thinking things are just the way they were, with no changes in Cosmo's condition. I want to believe and hope that's a good thing."

"I could never live here," Harry said as he tried to maneuver the Mercedes around a slow-moving Ford Focus with an elderly couple inside. "Lookie-looks, and they back up traffic for miles," Harry continued to grumble under his breath.

"The city that never sleeps. No clocks. City of dreams and crushed hopes. I agree, I could never live here either. This has got to be the mecca of all money. Did I say that right?" Not waiting for a response from Harry, he continued, "Millions and millions of dollars change hands in this town every hour of the day and night. I read an article once about some couple from Boise, Idaho, who saved their money for years and years because they thought they had a foolproof plan to quadruple their money and retire to some island and live happily ever after. The article went on to say they hit the craps table running and were wiped out in two hours. They didn't even have enough money for gas to drive back to Idaho. They had to panhandle to get home. Who does something like that?" Jack asked.

"Okay, we're here. I hate this place. I just want you to know that."

"I do know that, Harry, but we have to make the best of a really, really bad situation," Jack said irritably. Sometimes Harry made him crazy, and this was one of those times.

Jack and Harry registered and accepted their room

cards. They were next door to each other, one floor down from Annie's penthouse suite. The desk clerk had clarified that everyone except Fergus and Charles, who were staying in the penthouse, were on the same floor.

At the door to their respective rooms, Jack looked across the hall at Harry and said, "When you're ready, let's head up to the penthouse. I just hope one of the guys had enough sense to bring our bags when they checked in."

"Dennis was gathering them up when we left," Harry called over his shoulder. He gave a halfhearted wave and closed the door behind him.

Jack shut his own door and looked around. His bag was on some kind of fold-up table at the foot of his bed. A huge bed, big enough for him, Nikki, Cyrus, and six other dogs. He missed Cyrus as much as he missed Nikki when he was alone like this. He could hardly wait to call Abner to bring Cyrus down to his room. Cyrus didn't do well in the cargo hold when flying, so he'd made the decision for the big shepherd to ride with Abner, and that way Abner had company for the long cross-country ride.

Jack had his phone in hand when he stopped and listened. Was it his imagination or was he hearing a dog bark? Did Cyrus know he was here? Damn straight the dog knew, because in that moment he heard feet thundering down the hall and joyful barking. Jack opened the door just in time for Cyrus to slam up against him as he tried to hug, snuggle, lick, and bark at his owner all at the same time.

"Good to see you, too, big guy!" Jack laughed as he let the big dog drive him back to the bed, where both man and dog fell backward and proceeded to tussle with each other.

"That dog knew the minute you hit the building, Jack. How do they know that?" Abner asked fretfully.

"They're extrasensory is the best answer I can give you," Jack said, getting up off the bed. "So, talk to me, Abner.

What, if anything, do you know?" He watched as Cyrus prowled through the suite, sniffing everything, then pawing the carpet to make sure he put his scent in the room. He did the same thing each and every time they entered a room he'd never been in before. Marking his territory is what it was.

"I gotta tell you, Jack, Cyrus is real good company on a road trip. Thanks for letting him ride with me. I know you missed him. As to what's new . . . that tall doctor—surgeon I guess, the one in the cowboy hat—made us all leave when they took Cosmo back into surgery, which he himself performed. Some pretty long hours. I fell asleep. When I woke up, they made us leave. Charles said Cosmo was critical but holding his own. The cowboy stayed at his side and is still there, I think. When we asked why he was going back into surgery, the guy just said it was complicated and we wouldn't understand anyway, so we had to leave it at that. He did say he was cautiously optimistic. At this stage of the game, that's as good as we're going to get. Everyone is here now. Where's Lizzie?"

"We dropped her off at the hospital and drove here in her car. With her permission, of course."

"Okay, well, when you're ready, come up to the penthouse. Charles and Fergus are making breakfast."

"Hold on a minute, Abner. Harry and I were going to go to the police station to see if we could get a copy of the police report."

"Ted and Espinosa went and got it. No clue what it says, though. Guess we'll find out when we all meet up. See ya!"

Cyrus sprinted across the room and held out his paw to Abner, who dutifully shook it. "My pleasure. You can ride shotgun with me anytime, Cyrus." Cyrus woofed his thanks for the compliment, and then it was just Jack and Cyrus in the room.

Jack dropped to his haunches and eyed the big dog. "Damn, I really did miss you. That was a good thing you did, riding with Abner. Settle in while I shower and shave, then we'll go up to the penthouse and get some breakfast."

Cyrus leaped up onto the bed and stretched out. Jack laughed. God, he loved that dog.

Forty minutes later, Jack and Cyrus stepped out of the private elevator into the foyer of the penthouse. The scent of freshly roasted coffee and bacon struck his nostrils, reminding him of how hungry he was. Cyrus barked to show he was in agreement as he pranced into the huge penthouse and made the rounds so everyone could pet him and tell him how glad they were to see him. He waited just long enough to see where Jack was going to sit at the dining-room table before he found a spot next to his master's chair. He flopped down and closed his eyes just as Harry arrived and sat down next to Jack.

"Okay, we're all here now," Jack said, "so let's hear something. Right now, I'll take anything you all want to share. Abner told me that Ted and Espinosa got a copy of the police report. Somebody clue us in."

"Not much on it, Jack. The gunning down, the shoot-out, whatever you want to call it, went down in an area of town that is being, I guess the word is, refurbished. Renovated or whatever. It was originally an area off-limits to most people because of the crime and decay. The renovations have been going on for years, and real progress is being made. Cosmo owns it, along with a partner. Not sure whether it was gang related because their turf was invaded. No one has been arrested. Someone, no one knows who, called 911 when shots were fired. I did a little research on the area in question, and while originally seedy and less than desirable, it has never been known for gunfire. An ambulance came, and the first responders did what they had to do and whisked Cosmo to the clinic. He was able to tell the first responders where to take him, then he was out. As far as we know, he never said another word."

"That's it?" Jack said, disbelief ringing in his voice.

"Pretty much," Dennis said. "I did some digging, too, and that whole quadrant of the city is owned by Cosmo Cricket and someone named Zack Meadows. I googled him, and he's on the Gaming Commission, so it's a safe bet he's a good friend of Cosmo's. In addition, three blocks of buildings are inhabited by senior citizens. The buildings and their grounds are in tip-top shape. It's the only nice, decent part of that whole area, which is otherwise full of decaying buildings, but that's changing on a daily basis. Maybe an eighth of a mile up from the complex is a little park with benches, where the seniors go to play checkers, chess, people-watch, that kind of thing. As I said, the area is being refurbished, but slowly." Dennis spread his hands, palms up, as if to say, *There you have it.*

"I have a call in to Mr. Meadows, asking him if he'll meet with us," Charles said as he set a large platter of bacon and waffles in the center of Annie's long dining-room table. Fergus then placed a platter of scrambled eggs, toast, and pancakes at each end. Warm syrup and melted butter followed as the gang dug in. Charles's number one rule of not talking business during mealtime was paid no never mind as everyone started talking at once.

"I guess you're saying he didn't get back to you," Dennis said.

"Not yet," Charles agreed, taking his place at the table. "I'll put in another call to him when we finish here. If he doesn't take my call, then we might have to ask Lizzie to pave the way for a meeting."

"We should have heard something on Cosmo's condition by now," Jack said. "Lizzie swears Dr. Wylie is some kind of magical surgeon. Has anyone called him?"

"He told us not to call him. He said he was staying with Cosmo. He meant that literally. He was in the recovery room after surgery and planned to stay there until they moved him into ICU, and he promised he would stay there to monitor him no matter how long it took," Charles said as he crunched down on a piece of toast.

"Do the police have any kind of theory?" Harry asked.

"If they do, they sure didn't share it with us. We're outsiders, and this is Vegas. The police do not share or confide. You know what they say—'What happens in Vegas stays in Vegas.' As I said, we're outsiders, so that means we're on our own. Even our press credentials didn't help. If anything, they clammed up even more when we showed them," Ted said.

"What's your feeling about the gangs, Ted?" Jack asked.

"Did you get a feel one way or the other in that regard?" Harry asked.

"I couldn't read it, sorry to say. Dennis found out through his research that there are two gangs. Seems there are always two at war with each other. Everyone wants to be top dog. It's the same way back home. One gang is called the Cavaliers. The other one is called the Scorpions. When the renovations started, they had to relocate to another area, but before they did, the Scorpions raised all kinds of holy hell. They tried to burn down the senior complex. Then they blew up some cars. They messed with the city's earthmoving equipment to delay the renovation. The skinny is that the Scorpions did it. The Cavaliers simply relocated and didn't cause any problems. No arrests were made. It was rumored that the Cavaliers are the guardian angels and protectors of the seniors. The Scorpions don't like that. In other words, the Scorpions are the bad guys, and the Cavaliers are the good guys, if there is such a thing when two gangs are at war," Ted said.

"That's crazy," Jack interjected.

"Not if you really think about it, Jack," Charles said. "Cosmo and his partner purchased that property years and years ago. They renovated three city blocks of dwellings to provide homes for senior citizens. Who better to protect the seniors and their investment from a gang than another gang? Cosmo is no fool, we know that. This is Vegas. He would have hedged his bets all the way around. I'm sure he's funding the gang in some way. His own father resided in one of the buildings for a while before he passed away. I'm thinking Mr. Meadows might have had a parent there, too, at some point, and that might explain why Cosmo and he went into that venture together.

"Several years ago, I recall a conversation I had with Lizzie about everything and nothing, just a conversation, but she mentioned what she called Cosmo's project, and she said it was his, that she wasn't involved, just the way he wasn't involved in her activities with the sisters. She did say that after Cosmo's mother died, his father went dark and quiet, kind of the way Myra went when our daughter Barbara died. It was his way of getting his father back among the living, giving him a reason to carry on. I don't know if any of that is going to help us."

"Hanging out at the hospital isn't going to get us any-where. Maybe you should go out to Happy Village and talk to some of the seniors, or if you're lucky, the leader of the Cavaliers," Abner said. "While you guys are doing that, I can see what I can hack into in regard to the Village, the gang, and Mr. Meadows himself."

Jack looked at Harry. "You want to stay with your guys? I can take Dennis with me. Ted and Espinosa can hit the local papers and see what their colleagues are willing to part with. Reporters are a close-knit group but usually kind to one another. Fergus and Charles can hang out here or go to the hospital. How's that all sound to you guys?"

Everyone said it worked for them. They all agreed to

stay in touch and meet up back at Babylon at one o'clock
for brunch in one of the main dining rooms.

Jack was about to get up to help clear the table when his
cell phone vibrated. He looked down at the caller ID and
was surprised to see it was Little Jack. He knew instinc-
tively the boy had a problem and it wasn't going to be
good. He knew this because it was way too early in the
morning for LJ to get in touch. He showed the caller ID to
Harry, who rolled his eyes.

"What's up, little man?" Jack said, forcing cheer he was
far from feeling. He listened, then let out a huge sigh. Before he commented, he walked out of the dining room and
down a hall, to where he could have some privacy.

"Whoa. Whoa. Calm down now. Let me make sure I
have this right. LJ, take a deep breath. This is not the end
of the world. You went to bed last night and sometime
during the night someone went into your room and drew
sour faces on your knees with a black magic marker that
won't wash off. Do I have that right?" Jack listened as the
boy on the other end of the phone fought not to sob. "All
the girls are giggling. Well, of course they are. They're the
ones who did it. It's what kids do at summer camp, LJ.
You have to suck it up and pretend it doesn't matter. Take
the high road. Yeah, I get the part about the fat knees and
you have to wear shorts. Emily is waiting for you to ex-
plode, to retaliate. That's what girls do. Now listen up,
this is going to be really hard for you to do, but you have
to do what I tell you. I want your promise, LJ."

All Jack could hear on the other end of the phone was
sniffling. "Cut that out right now. Sniffling and crying and
tattling is exactly what Emily wants you to do. She's
counting on it, depending on it making you so mad you
lose your timing when you hit the water. What you're
going to do is turn the table on her. You're going to go
with the joke, show off your knees, laugh about it. Don't
blame her, don't even look at her. She's expecting you to

go all ape poop on her, and you aren't going to do that. If you do what I say, she will be the one who loses time in the water because she will be trying to figure out where she went wrong and why it isn't bothering you. You listening to me, LJ? Can you do it? Can you carry it off?"

"All I wanted was for her to like me, Uncle Jack. My friend Luke told me she likes Trevor, but Trevor likes Sally. See my point?"

"I do see your point, but you need to see *my* point. So, do I have your promise? And it wouldn't hurt to maybe show some interest in some other girl, just for fun. Okay, are we good here, pal?"

"We're good, Uncle Jack. Thanks. I'll send you a text later to let you know how the day goes, okay?"

"You got it. Good luck. Remember now, play it cool."

Jack ended the call. *Oh, to be that young with those kinds of problems.* He felt a bit guilty about continuing to keep LJ in the dark about Cosmo's situation, but he knew it was for the best. He shook his head to clear his thoughts. Right then, at that precise moment in time, Jack Emery wished he were ten years old again and in summer camp with all the drama that occurred twenty-four hours a day and loving every minute of it.

Cyrus nudged his leg. Time to get back on the stick with his own real-world drama.

Jack was happy to see that Annie's kitchen sparkled and everyone was on the move. Dennis was waiting, his backpack settled comfortably on his shoulders.

"Harry said to tell you he'll see you at one o'clock and to try not to get into any trouble, because he'll be too busy to get you out of said trouble," Dennis said.

Cyrus didn't like the sound of that. He woofed, then woofed again. Jack laughed as he looked around for his own backpack. "Guess we're taking Lizzie's Benz. Do you know where we're going, Dennis?"

"Got the address right here. Straight drive as the crow

flies. Forty minutes depending on traffic. I think we should drive around first, get the lay of the land before we tackle the senior citizens. What do you think, Jack?"

"Sounds good. Do we know who's in charge of the housing complex?"

"I'm not one hundred percent sure, but I think it's a man named Gentry Lomax. His second-in-command is a woman named Bessie Love. I got all that from the Happy Village newsletter they publish once a month. Another thing I learned was that there are no couples in Happy Village. It's for people who've lost a spouse. That's not to say that some of them might not . . . um . . . hook up from time to time, but from what I read it's frowned upon. It's a friendship kind of place, and if you stop to think about it, Jack, it's a great idea. No one can replace a wife or husband after, say, forty or fifty years of marriage. From that point on, it's all about friendship. At least that's what the newsletter wants everyone to believe."

"I guess we'll see for ourselves once we get there," Jack said as he followed the instructions on the navigation system.

It was barely ten in the morning, and the traffic was already bumper to bumper. Jack wished he were hitching a ride with Harry on his Ducati. If that were the case, they'd arrive at their destination in fifteen minutes.

As Jack muttered under his breath, he found his thoughts going to his godchild, Little Jack, and how he was faring with his decorated fat knees. He found it hard not to laugh that a ten-year-old girl named Emily could bring his godson to his fat little knees.

No pun intended.

Chapter 3

Dennis did his best to keep up a running conversation with Jack as they made their way to Happy Village in the stop-and-go traffic.

Jack took his eyes off the road for a moment to look across at Dennis. "If I counted right, that was about ten questions you just asked me, none of which I have the answers to. I got here when you did, so I know what you know. I don't see any point in speculating at this point. I'm still racking my brain to try to remember if I ever even heard about this project of Cosmo's. I know for a fact Lizzie never mentioned it, or if she did, it was in the vaguest of terms and didn't register as something I needed to remember. On the other hand, I think I can count on one hand the times I've been in Cosmo's company, so there's no reason for me to even know about his affairs. Lizzie and Cosmo are both very private people, or at least they try to be in a town like Vegas."

Dennis nodded as he stared out at the bumper-to-bumper traffic, the exhaust spiraling upward into the cloudless blue sky. "It's supposed to reach over a hundred today, Jack. Did you hear that this morning on the news?" Jack shook his head to indicate no, he had not heard about the temperature.

"Do you have a plan in mind when we get to Happy Village?"

"I wish," Jack muttered. "No. Do you?"

"No. I think we need to think about the possibility that the seniors won't want to talk to us. As a rule, senior citizens are very much aware that there are people who try to take advantage of them, scam them because they're up in years. We're going to be strangers to them, and we're going in cold, with no credentials. Yeah, we know Cosmo Cricket, and yeah, we know he's fighting for his life. All the more reason for them to clam up to strangers. I suppose we can bandy Zack Meadows's name about, but whoever is in charge will want to know why Meadows didn't get in touch with him or her to warn them we were coming."

"I guess we'll just wing it the way we usually do. By the way, did you have any luck researching those gangs we talked about earlier?"

"You mean the Cavaliers and the Scorpions?"

"Yes," Jack responded.

"The members of the Scorpions are all tatted up with scorpions on their arms, necks, the back of their hands, and the calves of their legs. They're a mixed bag, white, black, and Hispanic. They are some badass dudes, from what I read. Happy Village is in the area that used to be their turf. They were forced to move away—and managed to cause quite a bit of trouble before they did. A lot of them are still in jail, but their total membership somehow increased. Serving time in jail is a badge of honor with the gangs."

"What about the Cavaliers. They badasses too?"

"All gangs are bad, you know that, Jack. But to answer your question, no, not really. I could not confirm this, but it seems that Cosmo somehow, in some way, communicates with them, and they are more or less guardians of

Happy Village. We should have talked to Zack Meadows before we came out here to get the lay of the land."

"I tried calling him three times and left messages. He didn't return any of my calls. That is not sitting well with me. He didn't get back to Charles, either. I'd like to know if the guy is a silent partner or one with a voice, or is it Cosmo who calls the shots. I don't even know if Lizzie knows. My point is that the guy should be jumping all over himself to help us, and he isn't, is he? Why do you think that is?"

Dennis felt goose bumps race up and down his arms, and it had nothing to do with the chilly temperature in the car. "Are you thinking what I think you're thinking?" There was angst in the young reporter's tone that set Jack's teeth on edge because he knew exactly what the young reporter was thinking.

The robotic voice on the navigation system instructed Jack to make a right-hand turn two hundred feet ahead.

"I guess this will take us into Happy Village. Doesn't look too bad to me so far. It's been cleaned up quite a bit from the looks of things. Entrances to communities and the like are important. Landscaping will usually do it," Jack said, just to have something to say.

Dennis laughed. "I can show you some pictures of before and after. The after still has to be finished, and by that I think it means the landscaping. The before is a little hard to swallow. Rusted-out junk cars, greasy-looking mattresses, old appliances along with all the other junk people just dumped to get rid of it. Now it just looks like flat scrubland. Put in a few trees for shade, some flowering bushes, some hedges, grass, along with a few benches, and you have urban development. I think it will look really nice once it's all finished."

Jack kept his eyes on the road. "I think it was Ted, but maybe it was Espinosa, who said that all the cosmetic work is being done by volunteers and that's why it's taking so long. Not everyone has a green thumb, was the way he put it. And everyone isn't into gardening, so what gets done gets done and what doesn't doesn't.

"I'm going to find a place to park. Then we're going to hoof it. Our first stop will be to find Gentry Lomax or Bessie Love to see what they can tell us. Most of these buildings look like town houses to me," Jack said, eyeing the dwellings in front of him.

"They are. Three floors to each building. Six apartments to each floor, so that means the buildings extend into the back. Eighteen residents to a building. Ten of those buildings in all, which translates into one hundred and eighty residents. Assuming all the apartments are occupied. In addition to those buildings, as you can see, there are four blocks with small ranch houses on them, three on a side, including the corner houses, which adds another thirty-two residents, bringing the total to two hundred and twelve.

"Apparently Cosmo figured that some people would prefer living in a small house rather than an apartment and took that into consideration when he decided to put up this complex. That had to be a pretty massive undertaking on Cosmo's part to have all this built. Unless he did it slowly, a little bit at a time, and this is the end result. All the apartments are one-bedroom, one-bath units. To discourage coupling, I assume. The houses are only slightly larger but still only one bedroom." Dennis giggled.

"According to the floor plan, the rooms in the apartment are a good size and they have eat-in kitchens. The bathrooms are all those walk-in kind for the safety of older people. The houses have a larger living room and a dining area separate from the kitchen. I suppose the people who live in the houses figured they would have guests over, maybe their kids and grandkids, and wanted to be able to sit down comfortably for a meal. It's a good, safe environment as far as I can tell. If Cosmo is responsible for the design, then I'd say he did a good job."

Jack nodded as he parked the car and turned off the engine. "He put his father here, so yes, I would have to agree. Lizzie said that Zack Meadows's mother was here also, so I guess that's why the two of them partnered up. I know that Cosmo's father passed away a year or so ago, but I don't know about Zack Meadows's mother. No one said, or if they did, I missed it."

The blistering heat immediately attacked the two men after they exited Lizzie's air-conditioned car. Dennis immediately started to fan himself as sweat beaded on his forehead. The sky overhead was clear blue, and the sun was a bright golden orb in the sky as a flock of scrub jays swarmed down to nestle in a large oak tree at the end of the street before they squawked and descended to a patch of lawn that had a sprinkler throwing water in all directions. "I have this crazy urge to run through that sprinkler," Dennis admitted, grinning.

"Yeah, me too. No one is out and about," Jack said. "Guess it's too hot for any kind of outdoor activity. How do you want to do this, Dennis?"

Cyrus let loose with a sharp bark. *We need to get a move on here.*

"Yeah, yeah, we're gonna move, big guy, but first we need to see if there is some kind of central building, an office of some kind, maybe a community center, or at the very least a clubhouse. Let's walk down to the end of the block and see what's there. This area looks strictly residential. All the patches of grass are mowed, probably cut with manicure scissors, and the flowers aren't wilted, so the irrigation system obviously works. The buildings are well cared for, freshly painted—a really nice place, in my opinion," Jack said as he strode forward, Cyrus at his side.

"Maybe they have a lawn service that comes around once a week. I can't see senior citizens down on their knees pulling weeds, and I haven't seen a single weed," Dennis observed, peering down at the patches of lawn as they moved along.

"It might be my imagination, but I feel eyes on me," Jack said.

"Yeah, I have the same feeling. I wasn't going to say anything, thinking it was just my imagination," Dennis replied, his voice jittery.

"Look, Dennis," Jack said, pointing to a small plaque by the front door of the last building. "It says OFFICE. Looks like they have an intercom. Let's give it a whirl."

Jack marched up the five steps to a long, skinny porch that looked like a runaway rainbow with bright blue morning glories and clematis climbing up the walls and pillars that held up the narrow roof over the porch. There were clay pots full of petunias, Shasta daisies, and impatiens, all of which were thriving even with the brutal summer heat. Jack pressed his thumb on the doorbell and waited. A froggy-sounding voice blasted from the intercom. "Identify yourself."

"Jack Emery and Dennis West. We're here at the request of Mrs. Cosmo Cricket," Jack lied with a straight face. "We'd like to speak to Mr. Gentry Lomax."

"He isn't here right now," the froggy-sounding voice said.

"Is Ms. Love here? Ms. Bessie Love. We can speak with her if that's possible."

The froggy voice spoke again. "It's *Mrs.* Love, not *Ms.* Love. And you are speaking with her right now. What is it you want? We have a strict policy here, and we do not open the doors to anyone we don't know. You need to make an appointment. That's how we do things here."

"I can appreciate that, *Mrs.* Love, but Mrs. Cricket

asked me to come here. I don't think she would appreciate your policy of not cooperating when it concerns her husband, who is fighting for his very life and who owns this complex along with his partner, Zack Meadows. Are you seriously telling me you want me to go back and report this conversation to Mrs. Cricket?"

The bright blue door, the same color as the morning glories climbing over the door frame, opened suddenly—so suddenly that Jack had to take a step back and almost knocked Dennis down the stairs.

"That's not what I'm saying at all, Mr. Emery," said a tiny lady in a flowered dress that clashed with all the flowers on the porch, as she motioned for Dennis and Jack to enter the room. Cyrus barked to show he was part of the party. "All right, you can come in too, but do not pee on the carpet." Cyrus barked twice to show he was offended at the remark.

It was a real office, but it didn't look as if it got much use. Everything looked new and fresh, and even smelled as if it had just been painted. There were three desks with three bright red, futuristic-looking plastic chairs. A long table held three computers, an all-in-one printer, and a console telephone. Two bright red file cabinets stood next to the long metal table. Obviously, whoever sat at the desks had to slide a chair over to the table if they wanted to use the computers.

Completing the decor was a large, lush, and healthy-looking ficus tree that took up one entire corner of the office. Black-and-white prints of Las Vegas from the early days up to the present adorned the walls. A small television sat on the corner of what Jack assumed was *Mrs.* Love's desk and was tuned to a morning game show. Three old-fashioned ledgers were spread open on the long table, with a box of colored pencils next to them. Different-colored pencils were nestled in the open spine of each ledger. Probably some kind of code for the workings of the complex, Jack decided.

"What is it you want, Mr. Emery? Whatever it is, I'm sure I won't be able to help you. I just fill in here a few hours each day or when Gentry has other things to do. I do it for a reduction in my rent. Gentry is in charge, and I certainly do not want to step out of line."

"When will Mr. Lomax be back?" Dennis asked, speaking for the first time. He offered up his famous boyish smile, hoping she would respond to him the way that other elderly people did. She did.

"I'm not sure, honey. He just said he had something he had to do and I would see him when I saw him. He told me what he wanted me to do, and that's what I've been doing since I arrived at eight-thirty this morning. I can make an appointment for you for tomorrow if you like."

Jack took over. "As I'm sure you know, Mr. Cricket is seriously ill. What you may not know is that he had to be taken back into surgery yesterday. He is still in critical condition. Understandably, Mrs. Cricket is at his side and won't leave, of course. She was told virtually nothing about what happened on that tragic day. She wants to know what happened. That's why we're here, *Mrs.* Love. You live here, so you were here when the shooting happened. You must know *something.*"

"Well, of course the poor thing wants to know. I do, too. Everyone does. The thing is, we don't know anything; none of us do. I was napping that day because I wanted to stay up to see the guest Mr. Hannity had on his show that night. As far as I know, and all of us talked about it afterward in a special meeting Gentry called, not one of us knew anything had happened until after the fact. When the weather is as hot as it has been, in the upper nineties, we all pretty much stay indoors until the sun goes down. The air-conditioning units more or less drown outside noise, if you know what I mean.

"We only became aware that something was wrong when the ambulances and the police cars showed up with their sirens blaring. That's when we all ran out to see Mr. Cricket lying in the road. The police questioned all of us, but there was nothing we could tell them. I'm truly sorry about that. Mr. Cricket is a lovely man, and he takes care of this complex as if he lived here. His father used to live here, so that might have something to do with it. He held Gentry's job for a while, but that was all before I came to live here."

"What about Mr. Meadows?" Dennis asked, again paired with his boyish, winning smile.

She tilted her head to the side as she thought about the question. "I don't think I've seen Mr. Meadows more than five or six times in the two years I've lived here. I do know that the other tenants said he used to come quite often. But like I said, that was before I moved in. He doesn't attend our annual Christmas party or our Fourth of July festivities. Mr. Cricket and his wife and son always come. Sometimes Mr. Cricket plays Santa Claus. That's always a fun evening."

"What can you tell us about the gangs around here? Do you all think they had something to do with Mr. Cricket's shooting?" Dennis asked.

The little gray-haired lady in the flowered dress eyeballed Dennis for a moment before she responded. "Now, that is something you have to talk to Gentry about. If you're talking about the Cavaliers and Lionel, we don't consider them a gang. Lionel and his friends patrol and protect this complex, and one reason for that is that Lionel's mother lives here. I know Lionel, and neither he nor his friends would do anything like that."

"If they aren't a gang, what are they?" Dennis asked, going into reporter mode.

"Just . . . just Lionel and his friends. Someone said there are twelve of them altogether. Young men, early twenties.

They're always nicely dressed, they don't use bad language. Very respectful. Lionel looks out for his mother, who is a really sweet lady. He brings her food, buys her presents, and sometimes takes her out for a ride on Sunday afternoon. Or he'll take her to one of the casinos to play the slot machines for an hour or so. He's a good son. Much better than my own son, I'm sorry to say." Her eyes suddenly filled with tears, which Jack and Dennis pretended not to see. But not Cyrus, who stepped forward and wrapped his front paws around the little woman's shoulders. He woofed softly to show *he* understood.

"Oh, what a sweet doggie you are," Mrs. Love said, stroking Cyrus's head. That was enough for Cyrus. He backed away and dropped to his haunches next to Jack. *Sweet doggie indeed.*

"Do they work? Do Lionel and his friends have jobs?" Jack asked.

Mrs. Love threw her hands in the air. "I have no idea. I just assumed—now mind you, no one said this, it's just my opinion—but I more or less thought they were on Mr. Cricket's payroll. I suppose I could be wrong. I just don't know. Just so you know, we here at Happy Village might be old, but we do not—I repeat, we do *not*—gossip."

"What about the other group, gang, whatever they are?" Dennis asked.

"Ah, yes, the Scorpions. They are a bad group. This whole area used to belong to them, at least that's what they claim. They had to . . . I guess you would say relocate, to a less desirable area. They make trouble whenever they can. They have guns. Their leader is someone named Alonzo. There are a lot of them, and they ride motorcycles up and down the roads here in the middle of the night. They throw rocks at our windows, strew their trash all over our lawns. Sometimes they shoot their guns off. By the time the police come, they're always gone. Someone said that Lionel told

Gentry they have over fifty members and that a lot of them are girls. Don't know if any of that's true, it seems unlikely, but that's what I heard.

"You really need to speak with Gentry about all of this. I'm sorry I cannot be more help. Tell me this, if you know. How is Mr. Cricket? Please tell his wife we're all praying for her husband's recovery. He's such a good man."

"We'll do that. We'll come back tomorrow, probably late morning. One last thing. Do you know how many people live here in this complex?"

Mrs. Love pointed to the open ledgers on her desk. "I was working on that when you arrived. We have room for 216 people. We were full as of December of last year, with a small waiting list. We're down to 192 now. We have applications pending. We thoroughly vet all the applicants, and it does take a while; but it's worth the wait, as everyone says. This is a wonderful place to live, with people just like you."

"Where did the other twenty people go?" Jack asked.

Mrs. Love shook her head. "That's the sixty-four-thousand-dollar question. I don't know. No one knows. They just left. Not all at once but over a seven-month period. It's worrisome, I can tell you that. No good-byes. They were just gone. Gentry had a call in to Mr. Cricket to discuss it. I'm not sure, but I think that's why Mr. Cricket was here that day, to talk about it."

"Well, thank you, Mrs. Love," Jack said. "We appreciate your taking the time to talk to us. We'll be back tomorrow."

"I'll put you down in Gentry's appointment book. You all have a nice day; you too, you sweet, handsome doggie," Bessie said as she stroked Cyrus's big head. Cyrus woofed his thanks for the compliment and the ear rub. *Handsome was good, and he could overlook the sweet doggie bit.*

On the way back to the hotel, Dennis kept up a running commentary on their visit with Bessie Love. "I think she's just who she says she is. I didn't get the impression she was withholding information. She seemed open and aboveboard to me. Mr. Lomax might know more, but I wouldn't bet any money on it. What she said about Mr. Meadows did jar me a bit. I felt like I had an itch I needed to scratch when she said he doesn't go there much. I'm wondering what his total share is on that investment. Do we know anything about him? Like what does he do at the Gaming Commission? Is he Cosmo's right hand, his assistant, or are they just in this venture together as partners and his job at the GC is just a job? If he's a partner, where did the money come from? I think we need to know a lot more about Meadows. What do you think, Jack?"

"I agree with everything you just said. It's weird, but I got the same itch you did, and I'm not even a reporter. I wish Cyrus could talk so he could tell us his opinion."

The big shepherd woofed, then woofed again. "I think he's agreeing with both of us," Jack said. Cyrus woofed again. "Confirmed," Jack said.

Dennis nibbled on his lower lip as he squinted at the bright sunshine flooding the car. "There was one other thing that brought me up short. What did you think about the twenty people leaving? Mrs. Love said she thought that Cosmo and Mr. Gentry Lomax were going to discuss the twenty people who had left and that it was worrisome. Seven months is a long time not to question why that many people would suddenly up and leave without telling anyone. In this kind of environment, you would think elderly people look out for one another rather than wait seven months to do something, even if that something is just discuss possibilities among themselves. I don't like it when I can't come up with an answer." The young reporter's voice was so fretful, Jack found himself wincing as though in pain.

"That's something we need to talk about, but with who I have no idea. Cosmo is in no condition to talk to us, at least not right now. Lizzie doesn't seem to know anything about the workings of Happy Village. That leaves us to do our own research or possibly have a face-to-face with Zack Meadows. I don't mind telling you that I'm a little ticked that he hasn't responded to the three phone messages I left," Jack said.

"Let's call him again and see what happens," Dennis suggested.

Jack took his right hand off the steering wheel to dig in his pocket for his cell phone. He tossed it to Dennis. "Go ahead, make the call, and if it goes to voice mail, tell him we just left Happy Village, where we spoke to Mrs. Love, and it's imperative we meet and speak with him, on Mrs. Cricket's orders."

Dennis did as instructed. The cell phone on the other end rang four times before it went to voice mail. He held out the phone so Jack could hear the cryptic message and what the caller should do if they wanted to leave a message. Dennis left a precise, detailed message stressing the importance of a return call at Mr. Meadows's earliest convenience. He ended the call and handed the phone back to Jack. "I don't think we should hold our breath waiting for a return call. I'll take that one step further and go out on a limb and say I think the guy is avoiding us. The question is, why?"

"Quoting Mrs. Love, I think that's the sixty-four-thousand-dollar question. Why indeed?"

The rest of the ride back to Babylon was made in silence as both Jack and Dennis contemplated their next move.

Twenty minutes later, Jack, Dennis, and Cyrus stepped out of the private elevator that let them off in the foyer of

Annie's penthouse apartment. A babble of voices greeted them, and a buffet lunch was set out on the dining-room table. Everyone stopped talking and eating to stare at the trio. Cyrus barked, then barked once again as he beelined for the table, his way of letting everyone know that he was hungry. Fergus immediately fixed a plate for him while the others demanded answers to the questions they kept throwing at the two men.

"First things first. Good idea to serve lunch here so we can talk openly and not worry about someone listening to our conversation in a public place. Since you're all here, that has to mean Cosmo is, at the very least, holding his own, right?" Jack asked. "Am I right?"

"He's still in the ICU. Dr. Wylie is at his bedside, and Lizzie is with him. They both insisted we all leave. They promised to call with any news even if it's bad news. We had no other choice but to come back. We're just biding our time," Charles explained.

"You two probably know more than we do. We're still in the dark as to what really happened, not to mention why it happened."

"I will say this," said Charles, "Dr. Wylie said he is cautiously optimistic as to Cosmo's complete recovery, so I think we should all take that as a plus. Now, if you two don't mind, we'd like to hear what you found out at Happy Village."

Jack took the floor and, as he walked around the table filling his plate, gave a detailed account of their meeting and everything that was said. He ended his tale with, "And right before we got here, I had Dennis call Mr. Meadows for the fourth time, and the call went to voice mail like the other three calls. He has not gotten back to me. I find that strange and more than a little disturbing. We need to do a full check on that guy.

"For starters, I think we should talk to Annie's people

here at Babylon. They probably know everyone at the Gaming Commission and might even know Meadows, or at least something about him. Ted, you and Espinosa might be good at that. You want to take a crack at it? Just for the hell of it, Abner, check the guy's financials. Go back to the day he fell out of his mother's womb."

"Sure, we can do that right now. We're done eating," Ted said as he slung the backpack he was never without over his shoulders. Espinosa did a quick check before he slid his arms through his own backpack. He grabbed two egg rolls on the way out.

"Abner, hack into that guy's bank account and see what you come up with," Jack said, as he bit down into a crusty egg roll. "We also need to find out everything we can on those two gangs. Well, maybe one gang and one . . . whatever Lionel and the Cavaliers are."

"I can do that part when I'm done eating," Dennis volunteered.

"Where's Harry?" Jack asked.

"He left with his friends right before you two arrived," Charles said. "He said to call him if we needed him. He indicated that he wanted to spend some time with his friends but was just a phone call away. I think they would all like to see some action, but that's just my opinion."

"We're good for now. Let Harry enjoy his friends," Jack said, as he peeled the shell off a shrimp and popped it into his mouth. "Listen, if it's okay with the rest of you, I want to take a shower and try for at least a two-hour nap. I'm about dead on my feet here."

Charles made shooing motions with his hands, which meant, *Go already, we can look after things here fine without you and Cyrus.*

Jack looked over at Dennis, who was oblivious to what was going on as he tapped and tapped on his laptop. *Ah, to be that young again and know what I know now,* Jack thought wearily as he trudged to the door, Cyrus on his heels. "Call me if something goes down."

No one responded.

"Guess it's just you and me, big guy. You can sleep on the bed with me since we don't have your bed with us." Cyrus barked to show that he loved the idea.

Chapter 4

Once upon a time, it had been a decent neighborhood with families. Kids played outside on the manicured lawns and picked flowers for their moms, while neighbors chatted over their back fences or just sitting on their front steps. As the families grew, one by one they moved out slowly, and with that an influx of undesirables appeared almost out of nowhere until there was nothing left of the old neighborhood but run-down houses, many of which turned into crack houses in the blink of an eye. Gangs formed, then multiplied at dizzying speed.

The neighborhood was originally divided into four sections, each with four buildings, be they single-family houses or two-story town houses. They were separated by three mini gardens full of emerald-green grass and flowers of all the colors of the rainbow; the neighbors took turns caring for them all. A comfortable place to come home to at the end of the day.

But that day was now long gone.

The first house in the fourth section was simply referred to as Building One. It sat in a row of four buildings with nothing to differentiate it because there simply wasn't anything else for miles except three other shacks in the same condition. The emerald grass was gone and so were the colorful flowers the little kids picked for their moms. Cactus, scrub, desert weeds, and sand was all that remained.

Buildings Two, Three, and Four were identical and housed the members of the Scorpions. The word *squalid* was way too kind to describe the interiors of the buildings. There was no water, no electricity, and no plumbing of any kind because the shell company that had been created to hide the identity of the real owner had failed to pay the taxes on the properties, and all the utilities had been turned off. The buildings smelled of rot, decay, feces, urine, unwashed bodies, and cannabis, of which there was plenty. But the gang had jerry-rigged things so they had electricity for their computers and cell phones.

There was only one difference between the four buildings—Building One was the domain of the so-called supreme leader of the Scorpions. It was where he sat on his throne, made up of two milk crates held together with duct tape. A red rag covered the crates, and it was whispered among the gang that the rag was red because someone's blood had saturated it, then dried. Of course, those who did the whispering had probably failed high school biology and had no idea that dried blood is actually brown, not red, but they never let the facts get in the way of a good story. Another makeshift stand held a brand-new Apple laptop—stolen, of course, from the backseat of a high roller's Aston Martin at one of the casinos in town. Dirty, filthy mattresses, stolen from the Trump International Hotel, littered the floor. In this room, the supreme leader ruled his disciples with a dirty fist and a meat cleaver. His name was Alonzo Zuma Santiago. It was a name he had given himself when he was ten and living on the streets with no parents that he knew of. No member of the Scorpions dared question the title he'd bestowed upon himself.

There was jerry-rigged electricity; water pipes, also jerry-rigged; and outside, four porta potties. All stolen. The members took turns emptying them.

At the moment, Building One was filled to capacity, with runaway or homeless young thugs of all ages lining the ramshackle walls and filling the doorway. The stench was sickening to the point that several of the disciples had to go outside, where they choked and sputtered as they fought the bile threatening to erupt. The meeting continued without them. It was a given they would pay for their defection, but they were young and didn't care. Later, they would learn the hard way that, whatever the circumstances, when the supreme leader said attend a meeting, you attended the meeting—no matter what.

Inside Building One, Santiago raised the meat cleaver and waved it in the air for silence. The crowd instantly went quiet. "Okay, guys, listen up. We have fifteen minutes until our guest arrives. It's not going to be a pleasant meeting. We were paid only half the money promised, but that's on us, and Mother Nature. The other half was to be paid to us today. Since we failed to complete the job to Mr. Hot Shot's satisfaction, there might not be a payday today unless I can convince our employer otherwise." Santiago pointed to a metal box with a padlock, which was simply called the money box.

"See that! Inside our money box is a measly six dollars. Our food supply is almost gone. The last time I looked, which was an hour ago, there were two boxes of Cocoa Puffs, one can of Spam, and two cans of tuna on our food shelf. Since we share and share alike, that means no one eats until there is enough for everyone. That means Team One has to hit the streets and bring back either food or money. Go now!" Six gang members broke ranks and left the building.

Santiago's second-in-command, a twentysomething named Miggy, stood up, and asked, "So what's the plan once Mr. Hot Shot arrives? Why is he even coming here? I thought we were done with him. . . ." He looked around to see if everyone was listening, and said, "And his other project. Does he think we owe him a second chance? What?"

"I don't know. I don't like it when I don't know something," Santiago snarled in return. "I have it on good authority—and by that I mean Hot Shot himself—that several strangers showed up at Happy Village and were asking questions. He called a little while ago. I think that's the main reason he's coming here today, since he does not like people sticking their noses in his business. I want to know who those strangers are and what brought them nosing around Happy Village. That means Team Two needs to head out there right now. And don't come back until you have the answers I want."

The leader of Team Two, a scrawny teen named Juno, jumped up and demanded to know why they were being sent out in broad daylight, because that just meant they were looking for trouble. Then he grew bolder, and said, "If you're planning on forcing Hot Shot to pay the balance, why should we risk going to Happy Village?"

The meat cleaver swung back and forth in the stifling air. "Because I said so, that's why, and do not ever question my orders again. Go now, or this cleaver will be sticking in your back. Clean up a little before you go."

"Like we have running showers here with tons of hot water," Juno grumbled as he scurried after the other four members of his team.

Santiago looked around. With eleven members now gone, there were only the five members of Team Three left plus Miggy. He looked down at the knockoff Rolex on his wrist. Five minutes until he had to play host to his employer, Mr. Hot Shot himself.

"Okay, boys, split. I'll handle this from here on in. Miggy, you stay with me." To the others, he waved the meat cleaver and shouted, "Stay close but out of sight."

Miggy dropped to his haunches at Santiago's feet. He

looked up at him, worry lines etched in his dirty face. They were identical to the worry lines he saw etched in his childhood friend's face. They'd been like brothers, living on the streets since the age of ten, two throwaway kids society didn't know about or want. They'd lived by their wits and did whatever they had to do to survive. From day one, they'd had each other's back, and as Miggy said, he never expected that to change.

Alonzo had big dreams, which he shared with Miggy in the dark of night. Someday they'd score big. Someday the Scorpions would be so feared, even the police would respect them and leave them alone. Someday there would be so much money, they wouldn't know what to do with it all. Someday they'd live in luxury, with showers that never ran out of hot water, soap that smelled like flowers, clean clothes, silk sheets on real beds, and the finest food and liquor.

Someday.

That someday was supposed to be now except for a few minor glitches. Every plan ran into a few glitches along the way.

Miggy was tired of waiting for someday to arrive. He wanted it all *now*. He knew that Alonzo was tired of waiting too. The two of them had talked and whispered to each other in the middle of the night that Hot Shot was the answer they'd been waiting for. Miggy believed, and so did Alonzo. And it had *almost* happened. And then it all went to hell in a handbasket in a matter of seconds, and they were right back to square one. The here and now. He hated it. Sometimes life sucked, and sometimes it *really* sucked, and this time it *really really* sucked. But, Miggy consoled himself, they still had one ace in the hole. Like Alonzo said, you never show your hand until the last second, and that's when you hit them right between their squinty eyes. Alonzo was always right. He could almost feel those silk sheets. Almost.

Alonzo and Miggy both heard the sound of the car at the same moment. Alonzo squared his shoulders. Miggy jumped to his feet and hustled to stand behind Alonzo as a show of strength. He held a lead pipe in his right hand.

"Remember now, he has the money, but we have the upper hand. Let me do all the talking. Where's your gun?" Alonzo hissed.

"Back of my jeans. Where's yours?"

"Same place. No more talking. Remember, we're going to make nice. At first." Alonzo's tone of voice was full of menace.

"I don't like this," Miggy mumbled.

"Get over it. Be cool. How many times do I have to tell you, the enemy of our enemy is our friend. He came to us, we did not go to him. We have the power in this situation."

Miggy wasn't sure whether that was true, but for now he had no choice but to go along with Alonzo's theory if he wanted unlimited hot water, primo food, and silk sheets.

Mr. Hot Shot, as the Scorpions called him, entered the room and walked up to the makeshift throne in full swagger as if he owned the place. He looked more like someone's neighbor, possibly a postal worker or a man who worked in a supermarket stocking shelves than a criminal mastermind. He had no distinguishing marks. He had no tattoos and no piercings like the two men in front of him. He didn't wear glasses or any jewelry, not even a watch. His clothes were ordinary, off the rack—wrinkled chinos, a long-sleeved Izod T-shirt, and boat shoes. He looked to have a full head of brown hair, with just a tinge of gray at the temples.

Mr. Nobody.

Mr. Somebody.

Mr. Anybody.

Or the man with bags of money.

Just a man with no name except for the name that Alonzo bestowed on him, Mr. Hot Shot. Or so the man thought; but about that, he was so very wrong. Alonzo knew *exactly* who he was, where he lived, and what he did for a living.

Alonzo leaned forward, his eyes as black and shiny as marbles. He squinted now with the sunlight pouring into the stifling room. "Where's my money?" His tone was light and sounded almost playful.

"You botched the job. Cricket is still alive, and it looks like he'll make a full recovery. In other words, you didn't *finish* the job." The voice was strong and angry, conceding nothing to the gang leader.

"My house, my rules. We did the job you requested. You can't blame me for the flock of pigeons that took that particular moment to swoop down to look for food. In my book, that's an act of God. And just for the record, we do not do do-overs, so pay up!"

"Or what?" the man barked.

The light, playful tone disappeared as if by magic. Alonzo laughed, a mean, menacing sound that didn't seem to bother the man standing in front of him.

The meat cleaver, which was razor-sharp, sliced through the air so close to the man's ear that it sounded to the man as if the tide at the ocean had just rushed in before it hit its intended mark on the door frame.

"Or *that!*" Alonzo said, pointing to the wall. Miggy leaped forward, pried out the cleaver, and brought it back to Alonzo. "I missed on purpose. The next time, you might not be so lucky, so we should both agree right now that there will not be a next time. One more time—my house, my rules. Now where's my money?"

The bravado drained from the voice of the man standing in front of him. He started to shake. When he finally spoke, his voice no longer sounded confident. "I don't have any money on me. That should be obvious to you. I'm willing to compromise. I'll pay half of the remaining money, but you have to finish the job."

Alonzo laughed. Miggy joined in the laughter.

"Listen to me, Mr. Hot Shot. I don't *have* to do anything. My boys will escort you to wherever you need to go to get the money, and not half, either. I want the full amount. Didn't your mama ever teach you that a man is only as good as his word? Now, if you want to negotiate a new contract, the price is double. I'm done talking to you. Miggy, escort the man outdoors and have Team Three follow for the handover. Same place as the last time. Don't be late. You have two hours, Mr. Hot Shot!

"Oh, one last thing. Like I said, we do not do do-overs. Your man Cricket is under guard and will be for a long time to come. Right now he's safer than the president of the United States. No one, and I repeat, no one, will be able to get near him. I am not going to risk jail time for my boys to make you happy. Find someone else to do your dirty work. A deal is a deal. And remember this: Our original project is still on the books, so don't mess with me. I don't like it when people try to tell me what to do. And as long as we're having this discussion, I want to remind you that payment for our original contract is due in two weeks. That means the rubber meets the road two weeks from today, at which time I become a rich man. Tell me right now if that's going to be a problem."

"It's not going to be a problem," Hot Shot said through clenched teeth.

"Then you are free to go," Alonzo said imperiously as he waved the meat cleaver back and forth.

Outside in the fresh air, Hot Shot gagged and retched as

he sprinted to his car. Right alongside Hot Shot's dusty Saab SUV, a rusted-out Honda Civic rumbled and wheezed as the driver prepared to follow the SUV with the mud-covered license plates.

Inside the stifling, ramshackle building, Alonzo and Miggy high-fived each other.

"I can almost feel the hot water pouring all over my body from fifty high-powered jets," Alonzo said happily.

"I can't wait to feel those silk sheets," Miggy added, laughing.

"We're almost there," Alonzo said in a hushed voice.

Miggy turned serious and dropped again to his haunches so he was eyeball to eyeball with Alonzo. He licked at his lips, then asked in a harsh whisper, "Do you think we'll have nightmares over this down the road?"

"Absolutely not," Alonzo said.

Miggy wasn't so sure, but he kept his thoughts to himself.

Back at the hotel penthouse suite, the only sounds to be heard were tapping keys and low-voiced cell phone conversations.

The sun was dropping beyond the horizon when Charles called a halt as Jack and Cyrus blew into the room like a hurricane.

"Sorry, guys, I didn't mean to sleep so long, but I was really beat," Jack said by way of apology. "What, if anything, did I miss?"

Charles took the floor. "The last report we've had, and it was from Lizzie herself, said Cosmo was now semiconscious. Dr. Wylie is more than pleased and is still with him. Lizzie said he was trying to talk, but it was just gibberish because he's so full of drugs. She thinks he was trying to say something about Little Jack. He's in and out, as she put it, but Dr. Wylie said that was all right. Both of them are cautiously optimistic. I do believe that is a good sign. In other words, no brain damage."

Jack nodded. "Did that guy Meadows ever call back?"

"No!" Fergus said. "Dennis called again, and just like the other calls, it went right to voice mail. I've lost track of the number of calls we've made to that SOB. Something is not right where that man is concerned."

"What do we know about him? Who was checking him out? Has anyone given any thought to calling in Snowden?"

"That's three questions, Jack. Avery is on his way. He was in Seattle. He might even be here by now since I called him earlier. He's free to go on the payroll. I was just about to call for a status report from the boys when you arrived, so let's hear it, lads," Charles said.

Dennis raised his hand to go first. Charles nodded.

"Background here first. The Nevada Gaming Control Board, also known as the State Gaming Control Board, is a Nevada state governmental agency involved in the regulation of gaming throughout the state, along with the Nevada Gaming Commission. It was founded in 1955 by the Nevada legislature. The Board is composed of three members appointed by the governor. Cosmo is one of those three. Board members serve four-year terms in a full-time capacity.

"The Commission is responsible for administering regulations, granting licenses, and ruling on disciplinary matters brought before it by the Gaming Control Board. It has five members appointed by the governor. Meadows is a member of the Commission, and each commissioner serves a four-year term in a part-time capacity. One member acts as chair. Meadows is the current chair. The Commission is the final authority on licensing matters, having the ability to approve, restrict, limit, condition, deny, revoke, or suspend any gaming license.

"The Commission is also charged with the responsibility of adopting regulations to implement and enforce the state laws governing gambling based on recommendations from the Control Board.

"When the Board believes discipline against a gaming license is appropriate, it acts as prosecutor, while the Commission acts as judge and jury to determine whether any sanctions should be imposed. Cosmo, as a lawyer and former federal prosecutor—like you, Jack—wears two hats."

"Thanks for the tutorial, Dennis, but what does all that mean?" Jack demanded.

"I have no clue, Jack. Maybe Meadows and Cosmo had a falling out over something gambling related. On one hand, since the two of them jointly own the property, he would seem to be on good terms with Cosmo, or at least was on good terms. But on the other hand, professionally speaking, he's chair of the Commission, meaning that he serves as judge and jury when the Control Board prosecutes casinos and the like for infractions of the rules. So you tell me. The guy can't be that busy that he can't return phone calls."

"What about a personal relationship between the two of them? Did anything show up?" Charles asked.

"Aside from their being business partners in Happy Village, I can't find out anything about their personal relationship. I think we'll have to ask Lizzie, but I'm betting she'll say that's Cosmo's business and doesn't carry into their personal lives. We already know that while the Crickets routinely attend celebrations at Happy Village, Meadows doesn't. That certainly makes it sound as if they don't hang out together. Meadows is not married and has no family, as far as I can tell."

"Who is more important? Who carries the most weight in Las Vegas, Cosmo or Meadows?" Fergus asked.

"I would say Cosmo. Cosmo was born and raised here. Vegas takes care of its own, you know that. Meadows came here about eighteen years ago. He's originally from Tennessee. Cosmo was already established and has been honored as Lawyer of the Year for seven straight years. The guy is rock solid and sterling, as they say.

"If you dig deep enough, you'll see that Cosmo is the go-to guy for the casino owners. They respect him, and he's known as being able to 'fix' anything within the law. He is a lawyer, after all. There might be some envy there where Meadows is concerned. By the way, Meadows is also a lawyer."

Jack snorted. "We already know what a great guy Cosmo is, otherwise Lizzie would never have married him. What else do you have?"

"What? What? That's not enough? I'm trying here to learn as much as I can about Meadows, but I've only just gotten started. If that's not good enough for you, Jack, then do it yourself," Dennis snapped.

"Whoa, whoa! Sorry! I didn't mean to step on your toes, kid."

Mollified with Jack's apology, Dennis went back to tapping on his laptop. Jack flapped his hands in the air to indicate his apology a second time just as Ted and Espinosa bounded into the room.

Everyone shouted at once. "What did you find out?" Even Cyrus, who had been silent until then, voiced his question with a loud bark.

"We can sum it up in three words," Ted growled. "We were stonewalled."

"You went to Happy Village?" Jack asked. "I thought . . ."

"Yeah, well, hold those thoughts. We switched up assignments after you left. Espinosa got some good pictures. There was no sign of that guy Gentry Lomax, though we asked. Those senior citizens are a tight-lipped group, and you can't blame them for that. They do not take kindly to having outsiders ask questions. We started at the first apartment building in the complex and worked our way forward. We gave up before we got to the second building. They don't open the doors to anyone, especially the elderly ladies. Even when we showed them our press credentials. The men were a little more cooperative, but not by much.

"The long and short of it is, we came up dry except for one elderly man who remembers Meadows's mother being there, as she was two apartments down from his. He said she was a nice lady and baked the best chocolate cakes. He said she was there only three months before she passed away. He was a little taken aback by that, because he said she walked the complex in the morning and early evening for exercise, rode the stationary cycle at the gym, and swam two laps every day. He said she was fit as a fiddle. Oh, and she was rich. The old gent said someone else told him that but said you'd never know it by the way she dressed and all. Just a nice lady."

Jack frowned. "What did she die from?"

Ted shrugged. "The old gent didn't say other than that she died in her sleep. Contrary to what you might think, that place is not a gossip mill."

"How long ago did she die, did the guy say?"

"He characterized it as 'a while back.' It could be last year or ten years ago. Then he just clammed up, and that was the end of it. I know, I know, I'm going to be checking the obits starting right now," Ted said, sitting down at the dining-room table and opening his laptop.

Chapter 5

Maggie Spritzer stared into her bathroom mirror, wondering who the person staring back at her was. She looked like something the cat had dragged in and forgotten to drag back out. Yes, she'd come down with a killer summer cold, but she'd had colds before that never left her looking like the wrath of God. And she still felt like crap. Five days had passed since she'd taken to her bed with what she'd thought were the sniffles. Then came the fever, then the hacking cough, followed by the chills. She'd bought out the local pharmacy with treat-it-yourself meds. She knew she'd never be able to look at another bowl of chicken soup. Ditto for the garlic tea she'd read about online and Annie touted each time anyone was under the weather. Nothing had really helped, and she was forced to reconcile herself to the fact that the cold—or as she called it, the crud—just had to run its course.

Maggie leaned closer to the mirror to see if her eyes were glazed over and that was the reason she was looking so bedraggled. Nope. No glaze, eyes clear as crystal. She simply looked like hell warmed over. Even a ton of makeup wouldn't help. She smacked the vanity countertop with a balled-up fist, then wished she hadn't when a searing pain raced up her arm to settle in her shoulder.

A shower. Wash her hair. Clean clothes instead of these ratty pajamas she hadn't changed in almost a week. *I am a slob*, she thought as she leaned forward to turn on the shower. She corrected the thought. She wasn't a slob by nature; actually, she was neat and tidy for the most part. But once she'd come down with this rotten crud, she'd become a slob. How had she let that happen? Like she was really going to find the answer in the shower.

Forty minutes later, Maggie stepped out of the shower because she'd used up all the hot water. She dried her hair, brushed her teeth three times, and gargled with Listerine before she dressed in a set of fleece workout clothes even though it was July. It was all about being warm and staying warm, with no comeback chills. She wasn't going anywhere, so it didn't matter what she wore. All she wanted was to feel warm and better. A mere second later, she realized that she did feel better. So much better, her thoughts went to coffee and scrambled eggs, which she made and consumed in record time, her cat Hero watching her from his perch on the windowsill.

Maggie leaned over and turned on the television sitting on her kitchen counter. Time to see what was going on in the real world. She marveled at the fact that she hadn't turned on the set in almost a week. She hadn't checked her e-mail or voice mail either. The world could be coming to an end, and she'd never know. Or care. Just the sound of people talking hurt her head. She also hadn't talked to anyone on the phone. Strange, now that she thought of it, that no one had called her the whole time she was sick. None of the sisters, or the boys. Not even Ted. That was so unlike him. Then she remembered that she'd called in to the *Post*, said she was sick and was taking a few sick days, and the first person who called her or showed up at her door risked being shot. She grimaced at the memory. How weird that they'd taken her at her word. Especially Ted.

Unless he was off on assignment. But that didn't explain mother hens Myra and Annie, who normally would be fussing all over her.

Maggie poured a fresh cup of coffee as she pondered her circumstances. It was Friday. Nothing happened in the newsroom on Friday, or the weekend, for that matter. Especially in the middle of July. Somewhere in the back of her mind, she had a recollection of someone, maybe Annie, telling her to take the entire week off when she'd called in sick. If she was remembering correctly, that meant she had three days, counting today, before she was due back at work on Monday. She worried a stray strand of hair with her index finger as she mentally calculated how many hours she had to while away before she had to report to work on Monday. Counting today, give or take seventy-two. To her way of thinking, that was a lifetime. Almost eternity. She wasn't used to sitting around or being sick. She must be getting old. The thought was very alarming, and she jumped up so fast that Hero hopped off the windowsill and ran for cover.

Right then and there, Maggie decided her life pretty much sucked. Big time.

Maggie knew what she needed to do. Move. Do something besides eat. Maybe she needed some fresh air. Take a walk around the yard. Go outside, sit on the stoop, and wait for a dog walker to go by for some conversation. One look out the window told her that wasn't going to happen, since it was pouring rain.

Maggie plucked her cell phone from the charger to see if she'd had any calls that had gone to voice mail while she'd hibernated. She was stunned to see that she had forty-two messages. Listening to them would eat up an hour. "Better than nothing," she mumbled to herself as she made her way into her family room and flopped down on the couch.

No calls from the sisters or the boys. So they'd done

what she asked them to do; therefore, she couldn't complain. They'd left her alone to her misery. All the calls were from friends, tips on possible happenings, crank calls, political calls. A dental reminder. A call from Hero's vet to say his special cat food had come in and she could pick it up at any time. Well, there was no hurry on that, since she still had at least two weeks' worth in the pantry. Hero wasn't going to starve anytime soon.

Just because she couldn't go back to work until Monday didn't mean she couldn't call the gang. She hit her speed dial and hit the number 1 for Nikki. The call went to voice mail. Ditto Alexis. Okay, that probably meant they were in court. She called Yoko, and the phone just rang and rang. Knowing Yoko, she'd probably left the phone someplace and couldn't hear it ring. Isabelle was next on the speed dial, but a robotic voice came on saying her phone was timed out. Whatever that meant. The next call went to Kathryn, who picked up on the second ring. All Maggie could hear her saying was that she couldn't hear her and she was in a dead zone.

Maggie looked at the phone in her hand. Surely Myra or Annie would respond. She called Annie first. When Annie clicked on, Maggie sighed so loud that Hero popped his head out from under a pillow where he was hiding to stare at his mistress.

"How are you, dear? Are you feeling better?"

"I am. By Monday I should be good as new. Is everything okay? Anything going on? Did I miss anything?"

Annie debated telling her star reporter about Cosmo but decided it would only upset Maggie to hear about it. "No, dear, everything is fine. Just take care of yourself and don't overdo anything. Rest. Eat lots of chicken soup, and don't forget the garlic tea. You'll be right as rain if you do that."

"Yes, Mom," Maggie drawled. "Say hi to the girls for me."

"Well, that was a bust, Hero," Maggie said, as the tawny cat leaped onto her lap and started to purr. "I guess I can call the guys. Maybe they're up to something. You never know where they're concerned. I think I'll call Ted first."

Maggie hit the number 7 on her speed dial and was stunned when Ted picked up on the first ring. "Good Lord, where are you? It sounds like an amusement park."

"Vegas, baby," Ted said flippantly.

"Las Vegas! And you didn't tell me! What are you doing there?" Maggie screeched so loud that Hero flew off her lap.

"Give me five minutes to find a place that's a little more quiet and I'll call you back. Are you okay?"

"If I wasn't okay, I wouldn't be calling you," Maggie snapped. "This better be good, Ted."

"What? What? You specifically said not to call you or show up, and if any of us did, you would shoot us. Those are your exact words, Maggie. I just did what you insisted that everyone do. Now, give me five minutes and I'll call you right back."

Maggie had the good grace to wince at Ted's words. Yes, she did say that, and at the time she sort of, kind of, meant it, but Ted knew her. He should have at least *tried* to call her after three days. She seethed, then started to chew on her thumbnail, a terrible habit she'd had since childhood.

Five minutes went by, then ten, and finally fifteen before Maggie's cell pinged. She clicked it on bullet fast. "So what are you doing in Vegas?"

Maggie could hear Ted suck in a deep breath. "Well, you know we all went to Reno for the martial arts competition with Harry. We talked about that before we left, so don't go saying you didn't know about it," Ted said testily.

"Okay, okay, yes, you did, but Reno is not Las Vegas."

"Of course it isn't. Jack heard on the radio that some big VIP in Vegas got gunned down, and he said from what he heard he thought it was Cosmo Cricket. So on that alone we came here to see if Jack was right, and he was. This is Vegas, and they didn't mention names. Someone shot up Cosmo pretty bad. He's had two operations and is in the ICU. He almost died, Maggie, that's how bad it was. Is, actually. Lizzie is with him. They weren't sure whether he'd make it. The surgeon is cautiously optimistic. That's all I know, Maggie."

"And you didn't think that was important enough to tell me, Ted? How could you do that? I could have been praying for him all this time. That's just cruel of you. Plain old cruel," Maggie said tearfully. "How is Lizzie holding up? Why aren't the girls there with her?"

"She doesn't want anyone, Maggie. Just like you didn't want anyone. We were already here, so she has to put up with us. There's no point in getting upset, since there's nothing you could do even if you knew or even if you were here. We're all just more or less trying to find our way ourselves. No one seems to have the skinny on how or even why Cosmo was shot. Lizzie is totally clueless."

"You need me there," Maggie said. "More to the point, I want to be there."

"Yes, we do," Ted responded smartly. "Do you want me to ask Dennis if he can get his Gulfstream fired up to bring you here?"

"What kind of idiotic question is that? I can be ready in ten minutes."

"You sure you're up to it?"

Maggie clenched her teeth. "I'm up to it. Call me when the plane is ready, and I'm out the door."

Maggie popped up off the couch like her legs were spring-loaded. She had a bag packed in ten minutes, her backpack replenished, and notified her cat sitter that she was going out of town and to take over Hero's care. "Suddenly, I feel like a million bucks," she mumbled to herself as she made her way to the family room.

While she wasn't a bona fide Sister or a bona fide member of the guy team, she fit in right down the middle, which meant she helped out both sides whenever her help was needed. They all jokingly called her Miz Switzerland, meaning she was neutral and didn't favor the sisters over the boys or vice versa. The only thing any of them cared about was that Maggie could be trusted.

Maggie chewed her nails down to the nub while she waited for the call to leave for the airport. She hated waiting for anything. Patience was simply not in her DNA.

Eight hours later, Maggie ran across the tarmac at Mc-Carran International Airport in Las Vegas, straight into Ted Robinson's waiting arms. He hugged her fiercely, and she hugged him back just as fiercely.

"I'm glad you're here, Maggie," Ted whispered in her ear. "You sure you feel okay and are up to whatever is going to go down here?" he continued to whisper.

"I slept the whole trip. I'm hydrated, and I finished the last of my medicine. I'm good to go, Ted. This is just what I need. One more day cooped up in the house and they would be locking me up somewhere."

"As long as you're sure. Dennis has your schedule all mapped out for you. That kid is so generous, he blows my mind. Who do you know besides Annie who would send his Gulfstream to fly cross-country for one passenger? No one, that's who. But like he said, he inherited the money, and he still has trouble thinking of it as his. But he's willing to treat it as his if it can be used to do good for other people. My kind of guy. And he's a hell of a good reporter in the bargain."

"You're just saying that because you're his idol," Maggie teased. "Now, tell me what happened here. Tell me everything and don't leave out anything. I want to hear it all, every last word. Is everyone okay with my being here?" Maggie asked, her tone anxious, which surprised Ted.

"Everyone is more than okay with your being here. We've all been worried about you. We need your female input and viewpoint. We know very little because Lizzie knows nothing and is so consumed with Cosmo's condition that even if she did know something, she can't remember it. She refuses to leave Cosmo's bedside. Jack and Harry literally forced her home to shower, sleep, and eat. The last thing I heard was via Charles, who said the surgeon—a personal friend of Cosmo's, by the way—was also at his side. Cosmo had to be taken back to surgery a second time. I think he's out of the ICU, but I'm not sure. Jack said Cosmo was trying to talk about Little Jack. That, to me, is a good sign."

"Speaking of Little Jack, where is he? Who's taking care of him?"

"Summer sleepaway camp. He doesn't know anything, and Lizzie wants to keep it that way. Jack has been in daily contact with the boy."

Maggie closed her eyes and listened to Ted's reporter voice. Just the facts, ma'am. She was taking in and storing away all of Ted's words so she could piece together her own version to make it work for her.

"I'm having a hard time believing Cosmo has enemies. That someone would try to kill him. Whoever it was must be a novice if they had to shoot four or five times and not kill him. Or Cosmo is the luckiest man walking the planet. Does he have enemies? I don't know why I thought this, but I thought guys like Cosmo traveled with security. This is Vegas, after all. I must have heard that somewhere," Maggie fretted.

"We don't know. Lizzie doesn't really know much about the inner workings of her husband's job, and she knows zip about Happy Village. She did say that if she had to guess, she would say no, he did not have enemies. No one that we've talked to said anything about Cosmo's having security. Think about it, Maggie. A big guy like Cosmo would scare the hell out of anyone. At least the kind of enemy who does not kill people. We're talking gangs here. Then there's Happy Village. Add Zack Meadows, his fellow gaming regulator and coinvestor, who will not call us back, and that's where we are at the moment."

"Who's doing what?"

"The usual drill. Abner drove because of his ear problems with flying. Cyrus made the trip with him. He's doing what he does best, hacking wherever he can to find out whatever he can. I think he's hitting some stone walls. Remember, this is Vegas—better security than the White House. It's Vegas, baby, land of secrets," Ted said, his tone sour. "Just so you know, they hate reporters out here, especially reporters from back East."

Maggie hated the word *secrets*. She wanted—no, she *needed*—to know everything. That word simply was not in her vocabulary. "Well, we'll just see about that," she huffed. "What else?"

"Charles and Fergus set up headquarters in Annie's penthouse. We're all staying at Babylon. Dennis booked you a room. Charles called in Avery Snowden. He's here, I'm told, but I haven't seen him myself. When I left to pick you up, Jack and Espinosa were up at the penthouse, but I have no clue what they're doing."

"That leaves Harry. What is he doing? How did the martial arts trials in Reno go? Did he win?"

"Does the Pope pray? Of course he won, and so did his

guys. He's giving his five pals a tour of Vegas. They love gambling. Great guys. Those trials were something else. We were all mesmerized. If I told you those five guys with Harry and Jack leading the pack could take on an army, would you believe me?"

"Well, yeah, Ted. This is Harry and Jack we're talking about here. What's not to believe?"

"Okay, we're here. I'll drop you off at the front, park, and meet you up at the penthouse. You look tired, Maggie, and it's getting late your time. Say your hellos and go to bed. Don't overdo your first day here. We'll hit the ground running in the morning. You okay with that?"

Maggie was more than okay with it. She said so, to Ted's relief.

Once she reached the penthouse, she could feel herself starting to wilt, and if there was one thing she didn't need, it was a setback. Even though she'd slept the entire flight, she did feel tired. Maybe she'd had the flu and not just a summer cold. Maybe a lot of things. She was on the mend now, and there was no reason for her to slack off. She closed her eyes for a moment as she remembered Myra once telling her to pay attention to what your body is trying to tell you, and in this case, her body was telling her it was time to call it a day.

The meet and greet over, Maggie looked around and announced she would see them all in the morning, but right now she needed to go to sleep. Hugs, well wishes, and a few jokes later, Cyrus escorted her to the door but not before her eagle eye zeroed in on Abner Tookus. *Something is off*, she thought the moment Abner's eyes met hers. She wrestled with the strange expression on Abner's face, one she'd never seen there in all the years she'd known him, and they went way, way back. Maggie felt she knew Abner better than his wife, Isabelle, knew him.

Damn it, what was that strange expression? It came to

her only when she stepped out of the elevator onto the floor where her room was located. *Fear, that's what it is. Pure, unadulterated fear.* She started to shake and whirled around to step back into the elevator, but it was already going down. Abner didn't know the meaning of the word *fear* as far as his hacking abilities went. Plus, he had his backup guru in Philonias Needlemeyer. So where was the fear coming from? No answer found its way to her tired brain. Tomorrow was another day.

Maggie dumped her bags, stripped down, then crawled into the king-size bed without washing her face or brushing her teeth. She was asleep within seconds.

Maggie cracked one eyelid, saw the blood-red numbers 4:00 on her travel clock, and groaned. She could sleep for three more hours if she wanted to. She quickly calculated that she'd fallen asleep around nine-thirty Vegas time, which means twelve-thirty back East. Not enough sleep. Or was it? She squeezed her eyes shut, took a deep breath, and let it out slowly as she willed herself back to sleep. When she next opened her eyes the little clock said that it was nine o'clock.

It was definitely time to get up.

An hour later, with a robust room service breakfast and a shower under her belt, Maggie was ready to go. As in *go.* With that thought in mind, Maggie barreled out of the room and hit the penthouse apartment in record time.

Maggie blinked, then blinked again at what she was seeing. The penthouse could have passed for the war room back in the dungeons of Pinewood. The gang waved absentmindedly, but it was Cyrus who gave her the warmest welcome. He woofed softly and nuzzled her hand. Maggie fluffed his ears and dropped to her knees to whisper in his ear, telling him she had missed him and was sorry that she didn't have any treats. Cyrus stared at her for a long minute before he trotted back to where Jack was sitting.

Maggie threw her hands high in the air. She hated being ignored. "What can I do?" she bellowed. And then she remembered what had disturbed her the night before. "Where's Abner?" she bellowed again.

"When I got here at seven o'clock, he wasn't here," Dennis volunteered.

"I think he worked all night. Said he was onto something, so I would imagine he either found whatever he was looking for or just fizzled out and went to get some sleep. Why?" Ted mumbled, never taking his eyes off his keyboard.

As far as she was concerned, Maggie felt she was still being ignored. She puckered her lips and let loose with a whistle so sharp it drowned out Cyrus's loud bark of stunned surprise.

"Good! Good! Now that I have your attention, I'd like to say something."

"So say it already," Jack said.

"It's about Abner." The room went totally silent.

"What about him?" Charles asked, his face a mask of sudden concern.

"That's just it, Charles. I don't know." Maggie quickly related what she'd seen, sensed, and felt as she'd locked eyes with Abner before leaving the penthouse to go to her room the previous night.

"That's it! You think you saw fear on Abner's face. You were tired, Maggie. Maybe you—" Jack started to say.

"Don't even go there, Jack," Maggie snapped. "I've known Abner Tookus forever, and I know what I saw, so don't try to placate me." She looked around, her facial expression one of frustration. "Dennis said Avery Snowden was here. Where is he?"

"I do believe he left either with Abner or shortly afterward. That would be around two this morning. I'm not sure of the exact time," Charles said with a baffled look. "What are you reading into this, Maggie?" His tone was neither unkind nor accusing, and Maggie accepted it for what it was—genuine concern.

"Like I said, I've known Abner for a very long time. We all know he has no fear, no equal except for that guy Phil he hacks with, so why would he suddenly be fearful? I think he found out something and maybe shared it with Snowden, and Abner is waiting for his buddy Phil to get back to him. Whatever it is, it must be pretty terrible. Let's all remember where we are and how much money changes hands in this town every single day of the year."

Fergus Duffy leaned forward. "What would you like us to do, Maggie?"

Maggie's arms flapped in the air. "I don't know. I just got here. Send someone to wake him up. If he left at two, then he's had enough sleep. Someone call Snowden and see what he's up to or what he can tell us. I know he just got here too, but usually he has people everywhere and has a bead on things while we're still just thinking about it. Something. Anything. I know I'm not wrong. I know it!" she hissed.

Espinosa volunteered to head out to find Abner, while Charles could be seen pressing the digits on his special phone.

Maggie sucked in her breath and waited, watching Charles grimace as his call went to voice mail. She listened as he left a message for the old spy to return his call as soon as possible.

The room went silent.

Dennis broke the silence. "I could be wrong, and this is little more than a guess on my part, but I think Abner was on the dark web last night. I think he found out something that scared the *bejesus* out of him. Maggie's right when she says she saw fear in his expression. I noticed it too, but at the time it simply didn't register, and I haven't known Abner as long as the rest of you. I think he found out something, and he's reaching out to his friend Phil and maybe some other people he knows who . . . who are perhaps more proficient in dealing with the dark web. When you travel the dark web, you need to know what you're doing, and if you just dabble in it, you can suddenly find yourself in a whole boatload of deep trouble. If he somehow managed to get to the underbelly of the dark side, then we all need to be concerned. That much I do know because I've heard the horror stories. This is just my opinion, so treat it as such."

Maggie patted the young reporter's arm to show she totally understood what he'd said.

Cyrus ran to the door just as Espinosa opened it. "Abner is not in his room. I had one of the maids working the hall check in the room, and he's not there. The bed was slept in, all his gear is still there, but he's gone."

"Where does that leave us?" Ted demanded.

"Right where we were before Maggie arrived. Nowhere, that's where," Jack said.

Maggie flapped her arms again. "What? We're just going to sit here and wait till Snowden calls back or Abner decides to honor us with his company? We need to do something. What was the plan before I got here? Jeez, do I have to do *everything?*"

Charles rustled the papers in front of him. He cleared his throat and looked around the table at everyone. "This is the plan for now. With Maggie here, I think she and Dennis should go to Happy Village and interview the residents. Don't take no for an answer. Be as persuasive as possible. Jack and Ted will also be going to Happy Village to talk to Mr. Gentry Lomax and Mrs. Love. With Harry temporarily out of the picture, Fergus and I will head on out to see if we can arrange an interview with Mr. Meadows and try to find out why he hasn't returned our calls or if he's avoiding us. We need an answer to that. Espinosa is going to hold down the fort, so to speak, in case Avery or Abner returns. He will be checking in with Dr. Wylie and Lizzie on the hour to see if there are any changes in Cosmo's condition. If so, he will inform us ASAP, and we'll do whatever we have to do. Any questions?"

There were no questions.

"Then let's get to it," Charles said, smacking his hands together. "Everyone check in with Espinosa at one o'clock."

Cyrus was the first one at the door. His lean body quivered with excitement. At last, *action*.

Chapter 6

Lizzie Fox gently brushed at her husband's dark hair tinged with gray. Only God knew how much she loved this man. Tears rested on her lashes before rolling down her cheeks as she prayed, the same words over and over and over again. *Please, God. Don't let my husband die, please, God.* She brushed at her wet cheeks, aware of how quiet the room was except for the machines that beeped, pinged, and purred. She didn't mind the noise and had tuned it out days ago. Right now she was aware only of a presence in the corner of the room—Joe Wylie, aka Cowboy, her husband's doctor and personal friend. Like her, Wylie had not left the room since Cosmo's second surgery. Such a kind man. Like Cosmo.

Tears continued to spill down Lizzie's cheeks and sparkled like diamonds in the dim light overhead. She reached for her husband's hand and felt it tighten against her own. Lizzie gasped when she saw Cosmo open his eyes.

"Angel."

At least, that's what she thought he said. Joe Wylie was at his beside in the time it took her to take a deep breath, checking his vitals and then making a joke. "Hey, big guy, you ready for some racquetball?"

Lizzie was beside herself. "Joe, does this mean . . ."

"Shhh. Let's see where this goes, Lizzie. Easy, slow and easy. Don't do or say anything to alarm him."

"Water." The sound was strangled, but Joe understood.

"Ha! Figured you for a scotch-on-the-rocks guy," Joe said as he poured water into a glass and added a flexible straw.

Water dribbled down Cricket's chin. He didn't seem to notice as he tried to suck on the straw. "Okay, that's enough for now. Don't want you throwing up."

Another strangled, mangled sound. "Cowboy?"

"Yep, it's me in the flesh. I'm taking care of you. We can talk more later, but right now I want you to sleep. It's the best medicine in the world."

Lizzie felt her hand being squeezed. She smiled through her tears. "I'm here too. Do what Joe said. Sleep. I'll be here when you wake up." Another squeeze, this one lighter. Her husband's hand, which was as big as a catcher's mitt, felt dry and papery while her own was damp and clammy. She used both hands to squeeze back.

"Okay, he's out. And so are you, Lizzie. I want you to go home and get some rest. I'm going to take a shower and catch a few winks myself. Don't say it. There will be a doctor and a nurse in this room at all times. We're both going on pure adrenaline right now. Neither one of us will be any good to Cosmo if we can't function."

Lizzie looked up at the tall, gangly doctor, tears still shimmering in her eyes. "Does that mean he's out of the woods?"

"Let's just say he's at the edge and getting closer to the clearing. I wouldn't leave him if I thought otherwise. You need to do your part now and do what I tell you. Tell me you understand, Lizzie."

Lizzie brushed the silvery hair back from her forehead. "I hear you, and I understand you. I have to find a way to get home. I think Jack has my car. When can I come back?"

"Tomorrow."

Lizzie squealed her displeasure. Joe remained adamant until Lizzie simply nodded to show she would obey his orders.

"I don't think you need to worry about a ride home. There are two . . . ah . . . portly gentlemen waiting right outside this door. Friends of yours, I assume. I think I saw them yesterday."

Lizzie nodded. Her eyes searched those of the tall man standing in front of her. "You're sure, Joe?"

"Look at me, Lizzie. I'm a doctor, not God. I am as sure as I can be as a doctor that it is okay for you to leave. Your husband is in good hands. Now, goddamn it, *GO!*"

Lizzie struggled to offer up a weak smile. "Okay, Joe, I'm going. Call me if anything changes."

"You got it."

Outside her husband's hospital room, Lizzie literally fell into Charles's and Fergus's arms. "Can you take me home?"

"Of course. That's why we're here, to help," Charles said. "Might I make a suggestion, Lizzie?" She nodded. "Instead of going home and being alone, why don't you come back with us to Babylon?"

Lizzie shook her head. "I have to go home. I need my . . . I need to feel close to my husband. I want to hug his pillow. I want to sit in his chair. The house is alarmed out the kazoo, Cosmo made sure of that. I'll be fine, truly, Charles, I will. I just need to be alone right now."

"Do you want us or just one of us to stay with you?" Fergus asked.

"Please don't take this the wrong way, but I need to be alone. I need to think. I need to . . ." Lizzie tossed her head from side to side, her hands flapping in the air. "I need to get back to being who I am so I can deal with . . . with all this."

"Totally understood, Lizzie. We're just a phone call away if you need us."

"And I appreciate it. Tell me what you've all been doing. Has anyone found out anything?"

"Well, for starters, Maggie is here; she arrived yesterday. I'm not sure whether you knew about that. Right now she's with Dennis at Happy Village. The boys decided that those two had the best chance of talking to the senior citizens, who as a rule do not talk to strangers. If anyone can get them to open up and actually talk, assuming they have something to say, it's young Dennis, with Maggie at his side." Lizzie smiled wanly and nodded to show she was in agreement.

"Ted and Jack are also on their way to Happy Village to talk to Gentry Lomax and his assistant, Bessie Love, the ones in charge of the day-to-day operations at the complex.

"Harry is with his friends from the martial arts trials, showing them around Vegas. He's just a phone call away if needed.

"Avery is here, and I'm not one hundred percent sure about this, but I think he has teamed up with Abner. Both men seem to have gone off the grid, and we are not sure why. We think, and I stress the word *think*, that they both started to explore the dark side of the web and are not sure of their next move. I'm sure that Abner has enlisted the aid of his . . . ah . . . fellow hacker, the one he calls Phil. But that's all we know right now.

"Mr. Zack Meadows, your husband's partner in the ownership of Happy Village, has not seen fit to return our numerous phone calls, and that's starting to bother all of us. An eyeball-to-eyeball meeting is on the agenda. It was our job this morning, before coming here, to see if we could speak with him. We called, and of course the call went to voice mail, as did all the others. We tried calling the office, but the person who answered just said Mr. Meadows was not available and asked if we wanted to leave a message. We did. At that point, Fergus and I decided there was no point in fighting this abominable traffic just to be told that the man was unavailable, so we came here.

"Joseph is manning the apartment. Everyone checks in hourly with him, and we're to meet up at one o'clock, but if that isn't physically possible, then people will call in. I think that brings us pretty much up-to-date, and I regret that we don't have more to report. But rest assured, we are working it. We'll figure it all out, then take the appropriate action. We're dealing, I suspect, with gangs and some turf warfare."

"We're here," Fergus blurted as he swung the car into Lizzie's paved driveway, where the silver Mercedes Jack and Harry had borrowed and obviously returned was sitting. Both men got out and walked Lizzie to the door.

Lizzie hugged both men before she unlocked the door. She thanked them for bringing her home, her eyes filling with tears. The last thing she said before she closed the door was a heartfelt whispered "Find those bastards and make them pay for what they did to my husband." Fergus and Charles simply nodded.

"She'll be fine, mate," Fergus said on the way back to the car. "When we see her next, she'll be ready to take on the whole world. That is one woman you don't ever, as in ever, want to go up against. Especially when she's in top form. These past few days blindsided her. Stronger people than Lizzie would have crumpled too. Now she's mentally where she goes before she hits that courtroom to fight for her clients. This time, though, she's fighting for the love of her life, and I, for one, would not want to be on the other end of whatever she decides to do."

Charles agreed. "I guess it's back to Babylon to do

whatever we can. There must be someone who can turn us on to the group they call the Cavaliers to see what they're all about. Call Joseph to see if anyone has checked in or if he knows anything."

Five minutes later, Fergus shook his head. "Quiet as a church, in his words, mate. Meaning nothing has happened and no one has called in."

"Guess they need us to liven things up. What's your feeling on all of this, Ferg?"

Fergus shivered and hugged his arms across his chest. "Nothing good, that's for sure. I keep thinking about what Maggie said about Abner, and now he's off the grid. That's what happens when you mess around with the dark web. It's evil, Charles. Not for the likes of you or me or the boys. We don't live in that kind of world. I'm not sure we're equipped to take on the likes of what dwells in the underbelly of the dark web."

"Good will win out over evil every time, Ferg," Charles said. His tone of voice, however, sounded less than reassuring to Fergus, who simply shook his head and stared out the window. His thinking was, there was a first time for everything.

Back at the hotel casino, Charles turned his car over to the valet parking attendant, and the two men rode the elevator to Annie's penthouse suite. They looked expectantly at Espinosa, whose first word was *"Nada."*

Less than seven miles away as the crow flies, Maggie was ringing the doorbell of the first apartment building in Happy Village. When there was no answer, she rang the bell again and kept her finger pressed hard on the round button. "I'm staying here until someone opens this door. These people need to know we're the good guys, and I'm the one who is going to rally them together so they understand we mean no harm. You with me, Dennis?"

"Of course I am. It's not me you need to be concerned about. We have to win them over, and I think we can do that, but first they need to open the door."

Maggie leaned closer to the door, sensing that somebody was standing on the other side. She told herself she was a reporter and knew things like that. Besides, it was what she would do if she were the person on the other side of the door. She removed her thumb from the doorbell and gave it three zippy little taps. The bell bonged inside. Finally, she heard a voice say, "Who is it?"

"My name is Maggie Spritzer, and this is my partner, Dennis West. Mrs. Cricket asked us to come here to talk to you. Please, open the door. We can talk out here if that is more comfortable for you. I was hoping you'd invite us in for a cup of tea so we could talk."

No one was more surprised than Maggie and Dennis when the door opened and a pink-cheeked lady who looked to be in her early seventies, with pearl-white hair and wearing a purple-flowered dress, smiled at them. "Come in. A person living alone these days can't be too careful. We have classes here about how older people get taken advantage of. Mr. Cricket takes good care of us, along with those lovely young men of the Cavaliers. Still, we have to be alert at all times. That's why we all wear what Mr. Cricket calls our magic buttons," the woman said, pulling a chain out from under her dress. A white square with a blood-red cross in the middle served as the button. "And we don't have to pay for this service either. Help comes in under five minutes if we press the button."

"That's wonderful," Maggie said sincerely. Dennis nodded his agreement.

"Well, now that you're here, were you serious about wanting a cup of tea? I have some nice blackberry tea I save for guests. I get it from a specialty shop."

"No, not really. We just want to talk to you, Mrs. . . . I didn't get your name, ma'am," Maggie said.

"Frances Gossett. Well then, we can sit in the parlor and talk," the little lady said primly as she led the way down a short hallway to a neat-as-a-pin parlor with comfortable furniture. A fat tabby cat stared at them before it leaped off the sofa to land in Frances Gossett's arms. She laughed out loud as she hugged the fat cat. "I don't know how I can help you, but ask me whatever it is you came here to ask me."

Dennis spoke first. "Let's just cut to the chase and you tell us what, if anything, you know about the shooting that took place here, the one that landed Cosmo Cricket in the hospital fighting for his life."

Frances Gossett looked as if she was going to cry. "That's just it. I don't know anything. I was watching my soap opera, and I keep the TV turned up high because my hearing isn't what it used to be. To be honest with you, I'm vain enough not to want to wear hearing aids. I found out only when the ambulances swooped in, and Sawdust here about jumped out of his skin. In case you're interested in his strange name, I named him Sawdust because he used to like to stay with my husband in his woodworking shop, and he'd come into the house all covered in sawdust. However, I digress. I saw all the flashing lights through the windows and went outside to see what was happening. It's not all that unusual to see an ambulance here. We are, after all, a community of elderly people.

"All my neighbors from this building were already outside when I got there, and they didn't know anything other than that someone was shot. None of us knew that it was Mr. Cricket—who, by the way, is just the loveliest man in the world. Later, when we found out it was Mr. Cricket who had been shot, we all gathered in the chapel to pray. The police questioned all of us for hours and hours, but none of us could tell them anything. The police still have a presence here, and Porter, my next-door neighbor, told me that the police set up what he called a command post in a room off the main office, where Gentry Lomax and Bessie work. They more or less run the day-to-day business here at Happy Village.

"Now, I can't speak for the tenants in the other buildings, but I think I would have heard something by now if any of them saw or heard something. You'll have to talk to them directly."

Maggie smiled as the cat in Frances Gossett's arms purred so loudly she could hear it from across the room.

"What about the Cavaliers?" Dennis queried.

"Lionel? He wasn't here that day. But I think Gentry or Bessie called him, and he came over with his group later on. He checks on us three times a day. Or I should say his group does. Lionel is what we refer to here at Happy Village as our in-house security. Mr. Cricket pays him and his crew out of his own pocket to watch over us."

"Are you aware that Mr. Cricket has a partner where this complex is concerned? His name is Zack Meadows."

Frances Gossett's head bobbed up and down. "I know of him, but I have never laid eyes on him. I think his mother lived here at one point. At least that's what I heard. Contrary to what you might have heard about us old people, we do not gossip. No one talks about him. They just talk about Mr. Cricket."

"How long have you lived here, Mrs. Gossett?"

"I moved here five years ago, after my husband Ralph died. I had to wait seven months for an available apartment."

"How do you or the others get in touch with Lionel or his crew?" Maggie asked.

"We just call him, and someone shows up. Sometimes it's Lionel, and sometimes it's someone else. Lionel's mama lives here in Building Three. That's the building on the corner of Primrose Avenue and Lilac Lane."

"What do you think happened here, Mrs. Gossett? Do you know what the tenants think? Was Mr. Cricket at the wrong place at the wrong time? Someone must have seen or heard something. We know there are gangs all about, but we were told Happy Village was off-limits even though it had once been gang-held territory. Do the Scorpions come out in broad daylight? Do you think they're behind this?" Dennis asked all in one long, drawn-out breath.

Frances Gossett stopped stroking the purring cat to throw her arms in the air. "That's just it, we don't know. It's as if we were all struck deaf, dumb, and blind that particular day. I wish it weren't so, but I can't change what happened. I will tell you this—everyone in this building meets up at the chapel every day at four o'clock to pray for Mr. Cricket."

Maggie looked at Dennis, who just stared at her. His look said, *I think we got all we're going to get out of this lady.* Maggie stood up and offered her hand to Frances Gossett. "I would appreciate it if you'd give me Lionel's phone number, if you don't mind."

"Not at all, dear. I'm sure he'll help you if he can. He's studying to be a lawyer. Everyone in his group attends classes the casino owners pay for. At least that's what I was told." Sawdust jumped off her lap and raced out of the room. Frances got up and walked over to a small secretary, then rooted around until she found a small white card that had three inked-in phone numbers on it. "The top number is Lionel's, the second one is Sula's, and the third is Andy's. All lovely young men. They all treat us like we're their grandparents. It makes us feel safe. You can tell them I gave you the card. I have another one."

"Thank you for talking to us, Mrs. Gossett," Maggie

said as she led the way to the front door, Dennis right behind her.

"Ah, young lady, there is one other thing you might be interested in." The little woman in the flowered dress let her hands flutter in the air as her facial expression turned worried.

Those words were just what Maggie wanted to hear. She whirled around so fast she nearly lost her footing. "What?" she all but screeched.

Taken aback, Frances Gossett stepped back and stared at Maggie. She cleared her throat. "I don't know if it means anything, but I have been concerned simply because when I asked questions, no one had any answers to give me."

Maggie clenched her teeth. She wanted her to say it, spit it out already. Instead, she took a deep breath and then said, "What questions would that be, Mrs. Gossett?" She could feel Dennis's hot breath on her neck as he inched closer to make sure he didn't miss a word.

"It really is none of my business, but Ellie and I were friends of a sort. We were bingo buddies, and we always sat together when we took the jitney to the casino for lunch. We do that one day a week, you know. Each week, it's a different casino, and it's free to all of us."

"And . . ." Maggie prodded gently.

"Ellie Harper was her name. She was . . . is a widow like me. She lives at 202 Lilac Lane. Well, she did live there, but she's gone. She never said good-bye, and she didn't leave a note. It was like she disappeared into thin air. No one knows what happened to her. I wanted to file a police report, but Gentry Lomax said he would do that. I assume he did, but nothing came of it. Bessie Love said the police said Ellie probably just got tired of this place and moved on. I don't believe that for a minute. Ellie loved it here, and I know for a fact she had paid her rent through the end of the year. Her husband left her very well-off. She even had a *portfolio*." It sounded to Maggie's ears as if to Frances Gossett, a financial portfolio was right up there with the Holy Grail.

"Does she have a family?" Dennis asked.

"No. She had a son, but he died of leukemia years ago. People our age simply do not walk off into the sunset. Our goal is security. We like to surround ourselves with pets and friends, and Ellie was no different. I think something happened to her, and no one cares. That's what I think," Frances Gossett said, and sniffed.

"When did she leave?" Maggie asked.

"April 17 was the last time I heard from her. We were supposed to take the jitney to the dollar store, but she didn't show up at the clubhouse. That's where we board the jitney. When we got back, I went over to her apartment; I have a key, and she has one to my place too. I let myself in, but she wasn't there. Everything looked normal. Nothing was out of place. I felt like a sneak going through her things, but I felt as if I had to do it. I couldn't tell whether anything was missing. Her purse wasn't there. Ellie had this . . . what I call a satchel that she carried everything in—her knitting, personal things—and it was gone, and so was her cell phone. There was quite a bit of food in her refrigerator, and her pantry was well stocked. Her bed was made too. She had no pets, said she didn't want the responsibility of taking care of an animal.

"I went back every day for a week. I called her cell phone at least a hundred times during that week, then I asked Gentry Lomax to look into it."

Maggie felt like pumping her fist in the air. At last, something to sink her teeth into. She was about to ask a question when Mrs. Gossett continued, "And that's not all. Other people have left here in more or less the same way. My next-door neighbor Porter said his friend Will left too. He reported it the same way I did. Nothing came of it, either. Will's unit is also empty. Will was some bigwig in Silicon Valley, and he moved here, Porter said, about two years ago. Meaning he was wealthy. I don't know if he paid his rent ahead of time like Ellie did or not. That's one of the reasons Gentry gave for not being able to do anything. His mantra was they were free agents, older than twenty-one, in good health, and not answerable to anyone but themselves. Porter has a key to Will's place, and he still checks it every day, hoping to find that Will has come back. He and Porter used to play chess every day, and he misses him. It's hard to lose a friend. I miss Ellie terribly and am so glad I have Sawdust. Do you think you can do anything about this, young lady? Do you think it might have something to do with Mr. Cricket's getting shot?"

"I'm not sure what I think at the moment. So that's two missing tenants, and no one has done anything, is that what you're saying?" Maggie asked tightly.

"No, there's more. At least fifteen others who have gone missing, I think, but I don't know any of the details. I heard about the others at bingo during conversations that were casual. While I said we don't gossip, we don't. But when someone . . . ah . . . passes on, we talk about it, or when someone new moves in, we talk about welcoming them. That kind of thing."

"Would you be comfortable giving me the key to Ellie's apartment, Mrs. Gossett? I'll be sure to return it, and I will keep it safe until I do."

"I don't have a problem with that, dear. I keep it in my jewelry box. I'll fetch it for you."

Maggie was ready to jump out of her skin. Dennis shifted from one foot to the other. "Holy crap, Maggie, what did we just step into?"

"I wish I knew," Maggie mumbled as her mind raced at warp speed.

"Here you go, young lady," Frances Gossett said as she held out a shiny brass key. "You should talk to Porter. He lives right next door. I can call him if you like. Otherwise, he might not open the door when you ring his bell. He's a very nice man. He lives to play chess, and he's lost without his partner."

"Absolutely," Dennis said.

They waited while Mrs. Gossett returned to the kitchen to make the call. She was smiling when she returned. "Porter said he would be happy to talk to you. Thank you for stopping by," she said primly as she held the door open for Maggie and Dennis.

Maggie and Dennis stood for a minute outside the door as they heard all three locks snap into place. "I think it's the apartment to the left," Dennis said. He was proved right when they saw the door open and a man with gray hair and stooped shoulders step out. He looked to be in his midseventies. He wore a Vegas T-shirt that said WINNER on the front, baggy jeans, and boat shoes. "Come on in," he said cheerfully.

Maggie and Dennis were both stunned to see that the apartment was spotless. Delicious aromas wafted from the kitchen, including the smell of fresh-brewed coffee. "What?" He cackled. "You think only women know how to keep a tidy ship? My wife taught me everything I know." He cackled again. "I know how to cook, and I know how to clean. Coffee? I grind the beans myself. Ester says I make the best coffee she's ever had. Take a load off," he said, motioning to the chairs at a round oak table. "Tell me how I can help you. I can multitask—something else my wife taught me," he said as he got cups from the cabinet and poured coffee.

Dennis took the lead this time with hand flourishes along with elated and sour expressions. "And that's where we are. Mrs. Cricket asked us to look into things. Tell us anything you can that might help us figure out what is going on here, because clearly something is going on."

Porter Flannery, retired college professor, talked non-stop for twenty minutes. Maggie and Dennis finished their coffee just as he wound down. His monologue was basically the same as Frances Gossett's, almost word for word. With one exception. "I can't stand Gentry Lomax. He's full of himself. He's retired military, buzz cut, spit shine all the way, and he tries to run this place like the army. I'll give the devil his due, the man does a good job of it. Running the place, I mean. The man has no emotion, no social skills to speak of, and I don't think I've ever seen him smile. I don't know how Bessie Love can stand working for him." He answered his own question when he said, "I guess she doesn't have much choice since her salary works off part of or all of her rent. I'm not sure how that works. Her husband's medical bills left her with very little when he passed away. No one likes Gentry. I mean no one at all."

"Who hired him?" Maggie asked.

"I assume either Mr. Cricket or Mr. Meadows. He was here when I moved in six years ago."

"Did you ever meet Mr. Meadows?" Dennis asked.

"Once," Porter said, refilling everyone's coffee cup. "I wasn't impressed. He's what we would call back in my day a dandy. Nice-looking fella, pomade in his hair, everything he wears matches, or so I've been told. Like I said, I only met him once. Sharp dresser, high snoot factor. Charity Evans summed him up pretty good when she said he looks down on us renters and thinks he's better than everyone else. That's all I can tell you about him. Now, Mr. Cricket, he's totally different. Very personable, listens to you, always wants to know if there's more he can do for us. He cares. You can tell that the minute you meet him. He always calls us by name. How he remembers us all is beyond me. I hope they catch whoever it was that shot him, but I'm not hopeful. Frances told me when she called that Mr. Cricket is holding his own. Do you know any more than that?"

"That's all we know too. We're here looking around, trying to gain information at Mrs. Cricket's request."

"They say she's a real sweetheart. She'd have to be if Mr. Cricket picked her. So, what do you think of my coffee, youngsters?"

"It's the best," Maggie and Dennis said in unison.

Switching back to the topic at hand, Porter asked if they'd like to take a walk through Will's apartment. They both said that they would.

"Then let's go. You know it just eats at Gentry's ass—excuse my language, young lady—that I have the special keys to Will's place and he can't get in. I won't give them up, either. When I saw that Will wasn't coming back after a few weeks, I gathered up all his stuff, and by stuff I mean his financial papers from the company he worked for in Silicon Valley. I have it all in a box in my closet. Gentry even went to Mr. Cricket to demand I give him a key, but Mr. Cricket said no because Will was paid up till the end of the year. Same thing with Frances's friend Ellie Harper.

"Come along then, it's just a short walk. I wish I knew where Will was. I really miss that guy. He was a great chess player. I don't have a good feeling about it, and neither does Frances, but we try not to talk about it, because we get too upset."

"Does Will have a family, any relatives?"

Porter shook his head. "He outlived his children. He had two. He lost one to drugs, and the other was killed in a hit-and-run. He had a sister, but she passed away about a year ago. I guess I was the closest thing to a relative that he had."

Maggie and Dennis trooped behind Porter Flannery, mopping at their brows with the sleeves of their shirts. The hot Nevada sun was merciless.

Ten minutes later, with not a speck of perspiration on his brow, Porter Flannery announced that they had arrived at his friend's apartment. "This is it, 607 Lucky Drive!"

Chapter 7

"Man, this sun is brutal," Jack added, ringing the bell beside a quaint, multipaned door trimmed in white. Even though the sun was shining directly onto the window, making it shimmer like a huge diamond, Jack could see two forms inside the long, narrow office of Happy Village. "At least Lomax is here now. Maybe we'll finally get some answers. Let me do the talking, but feel free to jump in with anything you think might help. The little lady is quite nice, as well as helpful, but I think Lomax intimidates her."

The door opened wide. Bessie Love stood to the side. Jack didn't know why he thought she would smile when she recognized him, but there was no smile to be seen. Cyrus growled deep in his throat. Right then, Jack knew something wasn't right. His hand dropped to the big dog's head, his message clear to Cyrus. *I feel it too.*

"Good morning, *Mrs.* Love," Jack said, purposely using the title she'd corrected him on earlier. "We're here to talk to Mr. Lomax."

Mrs. Love stepped aside, then backed up a few steps to allow Gentry Lomax to take her place front and center.

Gentry Lomax was a presence, there was no doubt about it. He towered over Jack's six feet by a good four

inches. He wore his hair high and tight. *Military,* Jack sur-
mised. He had steel-gray eyes over brows that were manicured and totally gray. He was no youngster, but he was fit
and trim. He stood ramrod stiff, almost as if he had a
broom handle strapped to his back. He wore pressed
khakis with creases so sharp that Jack wondered if they
cut into his legs. He wore a collared T-shirt in olive green
with HAPPY VILLAGE stenciled on the front. Jack looked
down at the spit-shined shoes and swore he could see his
own reflection. The watch he wore was expensive and
probably did everything but cook a meal. "Jack Emery,"
Jack said, holding out his hand. "My partner is Ted Robinson. We're here at the request of Mrs. Cricket. And this is
Cyrus."

Gentry Lomax looked down at the dog, his eyes nar-
rowing. "We should talk outside. I don't want any dog
hair in the office."

"Cyrus doesn't shed, Mr. Lomax. Inside will be just fine,"
Jack said, authority ringing in his voice as he stepped past
the Happy Village manager, Cyrus at his side. Ted followed
and closed the door behind him.

Jack could see Lomax stiffen even further and his eyes
narrow. He looked as if he wanted to punch something,
preferably Jack.

"Mrs. Cricket would like to know what is going on.
That means she wants a report, and she wants to know
why you haven't been in touch." Jack waited for an invita-
tion to sit down. When none was forthcoming, his own
back stiffened. This was not going to go well; he could feel
it in his bones.

Gentry Lomax's voice was like his appearance, sharp
and clipped. "I don't see why. Nothing has changed other
than Mr. Cricket's being shot here. The police have all the
reports, and they're available to anyone who wants to pay
five dollars to get a copy. I file a report at the end of the

month for Mr. Cricket, and that's how we do things here."

"Well, that's going to change right now. Mrs. Love, please help us out here."

Lomax's hand shot upward. "Hold on. I don't take orders from you, and neither does Mrs. Love. You have no right to come in here and make demands."

Now Jack's ire was up. Cyrus started to fidget. Ted inched closer to Jack.

"We can call Mrs. Cricket, who has her husband's power of attorney. She herself is a lawyer, and a very good one at that, as I'm sure you know. That's if you want to put it to the test. So, let's have that report. I'm sure you keep a daily log. Just copy the logs from the day of the shooting and hand it over. Unless you don't keep a daily log."

"That's not how I do things here."

"You aren't in the military anymore, Mr. Lomax. You're overseeing a senior citizens' residential community, and that's how things are done in the private sector. Mrs. Cricket also wants to see a report for the past eight months or so on the tenants who moved out or relocated and the reasons why they left. Of course, you don't have to do anything you don't want to do, but let me be the first to tell you that no one is irreplaceable. Mrs. Cricket asked me to relay that message to you should you prove recalcitrant about honoring her requests, requiring her to stop asking and begin demanding," Jack outright fibbed. He did *not* like this guy.

"What? Are you implying I'm going to be fired?" The ramrod back stiffened even more. "I have a contract. Mr. Cricket hired me, not Mrs. Cricket." Jack almost smiled as he sensed the bluster in the tall man's tone and attitude.

"Power of attorney, Mr. Lomax. Power of attorney. Mrs. Cricket can do whatever she wants to do, including replacing you with someone who will honor her requests. She is a lawyer, as I pointed out earlier. All she wants to do is to get to the bottom of what happened to her husband. Why are you being so uncooperative? Could it be that you have something to hide? If not, I would think you'd want to do everything in your power to find out what happened that day."

"Our records are confidential. Privacy and all that," Lomax said in a more conciliatory tone. He turned to Bessie and instructed, "Make copies of what they want, nothing more. Is there anything else?"

"Are you in regular contact with Lionel and his boys?"

"Not if I can help it. Those boys are a thorn in my side. They serve no purpose. I understand that the tenants feel safe with them around, but all they do is get in the way."

"In the way of what?" Ted asked, speaking up for the first time. "How do they interfere with the operation of the community?"

"The day-to-day workings of the complex," Lomax snapped. "I run a tight ship here."

"And yet your boss, the owner of this complex, was shot and almost died on your watch as you ran your tight ship. How do you account for that?"

Lomax's lips tightened into a thin line. "I wasn't here when it happened, and Lionel and his boys weren't here either. Are you implying I'm to blame for Mr. Cricket's getting shot?" Jack shrugged. Cyrus growled, then showed the pearly whites that Jack religiously brushed twice a day.

"Where were you the day it happened?" Ted asked.

"I went to Home Depot to pick up two kitchen sinks on back order. When I got back, all hell had broken loose. I didn't even know Mr. Cricket was coming here that day. He always calls when he's coming, and he's never late. I respect punctuality, as does he. And yes, it is a military thing where I'm concerned. I can't speak for Mr. Cricket, since there are no clocks in the casinos. I assume he just likes to be on time."

Jack felt as if some of the wind had gone out of his sails. He moved on. "How many vacancies are there here in the village?"

"Normally, there are none, with a waiting list a mile long, but right now there are exactly twenty."

"Why?" Jack asked.

"Some of the tenants have moved or left. The apartments of those who paid their rent through the end of the year, which includes most of the twenty—Bessie can tell you exactly how many and which ones—even though vacant, cannot be rented until the year is up. No one knows where or why the tenants left. I consulted the police and Mr. Cricket as well. We cannot rent those apartments, that's the bottom line. It would be illegal to do so. And we are still considering the applications for the others."

Ted pursed his lips as he listened to Lomax and how his tone changed with the questions. He wished Maggie were here. She'd have a fix on this guy in five minutes. "Does Mr. Cricket make a habit of coming unannounced? Has he ever done that before?"

"No, he hasn't." Lomax sighed. "That's been bothering me too. For him to come out here to the desert in the middle of the day, something must have been important. And no, I have no clue as to what that reason would be. I cannot tell you something I don't know."

"What about Mr. Meadows?" Jack asked.

"What about him? I barely know the man. I know that at one time his mother resided here, but that was before my time. I met him once or twice for maybe a total of five minutes each time. I think it was Thanksgiving and one Christmas party. I'm not even sure I could pick him out of a crowd. My dealings were always with Mr. Cricket."

"And yet Mr. Meadows owns half of Happy Village?" Jack said, his eyebrows shooting upward to show how strange he thought that was.

"I find it strange myself, but that's all I know. I was never privy to how the two men manage the financial end of this complex. I did hear through the grapevine that some, maybe all, of the casino owners have a hand in it also. I have no way of knowing whether that's true, and it's none of my business. I don't ask questions. I do my job, and I expect everyone else to do theirs. Are we done here?"

"For now," Jack said as he reached out for the sheaf of papers Bessie Love handed him. "If Mrs. Cricket has any more questions, then we'll be back. You know what I find strange, Mr. Lomax?"

"Tell me," Lomax said through clenched teeth.

"You never once asked how Mrs. Cricket was or how her husband was doing."

"Why ask a question when you already know the answer? We learned that in the army, and I understand that's a rule for lawyers also. Mrs. Cricket is devastated. That's a given. I call the hospital four times a day for an update on Mr. Cricket. The report is always the same. He's in critical condition but holding his own. I'm a military man, Mr. Emery. We're trained not to show our emotions. Now, if there is nothing else, I have work to do."

Jack looked at Ted as much as to say, *We're done here.* Cyrus was way ahead of them, having headed for the door and barked.

Neither man spoke until they were a block away from the Happy Village office. "My gut and my reporter instinct are telling me Lomax knows something, or at the very least suspects something," Ted said as he wiped at his brow with the sleeve of his shirt.

Jack stopped and pulled a bottle of water from his backpack along with a fold-up bowl he carried for Cyrus. He poured water and waited while the big dog finished it all. "I feel the same way. I can't put my finger on what it is that triggered it either. Something is just *off*." Jack stuffed the empty water bottle and bowl back into his backpack. "We need to check in with Espinosa and Maggie and Dennis. They're here somewhere."

"I'm on it. You check in with Espinosa. I just sent Maggie a text. Ah, she said they're just now leaving someone's apartment. She said to meet them on the corner of Primrose and Lilac Lane. That's two blocks over. Damn, it's hot. I feel like I'm melting."

"Right now I'd like to take a shower with ice-cold lemonade pouring over me," Jack said, and guffawed. "How do these people handle this excessive heat?" he literally gasped.

"Who says they get used to it?" Ted roared. "We're the only fools out here walking around, or haven't you noticed? Plus it isn't even noon yet, the heat of the day."

"Come on, we have to get Cyrus out of here before he burns his feet on this red-hot concrete. I can feel it through my sneakers, so it has to be killing him."

Jack and Ted were breathing hard and Cyrus panting as they literally fell into the rental van. Ted quickly turned on the ignition and set the A/C to its highest level. At first, hot air blasted out of the vents, but delicious cold air followed. "We are not moving until we all cool down," Jack said as he stroked Cyrus's head. "We'll get you some ice-cold water in just a few minutes, big guy. Just hang on."

"I saw an Arby's about a mile down the road when we drove in here. Call Maggie and tell here to meet us there," Ted said hoarsely as he threw the van into gear and peeled out of the parking lot onto the paved highway. He burned rubber, not caring if he got a ticket.

Exactly three minutes later, having gone ninety miles an hour, Ted steered the van to the drive-through window. He bellowed at the young guy in the open window, "Six bottles of ice-cold water *right now!* Hurry it up, dude, we're dehydrating."

Jack had Cyrus's bowl in his hand and the icy bottle of water a second later. He poured, careful not to spill the lifesaving liquid. Cyrus fell to it and drank greedily, as did Jack and Ted. Jack opened the three remaining bottles and watched as Cyrus drank his fill. He pawed the car door to go out. "Two bottles of water will do that," Jack mumbled as he waited for the big dog to do his thing. Cyrus woofed and scampered back into the van just as Maggie and Dennis pulled up behind him in the drive-through.

Jack leaned out the window and shouted that they would order, and for Maggie to find a parking spot for her rental, and they would all eat in the van. He watched as Maggie backed up her Toyota rental and drove to the corner of the lot, where a tree offered a little shade.

Ted placed a huge order, to the young guy's delight. Twelve double-roast beef sandwiches with spicy brown mustard, five orders of fries, and five orders of onion rings. Five root beers loaded with ice and six more bottles of water along with four double-roast beef sandwiches, plain, for Cyrus.

It took a full twelve minutes for Ted's order to be filled. Money changed hands before bag after bag was handed through the small window. It took another seven minutes before everyone was settled and chowing down on the fast food. Between mouthfuls of food, the four of them took turns muttering about the excessive heat and how they were all sweating like Trojans.

"Now I just want to go to sleep," Maggie groaned as she finished the last of her sandwich and licked the mustard that had dripped onto her fingers. Cyrus barked to go out. Jack opened the door, and the big dog leaped down and sprinted off toward the back of the big tree, which looked as wilted as the rest of the straggly foliage surrounding the parking lot.

"Look, just make sure you all keep drinking. We have

to stay hydrated. This kind of weather is not something any of us are used to, so pay attention to what your body is telling you. Before we leave here, we'll go back through the take-out line for more water. Maybe if we pay the kid extra, he'll fashion some kind of container with ice. Now, what's next on our agenda? Are we done here at Happy Village, or are we heading back to Babylon?" Jack asked.

"Zack Meadows is still nowhere to be found. Charles and Fergus opted to go back to the hotel, so we could take a crack at seeing if he's in his office. We are here, and he's not located that far from where we are right now. There has to be someone there who knows something. I say we head there," Ted said. The others agreed.

"We have to be back here by two-thirty. That guy Lionel finally answered my text, said he was in class and just got my text. He is willing for a meet-and-greet at that building they use as a clubhouse," Dennis said.

"Then that's the plan. Give us time to go through the drive-through and follow us when we leave. Who has the address for Meadows?"

"I do. I'll program it into the GPS, so follow me when we leave."

Ten minutes and a hundred dollars later, a Styrofoam cooler loaded with ice and water was sitting next to Cyrus on the backseat. Ted raced the van across the deserted lot and followed Maggie out to the highway.

"Since this is Vegas, and if you were a betting man, Jack, what are the odds Zack Meadows is going to be in his office? My opinion for whatever it's worth is that the guy is avoiding us. The big question is, why? This whole thing is starting to smell more and more like a fish market. I don't mean to blow my own horn here, but I am an investigative journalist, and by now, under normal circumstances, I'd have a feel for what's going on. I don't. And I know Maggie doesn't either. Dennis, who has good instincts, hasn't said boo, so he's out there in left field with me and Maggie. What's your gut telling you, Jack?"

Jack scrunched his face into a grimace. "I can't read it either, Ted. About the best I can come up with is to say that something is off. I think we'll know more once we see what we come up with regarding Zack Meadows. I don't know why, but I think that guy is the key to what's going on."

"Are you . . . do you . . . are you thinking he wants to ace out Cosmo and take over, something like that?"

"Yeah, something like that. I could be really off base on that. For all we know, the guy might be out of the country or out of the state, but I don't care who it is or how important he is or thinks he is. In this digital age, the guy would be checking his e-mail and phone for texts. That's a given, don't you agree? Especially for someone who not only works for but is actually the chair of the Gaming Commission. He's got to be available twenty-four seven, I'm thinking. That means he has to check his messages. He's chosen to ignore all of ours, and we must have left at least a dozen. It smells, that's for sure," Jack said.

"I couldn't agree more. Did you check in with Espinosa? Anyone hear from Abner or Snowden?" Ted asked.

"I'm doing that now. Espinosa said Charles and Fergus are back in the penthouse. He hasn't heard from Abner or Snowden, and neither has Charles. That's it," Jack said.

"Maggie is slowing down. Meadows must hang out in that brick building on the right. Lots of cars. Busy place, I guess. She's turning so, yeah, this is it," Ted said, turning on his signal light to make a right turn to follow Maggie.

Everyone got out and immediately started to fan themselves. "The front door is over there," Maggie indicated, pointing to a green awning by a massive mahogany double door. Let's do it!" she said, sprinting ahead with Cyrus on her heels. The others followed and stepped into a small, beautifully decorated lobby that was so icy cold, they all started to shiver. There was no welcome desk, no one to ask for directions. But a monster bulletin board listed every office in the building. "We want 1102," Dennis said. "Where are the elevators?"

"Around the corner," Maggie said. "Looks like a ton of security. Get ready to shed everything but your undies." She forged ahead and plopped her backpack on the conveyor belt but not before she was asked for her ID. The others followed suit. Cyrus was the last in line after Jack.

"Sorry, sir, no dogs allowed," the guard said.

"He's a service dog. He goes where I go. Cyrus!"

Cyrus stepped forward and offered up his paw with a short, soft bark.

The guard blinked and turned to his partner. "Did you see that, Sid? Now ain't that somethin'? Well, okay then, big fella, you're good to go." Ham that he is, Cyrus barked again and dipped his head in acknowledgment.

The gang started off, Jack and Cyrus at the end of the line. Jack suddenly turned around and walked over to the guard. "Excuse me, but by any chance do you know Zack Meadows?"

"Well, I don't know him personally, but yeah, I know who he is. Is that who you're going to see?"

"I am. Do you happen to know if he's in today, or has he gone out to lunch yet?"

"I saw him about an hour ago. He usually comes in early, just when I start my shift at six-thirty. He could have left by the back stairway or taken the elevator down to the lower level where the garage is. I usually see him just in the morning. I hardly ever see him later in the day. He's not what you would call a friendly man. Doesn't even say good morning."

"Okay, thanks." Not to be outdone, Cyrus let loose with a sharp bark and offered his paw again. He allowed the guard to ruffle his ears. He was doing his part.

The elevator was small and smelled like Brut and some kind of flowery perfume. Cyrus sneezed. When the elevator stopped on the eleventh floor, Cyrus was the first one out.

The little group looked around the lavish waiting area, their eyes wide, their jaws dropping. "Furnishings, paintings, carpeting plus the mannequin behind the desk, three hundred thousand easy," Maggie whispered. "And this is just the waiting room. Well, it is Vegas, so I guess money is no object. Let me handle this," she hissed as she approached the shiny desk where a woman sat staring into space. Maggie summed her up in a heartbeat. Vegas showgirl gone to seed but fighting it every step of the way. Botoxed out the kazoo to the point that nothing moved on her face. There was nothing on the desk except a console phone and a computer that wasn't turned on. A game show with a shrill, squealing audience was on the color TV that hung suspended from the ceiling. Maggie eyed the wild Dolly Parton wig the woman was wearing, the blood-red nails that were so long she understood why the computer was off—the talons would get stuck in the keyboard. She took a second to wonder how she wiped her rear end. She answered her own thought by assuming the woman had a bidet. Maggie shook her head to clear her thoughts. "Ma'am, can you please help us?" When the woman didn't respond, Jack walked over to the free-hanging TV and pulled the plug.

"Ma'am?"

"It's Crystal. *Miss* Crystal Shine," the receptionist said, eyeing Jack, Ted, and Dennis.

"Of course it is," Maggie drawled.

"We're here to see Mr. Meadows."

"Do you have an appointment?"

Maggie was about to say no, then changed that to "Absolutely we do. Otherwise, why would we be here? Just tell us where he is, and we'll find our own way. That way you can get back to your game show."

The woman thought about it for a few seconds. "Go through that door on the left, go down the hall to the end, and Mr. Meadows's office is the last one. What did you say your name was?"

"Barbara Walters," Maggie said with a straight face.

"Really! You look wonderful for your age," Miss Crystal Shine said.

Jack developed a coughing fit that was so alarming, Ted had to clap him on the back. "Barbara Walters!" Jack gasped as he stumbled along behind Maggie and Cyrus.

"Obviously, she needs glasses," Maggie said, and giggled. "Ah, okay, here we are. Oh, lookie here, tell me that isn't a fancy-schmantzy nameplate. If you care to look around, this one is the biggest and the shiniest compared to the others. Guess that's why he gets the last office with the wraparound windows. Does his job pay that well?" she whispered.

No one knew the answer, but Dennis ventured a guess. "I would assume it pays very well, and remember, he gets a cut of the rents from Happy Village. And who's to say he paid for this pricey plaque himself?" When there was no comment, Dennis shrugged, and added, "I'm just saying."

Maggie whirled around and asked if she should knock or just open the door.

"Just open the door already," Ted said, irritation evident in his voice.

Cyrus growled low and deep in his throat.

Maggie opened the door. The four of them barreled through, Cyrus in the lead. The man sitting at the desk rose, a look of stark fear on his face. "What the hell . . ."

Everyone's hands hit the air, palms outward to say, *Whoa, whoa.* "Miss Crystal Shine said it was all right for us to come back here because you weren't busy and could spare a few moments. We're here at Mrs. Cricket's request."

In the space of time it took Jack to offer up his spiel, the gang had the luxurious office cataloged and priced out. The Jackson Pollock artwork that adorned the walls was way, way up into the hundreds of thousands of dollars. The Persian carpet alone could feed a city for a full year. The sofas and chairs were so luxurious, they screamed to be sat upon—custom crafted, undoubtedly, with an impossible price tag. The coffee table shimmered from the subdued overhead lighting. The only thing on the table was a massive basket of white lilies, white tulips, and white roses, with fern nestled among the stems. The desk looked as if it came from the White House, like a replica of the president's desk. The greenery, and there was plenty of it in the huge room, could have come straight out of a rain forest. Droplets of water could be seen on some of the leaves.

And then there was the man, who didn't bother to get up to greet his unexpected guests. It was hard to tell if he was tall, medium, or short, since he was sitting down. He had a full head of sandy-colored hair that was a tad too thick and styled; it couldn't be real. His nails were buffed and manicured. He wore a five-thousand-dollar Hugo Boss suit with a red power tie. His shirt was pristine white, with the cuffs monogrammed in the color of his suit.

Later, Dennis said any man who had to have his initials on his clothes had an identity problem of some kind.

"It's customary to make an appointment. That's how we do things here. All you have to do is call," Meadows said.

"We tried that, over a dozen times," Maggie said flatly. "You didn't respond to any of our calls, and that's why we're here. As my colleague said, Mrs. Cricket asked us to look into the attempted murder of her husband. In other words, she wants to know what happened, and for some reason she thinks you are avoiding her, the police, and even us. Is that true, Mr. Meadows? By the way, excuse my atrocious manners. I'm Maggie Spritzer and this is Ted Robinson and Dennis West. We're investigative journalists for the *Post* in Washington, DC. We just happened to be here when Mr. Cricket was shot. And this gentleman is Jack Emery, a former federal prosecutor and now a private attorney. Last but not least, this is Cyrus. We never go anywhere without him. He's a valued member of our team." Cyrus woofed softly to thank Maggie for his introduction.

"Your turn, Mr. Meadows," Dennis said, stepping forward. "Well, blow me away and let me land on my feet. Would you look at *that!*"

Everyone in the room said, "What?" at the same time.

"Mr. Meadows is a connoisseur of fine tobacco. Very, very fine tobacco. Those are Davidoff Oro Blanco cigars. They come in their own wooden box. Ten cigars to a box, and the box costs five thousand dollars. Each cigar, individually boxed, is worth five hundred. We did an article on tobacco a while back, so I know what those cost," Dennis chirped.

"I keep them on hand for the high rollers who come through here from time to time," Meadows explained. His tone was defensive.

"Uh-huh," was all Dennis said.

"Can we get on with this? I have to leave in a few minutes to attend a licensing meeting." Meadows shot his monogrammed cuffs to look at his watch, which made Ted's eyes almost bug out of his head at the sight of the Patek Philippe Swiss watch set in eighteen-karat gold with a perpetual calendar and sporting a genuine crocodile strap. If there was one thing Ted knew about in detail, it was watches. He'd been obsessed with them since he was a little kid and learning to tell time. He blinked, then blinked again, because he knew that the price tag on the bauble was $130,000.

Meadows got up from a chair that looked as if it would lull you to sleep the minute you sat down, and he came around to the front of the desk. Maggie looked down to see the distinctive boat-shaped Bettanin & Venturi loafers that were handmade in Italy for a thousand dollars a pop. She immediately calculated the cost of the apparel Zack Meadows was attired in and came up with the number $8,000. She felt as if she should let loose with a whistle but kept her cool. Serious money, for sure. They definitely needed Abner to look into this man's finances.

"I can't help you. And the reason I can't help you is that I wasn't here when Cosmo was shot. I was on my way to Reno. I've talked to the police ad nauseam. I call the hospital every day for an update, and they say the same thing—Cosmo is holding his own. I called Gentry Lomax the minute I heard. He manages Happy Village. Ironically, he wasn't on-site that day either. Other than that, there is nothing more for me to tell you. I wish I could tell you something. I can offer a suggestion. Talk to Lionel, Cosmo's version of security at Happy Village. He has an ear to the underground, and he might come up with something. Look, I really have to leave now. If you want to come back and talk at length, ask Crystal to make an appointment for you. It was nice meeting you all. I always enjoy meeting Cosmo's friends. Please, give Elizabeth my regards."

There was nothing the gang could do but follow Meadows to the door, where he quickly ushered them out. "I'll be along in a minute. I have to gather up some paperwork to take to the meeting. Since you found your way here, I'm sure you can find your way back."

And that was the end of that.

Chapter 8

A 1965 Mustang with more rust than paint on its chassis slid into a parking spot outside the clubhouse of Happy Village, its engine purring like a contented tabby cat. It was a totally rebuilt engine that Lionel Lewis and his friends in the Cavaliers had worked on for over a year, with the bulk of the parts coming from the graveyard of junked cars. It was unclear if the original paint job was red or blue, or possibly green. The reason Lionel left the ratty-looking exterior as it was was so that no one would want to steal the classic car.

Lionel Lewis stepped out from behind the wheel, his three best friends following from the back and passenger side. "Looks like we got here first," Lionel said as he mopped at the perspiration building on his forehead. "Dom, go on in and turn on the A/C," he said, addressing the friend who'd been sitting in the passenger seat. Lionel tossed him a set of keys. "Eddie, you and Nick stay right here until Mr. Cricket's people arrive. I see Gentry Lomax heading this way, and I want to head him off before he does something stupid. Go!"

Lionel started to squint in the bright sun. He'd removed his dark sunglasses, knowing Lomax would have some snide comment about not looking him in the eye. There were days, and this was one of them, when he wanted to beat the stuffing out of the pompous, know-it-all manager. Wanting to do something and doing it, however, were two different things. Lionel knew he'd never act on his feelings, because he didn't want Cosmo Cricket to ever think he'd made a mistake in hiring him and his friends. Instead, he conjured up as much respect as he could for the retired military man bearing down on him. He might defer to the man's position, but he never kowtowed to the man. Showing respect was one thing; letting the man ride roughshod over him and his friends was a horse of a different color.

The moment the two men were eyeball to eyeball, Lomax demanded to know what Lionel was doing at the clubhouse.

They were equally tall, equally muscled, both nicely dressed, both groomed, but Lionel was twenty-two and Gentry Lomax was sixty-two, which put Lionel at an advantage should things ever come to a showdown. The other obvious difference was that Gentry Lomax was white and Lionel Lewis was black. Lionel knew that Lomax was a racist. Bessie Love had confided in him that little factoid. And Bessie should know because she was also black and in constant contact with Lomax as his assistant.

"Mrs. Cricket's people asked to meet with me and my boys. I agreed. It's 110 degrees out right now, so I had Dom go in and turn on the air-conditioning. Do you have a problem with that, Mr. Lomax?" he asked coolly. "Mr. Cricket gave me a key to the clubhouse and said I could come and go as I please, as you well know. Just the way he gave me the master key to all the units at Happy Village. I have never abused the trust he placed in me, and you know that as well."

The boy's having a set of keys did bother Gentry Lomax. So much so that he'd asked Cosmo Cricket why and was told quite bluntly that it was none of his business. So, yes, it did bother him. "About what?" he snarled.

"Well now, Mr. Lomax, I won't know the answer to that question until I talk to them, will I?" Lionel replied, mustering the cool not to add "you fool" as he wiped at his brow with the sleeve of his shirt.

"You know you're supposed to check in with my office when you come on the property. You didn't do that, did you?" Lomax snarled a second time.

Lionel sucked in a deep breath of the hot, humid air and wished he hadn't. He was a hairbreadth away from losing it. "No, Mr. Lomax, I did not do that, because the moment I turned the engine off in the car, I saw your office door open and you walking toward me. I didn't see any point to it in this heat. If there's nothing else I can do for you, then, I'll go along to meet Mr. Cricket's people. They're parking their vehicles now, as you can plainly see." Lionel clenched his teeth so tight, he thought his jaw was going to crack. He didn't mean to say the words, but somehow they slipped through. "So am I dismissed?" he said, snapping off a sloppy salute. Without waiting for a response, Lionel turned and sprinted toward the clubhouse and the people Mrs. Cricket wanted him to talk to.

"Introductions can wait until we're inside," Lionel said as he ushered the small group ahead of him. "We need to get out of this heat."

"Did that guy back there give you a hard time? It looked like it from where I was standing," Jack asked.

Lionel snorted. "The man lives to make my life miserable. Nice dog. Does he need water or anything? It's 110 degrees, with the humidity in the high nineties."

Jack said Cyrus was good. Cyrus barked to show his appreciation of Lionel's concern for his well-being.

Even though it had only been a few minutes, the inside of the clubhouse was frosty cold. Dom offered cold Cokes from the kitchen refrigerator, and they all accepted as Maggie made the introductions.

"Nice room," Jack said, looking around. And that's all the clubhouse was, incorporating a huge kitchen, his and her bathrooms, and a pantry lined with shelves that held mostly paper products. A mini stage of sorts was raised against the far wall, with a portable podium pushed into a corner. Folding chairs and long folding tables were neatly lined up against the far wall. Eddie and Dom set up one of the tables and unfolded the chairs. Nick handed out napkins from the pantry for the dripping Coke bottles.

Maggie liked the look of the young men. They were all dressed in jeans, boat shoes, and button-down shirts, the sleeves rolled up. All of them had regulation haircuts, and she didn't see even one piercing or tattoo. A definite plus. She could tell they were all good friends and had respect for one another regardless of their ethnic background. Lionel was black, Dom appeared to be a mix of Italian and Asian blood, Eddie was Spanish, and Nick was a Brit.

Lionel took the lead. "I only have an hour, because I have a class at three-thirty. Nick has a class at three. So until then we're all yours. How can we help you? Anything Mrs. Cricket wants, we're up for. First, though, is there any news on Mr. Cricket? We call the hospital every day, and they just say the same thing—he's holding his own, or words to that effect. One day I did talk to the doctor. Nice guy. All he would say, though, was he was optimistic."

"Mr. Cricket is improving. They had to take him back into surgery, but he came through that okay. He was in a coma, but he came out of it. He's a fighter and has a lot to live for, so like Dr. Wylie said, we're all optimistic," Jack informed the young men. "Now, tell us what you know about this place and the day the shooting happened."

"See, that's the thing, Mr. Emery. We were all in class.

We usually don't come out here during the day, unless one of the tenants calls us. If we have a slow week, we will come out during the week, at least once or twice a day. We work in shifts. Basically, though, we're the night patrol. Mr. Lomax is in charge during the day. My boys and I take turns. There are nine of us on any given night. Sometimes all twelve of us are here. And Mr. Lomax doesn't want us out here during the day anyway. The guy hates us, hates the ground we walk on. None of us has ever shown him one ounce of disrespect. Never, not once.

"He wanted us gone from day one, but Mr. Cricket put his foot down. That settled things. We try not to get in his way. I just wish he would do the same thing, but he's determined to get in our faces every chance he gets. For some reason, he thinks this place is his. And he does run a tight ship. This place runs smoothly. I'll give him that. The tenants don't like him for a variety of reasons that are none of our business, and we try to stay out of it.

"But to get back to your question, no one here knows anything, and I made sure my boys and I talked to every single tenant. Most of these people are up in years, and they play their televisions loud because most of them don't have hearing aids, so the sound of a gunshot wouldn't register. Trust me when I tell you, if they knew anything, we'd know it before Mr. Lomax.

"To my knowledge, Mr. Cricket doesn't usually come out here much during the week. I've seen him pretty often on weekends, when we're all on duty. He's always trying to do more for the tenants. This is just a guess on my part, but the boys here agree with me. So for whatever it's worth, we think Mr. Cricket came out here that day specifically to see Mr. Lomax because he was upset about something. We *think* it was about the twenty tenants who have gone AWOL. But we don't have anything definite to base our opinion on. Bessie Love confided in me that Mr. Gentry gets a bonus at the end of the year based on the rentals. With empty units, his bonus goes down. He even squawked about Bessie's getting a reduction in her rent or maybe free rent to work in the office. I'm not sure how that works, and it's none of my business anyway. All she has to live on is her social security, and it isn't much. She's a kind soul, and Lomax treats her like a slave. One of these days, he's going to pay for that."

"So what you're saying is, you and your people really don't know anything. Do you *suspect* anything?" Ted asked.

Nick raised his hand. "I think—and this is just my opinion—but I think Mr. Lomax makes too many trips outside the village on a daily basis. Some of the tenants who are a little more alert and sharper started to keep track at our request. The day of the shooting was a legitimate trip to pick up sinks. That we verified. One of the tenants told us that one day Lomax left wearing his standard outfit, khaki pants and the Happy Village T-shirt, but when he returned he was wearing jeans and a plain white T-shirt. I don't know what if anything that means."

"Do you know anything about Zack Meadows, Mr. Cricket's partner? Does he come out here, do you know?" Ted queried.

The four members of the Cavaliers looked at one another and shrugged. All eyes turned to Lionel Lewis, who suddenly looked like a deer caught in the headlights. The young man cleared his throat, not once but twice, before he spoke.

"We met him, of course. Several times, actually. It's my understanding that he doesn't come out here during the day. Some of the tenants said he's been here on the weekends and huddles with Mr. Lomax. I have no reason to doubt that, but we've never seen him in the flesh. But I did see what I thought was his car. At night going as far back as maybe seven months ago. No one around here drives a Mercedes, so it was natural to assume it was Mr. Meadows's vehicle. We aren't able to run a license plate, but I'd stake my life that it was Mr. Meadows's car.

"The reason I say that is on Fridays I go to Mr. Cricket's office to pick up our paychecks, and this one time about two months ago, Mr. Cricket asked me to do him a favor, and of course I said yes. He wanted me to deliver a package to Mr. Meadows at his office. He just said he didn't want to send it by messenger, and I was right there and it was on my way home. I obliged. I'm pretty sure I saw the same Mercedes in the parking lot. I'm not one hundred percent sure, but I think it was the same license plate. Other than that, I don't know what else I can tell you."

Maggie looked at Jack and suddenly felt an itch between her shoulder blades. Jack gave an almost imperceptible nod, and she knew instantly that the young man sitting across from her knew or suspected something but wasn't going to volunteer it unless directly asked. She was trying to figure out how and what to say when Dennis West leaned over the table and asked, "There's more, isn't there? What aren't you saying? Whatever you say stays with us, and there will be no ramifications. In other words, we're on your side."

Lionel cleared his throat again and looked around at his friends, who shrugged. "I was taught from early on by my mother that if you don't have something good to say about someone, don't say anything. I have opinions like everyone else, of course, but that's what they are, opinions."

"Let's hear them," Ted said. "Let us judge if it's important enough to worry about."

Lionel looked around as his friends gave imperceptible nods. "Like I said, I go to Mr. Cricket's office every Friday. He has a nice comfortable office, like most corporate offices. Nothing to take your breath away, that's for sure. In a word, his offices are tasteful. I'm sure he makes a very good salary for someone in his position, and he has a sterling reputation, as you all know. Plus he has to have income coming in from Happy Village. He's just an all-around nice guy. He doesn't flaunt anything, dresses down, blends in, that kind of thing. Ordinary.

"Mr. Meadows is . . . different. I know he and Mr. Cricket are partners in Happy Village. I have no clue how much money they make or how all that works, and I don't want to know, because it's none of my business. The boys and I, we keep our heads down and do what we're paid to do. Mr. Meadows is what my mother would call *all flash*. He wears expensive suits and shoes, gets manicures, gets his hair styled, and his office blew me away when I got there. It was like . . . regal . . . imperial or something.

"I'm sure he is paid a decent salary, something I'll probably never earn in my lifetime, plus he has whatever monies he gets from the Village partnership. And he drives a high-dollar car. He appears to live high. He looks through you, not at you. My mother would say he's pretentious, and I guess that's as good a term as any I could come up with.

"I couldn't help myself when I was in his office, it was so . . . grandiose that I was looking around, and he said, 'I guess you don't see anything like this from where you come from, eh?' That kind of put my teeth on edge a little, but I didn't say anything. I just handed him the package, and it looked as if he knew what it was and didn't want to take it from my hand. I don't know, maybe it was me and he would feel tainted somehow if he touched something I was holding. I just laid it on the desk, and let me tell you about that desk. It's an absolute replica of the Resolute desk in the White House. Anyway, this might be just my imagination, but he looked . . . I'm not sure if *frightened* is the right word, but that was my first impression. I just got out of there as quickly as I could.

"Oh, there is one other thing. Mr. Cricket said I was to call him after I delivered the package. I did, and he just said thank you. Then I went home."

"Is Mr. Meadows married, do you know?" Jack asked.

The boys all burst out laughing. Nick laughed the hardest. "To every showgirl in Vegas is the rumor. He's a ladies' man. Everyone in Vegas knows that."

"Rumor has it he lives in a ten-million-dollar condo. Where's the money coming from?" Lionel asked. "Maybe he goes to Reno to gamble and maybe he made a killing," he answered himself. "Of course, he'd have to go in disguise, since employees are forbidden to gamble. I know this because Mr. Cricket told me it was in Mr. Meadows's contract. Well, he didn't exactly tell me that. I overheard him talking to someone about it. No, he did not mention Mr. Meadows by name, if that's your next question. It is my understanding that it's up to each casino if they want to allow their employees to gamble in their off hours. Likewise the Commission. Don't quote me on that, because I am not one hundred percent sure." Lionel looked down at his watch, his eyes widening. "I have to leave now so I can get Dom to his class and head off to mine. If you want to talk more, we'll be back here tonight by seven o'clock. I have to lock up now. I'm sorry we don't have more time."

"No, it's okay, I think you helped us a lot. I can't think of anything else at the moment anyway. If you think of anything, call one of us," Jack said, writing cell phone numbers on the back of his business card. "Call us anytime, day or night, if you think it's important. Don't be shy about the time."

"Will do," Lionel said as he waited for his friends to replace the fold-up table and chairs. Eddie picked up the

Coke bottles and stuck them in a trash bag he found under the sink. He carried them out with him.

Maggie wondered how it could possibly be hotter than it was before they entered the clubhouse, but it was. She mopped at her face and grimaced, knowing her hair was going to frizz to a fireball in the thick humidity.

Good-byes were said, hands shaken, then the boys were gone. The foursome, along with Cyrus, climbed into their respective vehicles for the ride back to Babylon.

"Nice bunch of guys," Jack said. "I'd take them over Lomax and Meadows any day of the week. I was hoping for . . . I don't know . . . maybe a bombshell, a smoking gun of some kind. We know less now than before we got here. I didn't get the feeling they were holding anything back that would be pertinent to the shooting."

"Not quite true, Jack," Maggie said. "We got the boys' impressions, that counts for something. True, they have skin in the game, but I agree and found them to be credible, and obviously so does Cosmo. Otherwise he wouldn't have hired them in the first place. Kids see things differently than adults, you know that."

Jack poured more water into the fold-up dish for Cyrus, who lapped it up immediately. "You're right, I do know that. You know what we forgot? We forgot to ask them about the badass gang. Well, if nothing else is going on tonight back at Babylon, we can come back here and get the skinny on what if anything they might know. It might be cooler, too, plus Lomax might get his jockeys in a knot if he sees us here at night. Three visits in one day for sure will make him a little antsy. I'm just saying. I really think there is something fishy, something off about that guy. It's not just that ramrod military thing either, it's something else. Right now I just can't put my finger on it, but trust me, it will come to me sooner or later."

"Go ahead, you can say it. The guy is an all-round prick," Maggie said.

"I didn't want to offend your delicate sensibilities." Jack guffawed. "But you're right, he is definitely that." Cyrus barked to show he also agreed.

Jack went back to staring out the window at the blistering heat that shimmered off the highway. His thoughts were everywhere as his cell phone rang. "Hey!" he said, turning to Maggie, who was driving. "It's Harry," he said, picking up the call. "Hey, dude, what's up? You guys winning big? Nice of you to check in."

Jack sat up a little straighter when he heard Harry's frazzled voice. Harry never got frazzled. Jack put him on speaker, and Cyrus immediately leaned forward so he could hear better. Maggie craned her neck to the right for the same reason.

"Oh, the guys are winning all right. Between the four of them, they've won over a million dollars."

"Wow!" was all Jack could manage to say. Finally, when there was no response, Jack asked, "So what's the problem?"

Jack closed his eyes and pictured Harry struggling to find the right words to convey whatever the problem was. "It's like this. . . . They're still winning. Big time. We're being watched to see if we're . . . hell, I don't know, using something or have some kind of system, but that's okay, not a problem. The boys haven't cashed in yet. They're hoping to win another million or so. This is where you're supposed to ask me why, Jack," Harry dithered.

Jack looked at Maggie and rolled his eyes. "Okay, I'll bite, why?"

"Because they want to turn it into gold. They want me to get in touch with that movie star William Devane, who does all those gold commercials for Rosland Capital. They even have the telephone number to call. They refuse to believe a celebrity such as me can't get in touch with the guy. They don't frigging believe me, Jack!" Harry said, outrage ringing in his voice.

Jack closed his eyes. He didn't know what he was expecting, but this certainly wasn't it. "Why? I guess my next question is whether they have given any thought to how they would transport all those gold coins or bars back to their home countries. Two million dollars will buy quite a bit of gold, and gold is heavy. And then there's customs."

"That's why they're still gambling. They want to win another million, plus enough to charter a private plane to take them and the gold home. They don't want paper money. They saw another commercial for gold by some other company, and the guy hawking the gold said, 'If you can't hold it, do you really own it?' They were off and running when they heard that. What that means is they want to hold it. They are taking what the huckster said literally. They're starting to draw crowds at the gaming tables, and the guests are cheering them on. They're loving all of this. Really loving it."

"So what are you going to do?" Jack asked out of curiosity.

"Me? Do? That's why I'm calling you. You always claim to have all the answers, so give me one before I pull all my hair out."

"My advice would be to put Charles and Fergus on it. You might have to make a few concessions, Harry. You know, offer, through Charles and Ferg, to have your picture taken with William Devane and pretend you're buying gold. I bet the guy and his sponsors would jump at the opportunity."

"You are crazy, you lunatic," Harry said before he broke the connection.

Jack burst out laughing. Cyrus let out a loud bark and

lay back down and closed his eyes. Maggie just giggled. "Ooooh, I can't wait to see how that plays out. For whatever it's worth, we have a directory at the *Post* of agents who represent various movie stars. It's yours for the asking if you want to help Harry."

Jack just rolled his eyes and shrugged.

The rest of the trip back to Babylon was made in silence. Maggie concentrated on the heat shimmering off the asphalt road, Jack stared out the window at the dry brush and dead grass, and Cyrus slept peacefully.

Jack almost jumped out of his seat when Maggie pulled into the underground garage. "I cannot wait to take an ice-cold shower and put on clean clothes that don't smell!" he bellowed as he opened the door and sprinted to the private elevator that would take him to the penthouse. Maggie was only a few steps behind, with Cyrus out ahead of both. He was also the first one into the elevator. He was panting as if he'd just run a marathon.

Inside Annie's penthouse apartment, Jack quickly filled a large bowl with cold water from the refrigerator. Cyrus lapped greedily.

"He drank almost the whole bowl, so give him fifteen minutes to cool down, then will you take him out, Espinosa? I have to take a shower and wash the stink off me. Just drop him off in my room when you get back," Jack said.

Maggie looked around at the laptops and papers spread all over the dining-room table. She itched to know what was going on, but like Jack, she needed to go to her room and shower and put on clean clothes. "I'm never coming back here in the summer. Never! So, you all hear me? This heat will kill you. How do people live here?" she grumbled as she headed for the door, Jack in her wake. "We'll be back shortly. What's for dinner, Charles?"

"Meat loaf, new potatoes, fresh peas and carrots, homemade crusty bread, and a blackberry cobbler with vanilla ice cream," Charles called to her retreating back. Cyrus barked to show that he approved the menu. "Dinner is at six, so take your time."

"Make lots of gravy," Maggie shot back. "Don't forget to put those little peppercorns in the gravy."

Charles threw his hands in the air the minute the door closed behind Maggie and Jack. He looked over at Fergus, who was holding up the bottle of multicolored peppercorns. He was grinning from ear to ear. "It's understandable, Charlie. You have a lot on your mind."

"Can you imagine the uproar at the table when the gravy is served with no peppercorns? I'd have to take the red-eye to somewhere to lick my wounds." Charles decided to change the subject, since he didn't want any visions of him climbing aboard the red-eye to parts unknown. "Any word from Avery or Abner?"

Fergus looked around the state-of-the-art kitchen as though he were expecting an answer from the four walls. When nothing was forthcoming, he said, "No, but I am starting to worry. I sent off two texts in the last hour and have gotten no response. It's like dealing with that guy Meadows. Or Jack's calls, which he didn't answer either. It's not like Avery, and it is certainly not like Abner to keep us in the dark. They know we're counting on them. You don't think anything has happened to them, do you, Charles? I'm not as worried about Avery, because I know he can take care of himself, but Abner is a numbers computer guy. He's a babe in the woods when it comes to fieldwork. He'd be mush if he were put in harm's way. My only consolation is they were together when they left us. I can only hope they didn't split up." Fergus waved the bottle of peppercorns to make his point.

"I think we need to think positive and decide that the

two of them are onto something and are following through on whatever it is. I'm also sure one or more of Avery's operatives would have been in touch if something had gone awry."

"Only if they *know* something went awry, mate," Fergus said glumly.

"There is that, Ferg. We also have to remember they work on Avery's payroll, not ours. Their loyalty is to Avery and only Avery. I'm certain Avery has some sort of protocol in place for situations like this."

"So what you're saying is that there is nothing we can do until Avery or Abner decides to grace us with their presence and share whatever it is they're both working on."

"That's pretty much how I see it, Ferg," Charles said as he stared down at the meat loaves he had neatly lined up in the roasting pan on top of the range. "As you can see, I made three meat loaves, knowing Avery's appetite. And Abner is no slouch, either. Just in case. If they turn out to be no-shows, Cyrus will be dining on meat loaf for the next few days. Since it's his favorite food, that shouldn't be a problem." Charles smiled just as Espinosa entered the kitchen, Cyrus at his side.

The big dog immediately went to the range and started to sniff at the roasting pan. "It's meat loaf, Cyrus! One for you and two for us." Cyrus barked happily as he wandered around the kitchen, looking for a spot that was out of the way but still gave him a clear view of what was going on.

"The dog wanted to come back here instead of Jack's room. I think he smelled the meat loaves," Espinosa said.

Ten minutes later, Jack arrived, smelling like a woodsy glen, with Maggie right on his heels. She was wearing a sundress, and her wet, kinky hair was pulled back and pinned into place with colorful clips that matched the rainbow of color on her dress. Jack wore flip-flops, khaki cargo shorts, and a bright yellow polo T-shirt. Both looked clean and refreshed.

"Anyone want coffee?" Charles asked just as Ted and Dennis entered the kitchen. They could have been Jack Emery clones, dressed in like attire, their hair still wet from the shower and slicked back. Everyone said yes.

While Fergus poured the coffee, Jack shared what they'd learned out at Happy Village with the two old spies.

"What was your takeaway, Jack?" Charles asked.

"That something is definitely off out there. I don't think Gentry Lomax is who he pretends to be. Having met Zack Meadows, I think he's also hiding something, and he's the one with the most skin in the game at this point. Lomax is just a hired hand. Meadows and Cosmo are nothing like two peas in a pod as we originally thought. I think Cosmo found that out somehow, some way. I sense there was dissension between the two of them, and Cosmo acted on it. That's just my opinion. Any news on his condition? Has anyone talked to Lizzie? Do we know anything more?" Jack asked, walking back to the counter to get a refill on the coffee that he'd gulped down in two long swallows.

"Well, I for one like your opinion. I'm gravitating toward the same one based on the little I know. Late this morning we went to the hospital, and Cosmo had regained consciousness. Dr. Wylie insisted that Lizzie go home and not come back until tomorrow. Dr. Wylie said Cosmo is not all the way out of the woods. He's still in the weeds. I guess that's doctor talk. But he was more encouraged than he was yesterday, which Lizzie is taking all the way to the bank, counting on Cosmo to make a full recovery. All good from where I'm standing," Charles said as he opened the oven door to slide the heavy tray containing the meat loaves onto the rack.

The conversation turned to Harry and his friends and

their current dilemma, then to the missing Avery and Abner, then back to who was going to set the table.

Maggie sighed, knowing she was the designated table setter. She smiled at Ted and winked. He immediately jumped to oblige, which had been Maggie's intention all along.

Chapter 9

Avery Snowden pushed his chair back from the make-shift table and rolled his shoulders, his eyes on Abner Tookus, who looked like a zombie. They'd been locked in this room way too long. He looked down at the watch on his wrist. Yes, way too long. He snapped his fingers in Abner's direction. "C'mon, kid, we're heading out for some fresh air and a bite to eat. I'm full up of trail mix. I need real food. Like *now* would be good, Abner!"

Abner stirred, struggled to focus, and finally stood up. "Okay," he muttered. He looked around as though seeing the room for the first time. He squinted and took a deep breath. "What about them?" he asked, pointing to Snowden's operatives, who were busy tapping away on computers. "I still don't know how you managed to secure this room and set up this makeshift station in less than three hours. I know for a fact these rooms are booked a year in advance, and yet here we are, six computers, four printers, three fax machines, and five different telephone lines. How'd you do it, you crazy Brit?"

The old spy whipped out a card from his pocket and waved it about. Abner grabbed for it. "Ah, I see," he said, eyeing the platinum courtesy card signed by Countess Anna de Silva, with a handwritten message underneath her signature that said every courtesy was to be shown to the holder of the card immediately on presentation.

"It's all in who you know, you know that, Abner. You okay, kid?"

They were on the way down the long hallway to the main lobby of Babylon before Abner trusted himself to speak. "No, I'm not all right. I wish I had listened to you. I can't get those pictures out of my mind. You should have kicked my ass out of here."

"I tried. I warned you. You wouldn't listen to me. You wouldn't listen to your friend Phil, either."

It was true, and Abner had no comeback as he pushed through the revolving door. He waited to see which way Snowden wanted to go. Snowden moved right. "There's a gourmet hot dog emporium a block away." They made the trek in silence. Neither man spoke until they were settled in a bright green leather booth that was roomy enough for six. Snowden gave his order: four dogs with the works and a pitcher of ale. The waiter looked at Abner, who ordered a soft roll and coffee that he knew he wasn't going to eat or drink.

"This is Annie's favorite eatery, did you know that?" Snowden asked.

"No, I didn't know that, but it doesn't surprise me since hot dogs are her favorite food. How the hell can you even think about eating after what we've been doing?" Abner grumbled.

"I'm a field agent, Tookus. I had to learn early on to eat when the opportunity presented itself and to sleep when and if I could, even if it was for just ten minutes. You're a desk jockey. Therein lies the difference. Like I said, I warned you, and you refused to listen. Phil warned you. If you wouldn't listen to me, I thought for sure you would listen to your old pal. Look, Abner, I've been in this game my whole life. I won't say I'm immune to what I have to deal with, but I have learned how to deal with it. You are not in the minority. You are very much in the majority, and thank God for that."

"I've been on the dark web before. I just never . . . I didn't think . . . stupid me thought that was it. I never . . ." Abner threw his hands in the air and let his eyes glaze over again.

"Explored the *underbelly* of the dark web. There, I said it for you. That's where evil lives and *thrives*. Anonymously. The Devil's personal recruitment center."

"Now what?" Abner asked in a voice that cracked just as the waiter set Snowden's platter of food in front of him. He watched in pure amazement as the old spy tucked into his first foot-long hot dog with the works that dripped all over his hands.

Between mouthfuls of food, which he appeared to relish, Snowden tried to divert Abner to a more pleasant topic and started to make observations about the weather, which Abner totally ignored.

"We need to check in with Charles and the others. We've been off the grid too long. They are not going to believe this."

"Yes, Abner, they will believe it. They're pros. You're excused because you're a sheltered desk jockey. No shame in that. You've proved your worth a thousand times over. We each do what we do, and we each learn to live with the hand we're dealt." Snowden wolfed down his second hot dog as he spoke. "You should eat something, kid. At least drink the coffee."

Abner dutifully brought the coffee cup to his lips and took a sip. Snowden was right, and he knew it. "So what's our game plan here?" he asked as he cleared his throat. Abner knew he had to get a grip on his thoughts and emotions or he wasn't going to be any good to anyone. He picked up his coffee cup and drained it. He appreciated Snowden's slight nod of approval.

Snowden reached for his third hot dog. "I'm going back

to the conference room, and you are going to join the others and tell them everything we found out. I'll continue with the team and check in every three or four hours. Take some advice, kid. It's late. Take a shower and hit the sheets for a few hours. You need to be fresh as a daisy when you talk to the gang in the morning. You're dead on your feet and you know it, so don't deny it."

Abner wasn't about to deny anything, because he was as mentally exhausted as he was physically tired. He'd been operating on pure adrenaline for the past few hours. He didn't know how the old spy sitting across from him could still be alert, eating, and able to carry on a coherent conversation.

"Go along now, Abner. I'll take care of the check and send off a text to Sir Charles saying we'll meet up for breakfast at eight in the penthouse. It's three o'clock now, so that will give you a nice little nap. Skedaddle."

Skedaddle! Abner grinned. He supposed the strange word meant split or something similar to get the hell out of here. These Brits. They were so weird. He felt the urge to say something, to apologize for his shortcomings, but the words wouldn't come, so he simply got up and left. He realized just how bone tired he was as he wobbled his way to the elevators that would take him to his room. If he hadn't been so tired and had had his wits about him, he would have seen Jack Emery and Dennis West racing through the lobby.

Outside, in the hot humid night, Dennis West pulled up short and grabbed Jack's arm. "I am not going one step farther until you tell me what's going on and why we're outside this fine casino at three o'clock in the morning and getting ready to go God knows where. You call me up and yell at me to get dressed and meet me here in the lobby. I listened. I did it. Here I am. Now talk, damn it!"

Jack and Cyrus loped ahead to the entrance to the underground parking lot, where they'd parked their rental earlier. He was talking as fast as he was walking. "Lionel Lewis, the head of the Cavaliers, called to tell me that two of his boys spotted what he thinks is Zack Meadows's Mercedes parked at the back end of Happy Village. He said he swears it's Meadows's car, but with a Kansas license plate on the back. Charles ran the number Lionel gave us earlier, and the Benz is registered in Zack Meadows's name. It's a simple matter to lift a plate and put another one in its place. He thinks that's what Meadows did. The question is, what is Meadows doing at Happy Village at three o'clock in the morning? That's all I know, so if you have any other questions, I do not have the answers for them."

"So nobody knows we're going to Happy Village?" Dennis said uneasily.

"That would be correct," Jack said, sliding behind the wheel. He waited for Cyrus to buckle up before he started the engine. "Buckle up, Dennis, then send off a text to Maggie and Ted. They won't get it till later, but by then we should be back at Babylon. Or not."

It was the "or not" that was bothering Dennis. He immediately sent off not one but three texts, including Espinosa at the last minute. It didn't make him feel any better.

"Lionel told me to park behind the second building on Lilac Lane. He said there is a carport there with two vacant spaces. One belongs to his mother, who drove to her sister's to help her out because she broke her arm. We're to park in her space. The other space he said belongs to one of the tenants who mysteriously disappeared. He'll be waiting for us when we get there."

"This could be a wild goose chase, you know that, right, Jack?"

"Of course I know that, but then again, as Lionel pointed out, the tenants—even the ones who are well-off financially—do not drive Mercedes. He also pointed out that people do not come calling at Happy Village at two o'clock in the morning, and yes, it means whoever it is has been there for over an hour. That's why he called us."

"To do what?" Dennis asked.

"I don't know, but it has to mean something. Meetings in the middle of the night have the ring of clandestine to them. You know, CIA, FBI. Spook stuff. No peering eyes, no chance encounters, secrecy, that kind of thing. We're not going to *do* anything, if that's what is worrying you, kid. We're just going to observe, try to figure out what's going on, and document it all. As well as run the Kansas plate to see if it's legit. We'll check in with the team in the morning when we get back and run it all up the flagpole."

Dennis relaxed and let his mind go blank. Whatever was going to be was going to be, and there was nothing he could do about any of it. At least for the moment. "This is a weird case, in my opinion. I know I've been on board only a few years, but it seems to me we always had some clues, something to point us in the right direction. We really don't have anything. We could be wasting our time right now, for all we know. I refuse to believe some bunch of gangbangers are smarter than we are. What did we miss, Jack?" he asked as he typed in the Kansas license plate to see what he could find out.

"I don't think we missed anything, kid, for the simple reason there was nothing to miss. We're a little further ahead than we were when we got here. We all feel Gentry Lomax is not what he seems and might possibly be racist in the bargain. Then we have Zack Meadows, who is Cosmo Cricket's partner at Happy Village, who might or might not be involved somehow in Cricket's shooting. We just have to sit down and figure out the why of it all."

"We're coming up to the turnoff for Happy Village. Lionel told me to turn off my lights, cut my speed to ten miles an hour, and park. He said the elderly don't do a lot of sleeping at night and instead spend a lot of time looking out their windows. I assume he knows what he's talking about, so we're going to do what he said. Watch for the street and building signs."

Dennis laughed when he heard Cyrus unbuckle his seat belt. "He knows where we are, so make a right turn and go one block. There it is, Lilac Lane! Coast around the back. I hope your guy wasn't yanking your chain and is here to meet us."

Lionel Lewis stepped out of the shadows the moment Jack turned off the engine. Jack opened the door and stepped out into the velvety, humid darkness. Cyrus inched closer to Jack's leg but allowed Lionel to stroke his head.

"Anything happen since you called me?" Jack asked.

"Yes and no. As I explained earlier, we take turns patrolling at night, so some of us can catch a few hours' sleep. Dom was watching Gentry Lomax's place. The guy doesn't believe in closing his blinds, so Dom could see him clearly. He was in for the night, watching wrestling. His lights went out at 1:37. Dom hung around for fifteen minutes to see if he'd make an appearance, but he didn't."

"If the driver of the Benz is Zack Meadows, then who is he here to see? I was under the impression he didn't have much of a relationship with the tenants."

"And that's true. But it doesn't mean he couldn't meet someone here at one of the empty units. He has access to all the keys. Lights usually go out for the night around eleven, give or take a few minutes. Except for Miz Louise. She leaves her porch light on all night in the hopes her wayward son will come for a visit. He's in jail, but she doesn't know that. It's the only light that's on in the whole complex, discounting the sodium vapor lamps at the end of each street."

Dennis strained to see in the darkness. "So then, what's our game plan here? Or don't we have one?"

Lionel shrugged. "My boys are on foot patrol. They check in every ten or fifteen minutes. So far, no one is out and about, so whomever Meadows is visiting, they're indoors, probably sitting in the dark, hatching some devious plan. I'm assuming it's Meadows. I could be wrong. Stay close, and I'll lead the way to where the Benz is parked."

"Let me make sure I have this right," Jack said in a deep whisper. "We're going to stake out the car and see who drives off in it, is that your thinking?"

"Yep. No sense running around like clueless chickens. We wait him or her out, as the case may be. At least we'll know for sure if it's Meadows."

"And then what?" Dennis hissed.

"Then I don't know. That's up to you and your people. I'm just doing my job here to the best of my ability. You guys are the investigators. We'll help in any way we can, but our help is limited to this immediate area."

Jack looked down at his watch. "It's after four now. Another hour and it will start getting light out. I'm thinking whoever is driving that car will want to be long gone before that."

"I agree," Lionel said. "What are you going to do if it turns out that it is Mr. Meadows?"

"You mean other than confronting him? No clue," Jack said. "For now, we just tuck that little factoid away for the future. Dennis, you having any luck running that Kansas plate number?"

"Actually, it's coming through right now. That plate was issued to one Ethel Farmington, and it belongs on a 2012 Ford Explorer. I'm googling Ethel right now. Ahhh, okay, here we go. Ethel has worked in the passport office for the past thirty-nine years. She is set to retire next month. She posted on Facebook that she was driving with three friends to Las Vegas for a preretirement party. If she stuck to her plan, she got here two days ago and is staying at the Luxor with her friends. According to her post, she will be here for an entire week."

"Makes sense," Lionel said. "She arrived, parked her vehicle, and takes either a taxi or an Uber to get around. You saw how clogged the roads are. It's stop-and-go twenty-four seven, and usually more stop than go. She'd never know her plate was switched. The driver of the Benz will replace it shortly, and no one will ever be the wiser."

Jack looked at Dennis, who nodded that he understood. "You want me to go to the Luxor and scout out the Ford Explorer, right? How am I gonna get there? I don't see a bunch of taxis or Ubers lined up waiting for me."

"Take the van. Lionel can give me a lift back once we make a clear ID on the driver of the Benz. Just be sure you're in a good position to take a picture of the guy putting the plate back on the car. There will be light in the garage. I'll do my best to take a shot of him getting into the car here, but I'm not hopeful it will satisfy Charles. He likes everything verified one hundred percent, so do your best. Go already!"

Dennis hit the ground running.

Cyrus suddenly bounded upright from where he'd been dozing at Jack's feet. "He's coming like *now*," Jack said.

In the blink of an eye, Lionel ripped into his backpack and pulled out two sets of night-vision goggles. "You know what these are, right?"

"You betcha," Jack said, slipping them on. The world immediately turned green, but the images were crystal clear. His hand dropped to the big shepherd's head to calm him. "Easy, boy, easy." Cyrus calmed immediately.

"Here he comes," Lionel whispered.

Having met Zack Meadows only once, Jack wondered if he would be able to ID the man. Black hoodie, black pants, black shoes. The dark-clad figure turned to look around. Beard. Meadows did not have a beard. He blinked when he saw the hooded figure press the key fob to open the door at the same moment he reached up to rip off the beard on his face. Bingo! Jack held his phone out and snapped picture after picture, hoping at least one of them would be worth something in Charles's eyes.

"It's him. It's really Mr. Meadows!" Lionel all but squealed.

"Sure is," Jack whispered in return.

He quickly sent off a text to Dennis, telling him they had confirmation the driver of the Benz was indeed Zack Meadows.

"Back, back," Lionel said as he pulled at Jack's arm. "His headlights will light you up like a Roman candle. Move, damn it!" Cyrus moved, then Jack simply dropped to the ground, as did Lionel. "We're good," Lionel said, packing up the two sets of night-vision goggles. "That was close for sure."

"Too close," Jack said, his nerves twanging all over the place.

"I have to check in with the guys. Ten more minutes and it will start getting light out. I can take you to town and be back here to write up my report just in time to end my shift. Does that work for you and Cyrus?"

"Sure. Take your time. What are the chances that one of your guys saw who Meadows was meeting?"

"Not good. They would have been in touch right away if that had happened. Whoever it was got away, so that has to mean he knows this complex, knows we patrol, and knows how to make a quick, quiet getaway. We can't be everywhere. I wish I had more people, but I don't, so we just do the best we can. Ten minutes and we can head to town."

Jack sat on the ground, his back to a spindly young tree, and hugged his knees, Cyrus at his feet. His thoughts were flying in all directions as he tried to make sense of what had just happened. Who was the nameless, faceless person Zack Meadows met here at Happy Village? That fact alone had to mean that Gentry Lomax was in the clear where Cosmo Cricket was concerned. And yet . . . his gut was telling him that Lomax was not what he appeared to be. Maybe there were two factions working against Cosmo.

Charles and the others were going to want answers, and he didn't have any to give them.

What the hell am I missing here?

Lionel was as good as his word. Exactly ten minutes later, he led Jack and Cyrus to his car. He grinned at the expression on Jack's face. "If I told you what this baby could do on the open road, you would pass out cold. Everything under the hood is brand-new. Took me and the boys over a year to finish it. We left the outside looking as it does on purpose, so no one would steal it. So far, we've been lucky. Mr. Lomax, however, insists we hide it when we bring it here. Said the optics are not good as far as advertising the place goes. He does have a point, I guess. When we're here, we can use the Jeep, and there are three golf carts. He doesn't like that Mr. Cricket gave me a set of keys to all of them. I wish I could figure him out. By the way, where am I taking you, Mr. Emery?"

"To the underground garage at the Luxor. I sent Dennis a text to wait for me there. I appreciate the ride. You're right about that engine. Purrs like the proverbial kitten."

Jack leaned back and closed his eyes. He knew Lionel wanted to pick his brain, but even if he was willing to share, there was nothing worth picking inside his head. He felt as if he were surrounded by brick walls with no exit anywhere in sight. He hated these moments, because he felt he wasn't doing *something*. What that something was, of course, he had no idea. That, by definition, is what makes it one of those moments.

Jack was jarred from his thoughts when Lionel said,

"We're here, Mr. Emery. I'm going to drop you off here on the side. Just walk to the left, go down the ramp, and scoot under the bar. Cyrus won't have a problem. Call me if you need me to do something for you. Just remember, we don't go on duty till seven o'clock. I probably shouldn't tell you this, but since you're one of the good guys, I will. Bessie Love checks in with me to let me know what's going on. Usually, she texts me twice a day. Even if she has nothing to report, which is pretty much the case every day."

"Okay, and thanks again for the ride. I'll be in touch, Lionel. I'm going to make it my business to go out to the hospital at some point. I'll send you a text on what the doctors tell me."

"Thanks. Good luck."

Jack and Cyrus watched the rickety, rusty car until it was out of sight. "I like that kid, Cyrus, I really do. He's got his head on straight for sure. Let's go see what Dennis has for us. When we get to the middle of this level, I want you to bark your head off so Dennis knows where we are, you got that?" Cyrus let out a soft woof to show he understood what he was to do. And he did it right on cue. The sound bounced off the cavernous walls, then bounced again. Jack thought his eardrums would rupture. Within seconds, Jack could hear Dennis shout, "I'm on three and coming down. Don't move. Stay where I can see you."

Jack winced when he heard tires squeal as Dennis put the pedal to the metal. When he slammed on his brakes and skidded to a stop, Cyrus let loose with a mind-blowing howl of outrage. The van's doors slid open, and Cyrus hopped in, still indicating his displeasure with a low growl as Jack slid onto the passenger seat next to Dennis.

"I got pictures. The lighting on three is bad. Some of the lights were burned out or turned off, which I'm thinking Meadows did beforehand. The third floor is full, not a space to be found."

"How did you find out where Ethel was parked?"

"Called the desk and asked. I told them I tapped her fender and wanted to leave a note with my insurance information. They were okay with that. She has a handicapped sticker, so she was assigned a spot closest to the elevator and service door. Which, by the way, is usually very well lit. Today, it was dark as Hades. My phone has a built-in something or other for extra lighting. Here's the kicker, though, Jack. I don't know if Meadows could see the flash. It didn't look like he did, but you never know.

"The other thing is that he had that license plate off and back on within seconds, and he was out of there like a bat out of hell. He knew what he was doing, that's for sure. We're making good time here. This must be the time of day you can go out and actually arrive at your destination in a reasonable time. Let's grab some breakfast in that café on the mezzanine level at Babylon. I'm starved. We can bring Cyrus, since you have all his service credentials," Dennis babbled until he was out of breath.

"Sounds good to me. I'm sure Charles will make breakfast when we all show up at eight o'clock, but it will be nine before we eat, so yeah, let's head to the café. I see a stack of buttermilk pancakes with my name on them. I don't know why I'm so hungry," Jack said.

"It's the adrenaline rush we've been dealing with since three o'clock this morning. Even Cyrus seems antsy. A nice, leisurely breakfast is a good way to wind down," Dennis said as he brought the van to a stop in front of the casino and turned it over to the valet.

"You go in and get us a table. I'll walk Cyrus and meet up with you in a few minutes. I'll wash up, then you can take your turn when I get in there."

Jack looked left and right. "Okay, big guy, pick a direction and let's have at it." Cyrus dutifully sauntered off and returned in seven minutes.

Business taken care of, Jack sat down at a table and savored his first cup of coffee of the day. It was always the best. They gave their order and just stared at each other. Dennis spoke first.

"I know you must have some thoughts swirling about inside that head of yours, Jack, so let's hear them. Tonight was definitely not a waste of time, but I have no idea what it all means other than that Zack Meadows is fully professional at lifting license plates and doing things he shouldn't be doing at three in the morning. Do you think there's a mole, a ringer, a plant of some kind, someone living in Happy Village who is tied to Meadows?"

"I'd say that's a pretty good bet since nothing else makes sense. How would anyone know? He could have had whoever it is moved in years ago, months ago. In the business, we call them sleepers. They operate legitimately, have jobs, go about their business until they're called upon to do something. It's all about blending in so no one gets suspicious. If that's the case, the next question is why? What's the end game? What is it they're aiming for? Was it to shoot Cosmo Cricket? That doesn't even make sense, since no one knew he was going out to Happy Village that day."

"I don't think we're going to know anything until Mr. Cricket is able to talk and make sense. For all we know, he might know nothing and was simply at the wrong place at the wrong time. Ahhh, here comes our food."

Jack blinked at the stack of a dozen fluffy pancakes with melted butter and warm syrup dripping down the sides and onto his plate. He sighed mightily as he wondered if he could possibly eat all of them. Then he eyed Cyrus's plate—four scrambled eggs, one sausage patty, and four slices of bacon, extra crisp, along with two side dishes of carrots and apples. A metal water bowl with a few tinkling ice cubes was set on the floor by the waiter. Cyrus waited patiently, knowing his food had to cool before Jack would let him eat.

Jack eyed the food on Dennis's plate. Waffles smothered with sliced chicken and gravy, applesauce, and skinny string beans on the side. "How can you eat that for breakfast, Dennis?"

"I grew up on it, that's how. My grandpa said it would grow hair on my chest, and he was right. Soon as I started eating it, I got hair on my chest. Also, it is delicious. My question is, How in the hell can you eat a stack of pancakes that's a foot high?"

Jack stuck his finger in the mound of scrambled eggs and decided they were cool enough for Cyrus. He set the plate on the floor and tucked into his pancakes. He ate them all. Cyrus licked his plate clean, and Dennis polished off his food in record time.

"Now all I want to do is go to sleep," Jack grumbled. "I'm stuffed, and it's all your fault, Dennis. This was your idea. We should have just gone with coffee and toast and waited for Charles to make something." Cyrus growled deep in his throat to show what he thought of that particular idea. Dining out meant he got a real meal as opposed to what Charles fed him—a skimpy, lean, and mean meal on Dr. Pappas's orders.

Jack dug around in his pockets for money to leave for the waiter. Then he signed the check, knowing the hotel would pick up the tab. Thank God for Annie and her generosity. "Dennis, let me see those pictures again."

Dennis took out Jack's phone, which Jack had given him earlier; clicked it on; and scrolled through the apps till he found what he wanted. "If you dare tell me that isn't Zack Meadows, then I am a monkey's uncle. That's him! The lighting isn't all that good, but you can still make out his features. Charles will have to agree, Dennis."

"You know what, Jack. I bet if we went to wherever it is

that Meadows lives and broke into his car, we'd find that damn beard he ripped off back there at Happy Village. You wanna go for it?"

"Nah. These pictures are good enough. I caught him ripping it off, so that's just as good. C'mon, I want to take a shower and wash the stink of the night off me. I'll meet you up at the penthouse when I'm ready."

"Works for me," Dennis said, pushing his chair back under the table. "Do you want me to take Cyrus out for you?"

Jack looked down at the big dog. "You need to do anything?" Two short woofs. No.

"Thanks for a fun night, Jack," Dennis said, a wicked grin playing around the corners of his mouth. "Let's just not make a habit of middle-of-the-night trysts."

Jack laughed out loud.

"What's so funny?" Dennis demanded.

"I was just thinking of Maggie and how ticked off she's going to be when she finds out we went without her."

"Yeah, that is pretty funny." Dennis chortled as he stepped into the elevator. "But five will get you ten she had more fun than we did."

Jack scowled. "There is that."

Chapter 10

Cyrus was the first off the elevator. He bounded through the foyer and headed straight for the state-of-the-art kitchen, where everyone was seated at the large round table, drinking coffee. The big shepherd made the rounds to get his ears tickled, his belly rubbed, and a few treats, which he devoured before settling himself next to Jack's chair.

Maggie handed Jack a slip of paper with a wild flourish, and said, "Ta-da!"

"What's this?" Jack asked.

"William Devane's agent's number for you to give to Harry. I told you yesterday we have a book of agents at the paper. Well, here it is. One big question: Is Harry going to call him? I did my part," Maggie said, smacking her hands together dramatically to make her point.

Jack snorted. "Like Harry is really going to do that. He's going to dump it right back on me. Harry doesn't do commercials no matter how much they offer in payment, so it's a moot point even if that guy would agree to the deal."

"Run it up the flagpole and see if he salutes," Ted said, laughing out loud. When Jack didn't make a move to pull out his cell phone, Ted reached for his own and pressed in the number 4 for Harry's phone. The gang stopped what they were doing to listen to the conversation the minute Ted pressed the SPEAKER button.

"Hey, Harry, you winning big?" Ted didn't bother waiting for a response. He dived right into the conversation. "Listen, Maggie came up with that gold guy's agent, and I have the number right here for you to call. You got a pen, or can you type the number into your phone?" The gang listened to a string of Chinese that literally bounced off the walls of Annie's kitchen. Doing his best not to laugh, Ted said, "I don't understand Chinese, Harry, so let's go with English. But before you do that, know this. You gotta give a little to get a little, so be prepared to . . . you know . . . maybe make some concessions to help out your friends, and they are *your* friends, aren't they? You want to talk to Jack, is that what you said?"

A gleeful look on his face, Ted handed the phone to Jack. If looks could kill, Ted would have expired on the spot. Everyone in the room leaned forward to hear what they all thought was going to be a one-of-a-kind conversation.

"So, how much did your friends win last night?" Jack asked in a jittery voice. "Uh-huh. Yep, that is a lot of money! They can't stop the boys from gambling if they aren't doing anything wrong. Yeah, yeah, yeah, I get that security is tight and they are being watched. So what? Some people are just out-and-out lucky. You could pull the discrimination card if it's getting out of hand. I guess. I'm not up on casinos and how they operate and do things. I'm talking to you now from a lawyer's perspective. Just call the guy and see if it's even possible? Or have your guys call the 1-800 number and place an order for the gold.

"How much longer are the guys here for? Timing is everything, Harry. Talk to them, Harry, then call me back. Did I just hear you right? The boys have a charter plane at the ready! Well, damn, Harry, do you or your friends really think a Brink's truck is going to pull up alongside a charter plane bound for someplace in Asia and unload five million dollars in gold without anybody saying a word to anybody? I get the part where they believe if they can't hold it, then they don't really own it. Truth in advertising. That's crap, Harry. I'm hanging up now because this is giving me a headache."

Jack handed Ted back his phone and snarled, "Don't anyone say one word. Not one word." He massaged his temples as he looked at Dennis and nodded. "Dennis will fill you guys and Maggie in on our night's adventure while I try to figure out Harry's next move." Jack continued to massage his temples as Fergus poured him a fresh cup of coffee and Dennis recounted their nonadventures of the early morning hours.

After letting the coffee cool down some, Jack was about to take his first sip, but he almost jumped out of his skin when Maggie shrilled at the top of her lungs, "You two went without me?! How could you do that?" The cup Jack was holding flew into the air, the coffee splashing everywhere.

Jack knew he needed to get a grip, or things were going to go to downhill very quickly. He almost passed out in relief when he heard Dennis say, "Maggie, be reasonable. You are just getting over the flu, and you also just traveled cross-country. Furthermore, when you left, you left with Ted, which meant to all of us that you were going to . . . um . . . spend the night with him. It's not like Jack or I participated in any kind of action. We pretty much just stood around and watched what was going on. You really didn't miss anything. I just told you all what happened and showed the pictures we took. There was nothing you could have done even if you had been there. So get over it and let's move on here and make some plans."

Slightly mollified because her young colleague made sense, Maggie started to chew on her thumbnail. She nodded, meaning she was okay with Dennis's explanation. For now. With Maggie, it was always *for now*.

Before anyone at the table could decide what to do, the elevator pinged. Cyrus was like a black streak of lightning as he sprinted forward to meet Abner and Avery Snowden.

"Well, it's about time," Maggie exploded as she took her frustration out on Abner and Avery. "Where have you guys been all this time? You know the rules. You don't go off the grid for more than a few hours at a time. What's going on? Why do you look like . . . like . . . someone just died."

"Coffee anyone?" Fergus asked, just to have something to say.

"I think I could use a cuppa tea, mate," Avery said.

"Tomato juice," Abner said.

Charles did his best not to stare at his old friend Avery. In all the years they were in service to Her Majesty, he'd never seen the old spy look like he looked at that moment. Not even during their stint serving in MI-5. He felt his gut start to churn, and then he looked at Abner, who in another minute was going to lose the tomato juice he'd just consumed. "The lavatory is over there to the right off the short hallway. Go!" Abner sprinted as fast as his legs could carry him.

Everyone at the table shouted at once, "What? What?"

Charles decided to take the lead the minute Abner returned to the table. He deliberately kept his voice neutral as he brought the two newcomers up-to-date. "And that's where we are at the moment. Of course, we also have to contend with Harry's friends' problems, but that is separate and aside from what is going on at Happy Village. The two of you have been off the grid for a day and a half. You both know the rules: Three hours is the max you can be off grid. You both broke that rule. There are consequences to rule breaking. This is not like either one of you, so that tells me something very unexpected happened to keep you from checking in. Speak up and tell us what you found, what you know, and where the rest of us fit into the equation." One look at Abner's white, drawn face forced him to choose Avery to tell the tale.

"I took over one of the conference rooms off the mezzanine. We've been here at the hotel the whole time. It took us a few hours to set up shop and get my five operatives on board. We've all been at it from the time we split up. There were eight of us in total, if you count Abner's friend Philonias Needlemeyer, who, by the way, was a godsend. He got us to places no one but the Devil goes. I'm not just talking about the dark web; I'm talking about the ugly, black underbelly of the dark web. That's where the Devil and his disciples reign supreme. As you can see, I'm up there in years and I thought I'd seen everything, thought nothing could shock me or shake me. I was wrong. I regret that young Abner here had to see what I saw, because he will have to carry those images with him for the rest of his life."

All eyes turned to Abner, who just looked sick to his stomach. Maggie offered him a stick of gum. "Chew it, Abby. It will settle your stomach because it's peppermint, and mint is good for sick stomachs." Abner reached for the gum and nodded in thanks.

Cyrus, sensing something not right with his travel buddy, got up and walked over to where Abner was sitting and nuzzled his leg. Abner looked down, smiled, and started to stroke the big shepherd's head. He felt himself calm almost immediately. He wondered what it was, the gum or the dog—maybe the combination of the two.

Avery said, "I might be able to answer some questions, but I'm going to leave you all for an hour or so to go shower and change into fresh clothes. I want you all to use that time to decide if you want to hear what we saw and read and heard. We do have some very graphic pictures. I will tell you this. At least five of the tenants from Happy Village who disappeared are dead. I'm sure the other fifteen are, too, we just didn't . . . um . . . see them. But what we heard indicates they are also dead. Think on this. I'll be back in an hour, and we'll talk more. Abner can answer any questions you might have in the meantime."

No one moved. No one spoke. Cyrus continued allowing Abner to stroke his head.

Maggie finally took the initiative. "Is anything you and Avery know or saw gang related?"

"Yes, very much so, sad to say," Abner said quietly.

"Can you be more specific, Abby?" Maggie asked gently. "If you would rather wait for Avery to get back, we can deal with all of it then. It's not like we're on deadline here. In the meantime, I guess we could look at the pictures you guys have. Ted can put them on the TV for better clarity if you give him your phone."

Abner exploded off his chair, his arms waving wildly. "Good God, no! Don't put those pictures up till Avery gets back. Look, I'm no more of a wuss than any of you, but I have my limits, and I know you do, too. Yes, I lost my cookies a few minutes ago, but Avery lost his earlier, so don't go thinking I'm less than he is. My best advice to all of you is not to look at them and just go with what we both tell you."

"C'mon, Abby, we've all seen dead bodies before, if that's where this is all leading. Let's get this show on the road. Ted, put them on the TV!" Maggie ordered.

"Wait just a damn minute," Jack growled. "Who put you in charge, Maggie? We should at least give some credence to what Abner is telling us and put it to a vote. Raise your hand to see the pictures." Maggie's hand shot high in the air. "You're outnumbered, so give it up already. We're waiting for Avery."

And that was the end of that.

Disgust ringing in her voice, Maggie said, "So I guess that means we wait for Avery, okay, I get it. But I would be terribly remiss if I didn't remind you all that a picture is worth a thousand words. That's why I'm having a hard time understanding your reticence. Men!" she snorted, as if that one word summed it all up.

Annie's beautiful kitchen suddenly exploded in a whirlwind of activity. Charles turned the water on in the sink, Fergus started banging pots, while Ted and Espinosa circled Dennis and whispered in his ear. Jack got up and started to pace the long, narrow kitchen, his thoughts on Harry and his immediate problem, along with worries about Little Jack and his upcoming swim meet on the weekend and wondering if he would be able to make it to the swim camp to see his godchild perform. On his third lap around the kitchen, he zeroed in on Dennis, who was doing his best not to laugh out loud.

"What's so funny?" Jack demanded.

"I think we just came up with a solution to Harry's problem," Ted said. "All we—meaning you, Jack—have to do is convince Harry that this is a better solution."

Miffed that her colleagues didn't see fit to include her in whatever was about to come out, Maggie snarled, "Well, what is it?"

"That guy on the TV with the pillows. The one who is all over television twenty-four seven. I just saw his newest commercial, and if you buy one of his pillows, you get two more. All for the price of *one!* Think about it! Harry's buddies have millions. They could buy hundreds of thousands of pillows and get hundreds of thousands more for free, and Lizzie could handle the export end of it as opposed to trying to buy gold and sneaking it out of the country. This way Harry won't have to worry about the Treasury Department and the IRS going after him or his buddies. Or them. Buying pillows is legitimate. Everyone sleeps on a pillow."

All activity in the kitchen came to a standstill as Dennis's words were processed. Cyrus let loose with two sharp barks, which indicated he approved of the idea. Jack whistled. "Ya know, that just might get Harry off the hook. Good thinking, Dennis. Now, who wants to call Harry with the good news?" There were no takers on Jack's offer, and he knew there wouldn't be, so he pulled out his phone and punched in Harry's number.

"Speak," Harry said.

Jack sucked in a deep breath. Harry was such a card sometimes. Never saying two words when one would do.

"I have an idea, Harry. As I told you earlier, buying and moving the amount of gold your guys want is a serious problem. You know it, too, and are just being a stubborn ass over all of this. We, as in all of us here in Annie's kitchen, came up with what we think might be a solution to the problem. You ready to hear it?" Jack sucked in another deep breath as he waited for Harry's response.

"Hit me!"

"Pillows!" Jack said triumphantly. "The guy who is all over television and advertises on just about every channel all day and all night. Right now he has a promotion going on where if you buy one pillow, you get two for free. And remember this, the guy guarantees a good night's sleep on his pillows. He manufactures the pillows here in the good old US of A! Lizzie can do all the paperwork, the export end of things, and it keeps it legal. *Legal* is the key word here. Think about it, Harry, hundreds of thousands of pillows! They buy one and get two free ones to sell. Think of the profit margin. Your friends will be so rich, they won't know what to do with all their money."

As Jack said good-bye to Harry, Dennis tried to calculate the profit margin on the pillows. He waved the calculator app on his phone around so everyone could see the numbers. "They might have to do some promotion, give away a few thousand at first. Then everyone will want one. There's no way this won't work, and it's all legal!"

"Good! Good! You can give Harry the numbers and see what happens. I hear the elevator, so that means Avery is about to arrive. Do it now, Dennis, so it's not hanging over our heads with what we are going to be dealing with in regard to Avery and Abner," Jack said, only too glad not to have to argue with Harry again.

Dennis nodded and started to tap out his text to Harry.

Charles motioned for everyone to take a seat at the table. Fergus poured fresh coffee, and Charles called the meeting to order.

Jack narrowed his eyes. Something was wrong here. In all the years he'd known Sir Charles Martin, he had never seen the big man who had all the answers looking so rattled. And while he hadn't known Avery Snowden and Abner Tookus as long, he was seeing something in their expressions that defied words. *What the hell is going on?*

He looked down at Cyrus, who was picking up on something because he had his head pressed tight against Jack's leg, not for a head stroke or a belly rub or even a treat. The big dog sensed what Jack figured they were all feeling. He just didn't know what to do about it.

"The short version will do nicely for the moment, Avery. Later we can delve into the intricacies." While Charles was speaking to Avery Snowden, his gaze was on Abner, who was leaning back in his chair with his eyes closed. He looked drawn and haggard, but then Avery looked the same way. A shiver of something he'd never felt before rushed over him.

"How short is short, Sir Charles? Before I share anything, don't you all want some background so you fully understand where Abner and I are coming from?"

"I think the highlights, then the guts, then back to highlights will work for all of us," Maggie said, impatience ringing in her voice. The others mumbled their agreement, even Abner, whose eyes snapped open as he bolted upright.

Snowden cleared his throat. "Almost everyone knows or has at least heard of the dark side of the web, where nefarious things go on. There are layers and layers to go through, and you literally need a map to traverse it or someone who has already traveled there. I personally did not know there was such a place. It's hell. That's the bottom line. The dark web is like an onion: You peel back the layers until you reach the underbelly, which is where the Devil and his disciples live. I'd never been there, nor had Abner, but his friend Philonias has. He traveled it with ease and took us along for the ride."

"It's not something I ever want to do again," Abner said quietly.

"Nor I," Snowden said, just as quietly.

"Everyone seated at this table is a grown-up, Avery. I think we can handle whatever you are about to tell us. Ted, Dennis, Espinosa, and I have seen it all. We're investigative reporters. You learn to deal with the unreal, the unthinkable, then you move on. It's what we're trained to do, so would you please just tell us what you found out. Is all of this gang related?" Maggie said, a definite edge to her tone.

Dennis was only half listening as he concentrated on texting Harry his hard sell of pillows. He stopped what he was doing when he heard Maggie's comments about the gangs. He made a face, clicked SEND, turned his phone to vibrate, and gave his full attention to what was going on at the table.

"Of course it's gang related. Only the depraved reside in the underbelly. We came in contact with, or I should say Phil came in contact with, members from Crips, the Bloods, and the Lobos gangs. I can give you a few statistics on the Lobos and leave the others to talk about later. Lobos seems to be front and center in this area. Nevada is rated seventh for most wanted gang members per capita. The FBI crime statistics report states they have about a hundred thousand members. Vegas Metro has the highest reported crime rate."

Snowden looked down at his notes and said, "There were 7,277 violent crimes, 83 murders, 2,537 robberies, 3,922 aggravated assault cases, and 22,234 property crimes this past year. Not good."

"I think Chicago is worse than that," Ted said.

"We aren't in Chicago, Ted. We're in Vegas, where Cosmo Cricket got shot, so we have to work with what we have. Early on, Abner came up with a theory, and I think he's spot-on. To join any of these gangs, you have to be initiated. Gangs like the Scorpions, the Rats, and the Snakes are small-town-gang terrorists hankering to join the big boys, have their own cells. If you can't pass the initiation test, then you might as well pack up and leave town. You lose face, and no one fears you. That's how they survive, through fear. Their motto is, rape, kill, control.

"The Lobos gang is known for cutting off limbs, murder, and drug trafficking. Right here in southern Nevada, they are actively recruiting, and every member of the Scorpions has applied for membership. In anticipation of being accepted, they've all gotten Lobos tattoos on their chests. Looks to be maybe around eight thousand Lobos members in Nevada, and they're ready to branch out by recruiting from other gangs. While they're the deadliest, the Mexican gangs recruit more actively.

"Their weapons of choice are firearms, heavy chains, machetes, and clubs. Their favorite targets are middle school and high school students.

"I think that's enough background for now. We can beat it to death later, when we fine-tune it all for background. Right now, this is what we all need to know. As I said earlier, Abner has a theory he'd like to share."

"I think—and this is not just my opinion but Phil's as well—we think killing Cosmo Cricket was the Scorpions' initiation exercise and they botched it. The Scorpions have lost face among the various gangs. In other words, they aren't worthy of being invited to join the Lobos, which was and probably still is their goal."

"Are the Lobos here? I mean here in Vegas," Jack asked.

"We think so. They're swallowing up the smaller gangs, indoctrinating them, and still actively recruiting," Snowden said.

"Phil thinks something else is going on. The missing tenants. Avery and I didn't think so until he took his search down to the bottom level. We have the pictures that he took."

"What does that mean?" Maggie demanded. "Do you mean two separate gangs working at cross-purposes? What?"

Up until now, Charles had remained quiet. He locked his gaze with Snowden and said, "The tenants are separate and probably kidnapped for their money. As I understand it, those who left had robust portfolios and probably large insurance policies. It's all about money. It's one way of looking at it, and the only one that makes any kind of sense, at least to me. The big question is, who called the shots on that one and who collected the payouts, if there were any. I think that the gang angle, and Cosmo's getting shot, are exactly what you stated—an initiation exercise to get accepted into the Lobos. Unfortunately for them, they botched the job. If I am right, shooting Cosmo was about prestige and no money changed hands. Since I could be wrong, I'm open to any and all theories."

An eerie silence settled around the table, but no one said anything.

"This might be a good time to . . . um show you the pictures Phil took. If you'll give me just a minute. I can bring them up on the TV. Ted, bring it here to the table, then we'll all be able to see what goes on the dark web. Be warned, it is not pretty."

Jack felt his stomach start to rumble. He looked over at Abner's ashen face and said, "Hey, Ab, you mind taking Cyrus for a walk?"

Cyrus was at the door before Abner could get out of his chair.

The silence was total as Snowden fiddled and diddled with his phone and the memory stick and with situating the TV. Jack coughed, just to hear some sound.

"Just a few seconds. Phil didn't keep the camera on any one shot for more than a second, so what you're going to see is what he saw and was able to capture. Okay, gentlemen and one lady, here we go."

The TV came to life with images so ugly no one was able to utter a word until Maggie gripped the edge of the table and said, "What is *that?*"

Avery Snowden looked across the table at Charles and said, "*That*, my dear, is the head of Ellie Harper, who lived at one time at 202 Lilac Lane. She disappeared on April 17. I believe you said you were in her apartment, that her friend and neighbor took you there."

Maggie bolted from the table and ran to the lavatory, where she slammed the door shut.

"I think the rest of the pictures tell their own story. The bodies were cut up. Legs in one pile, arms in another, feet in a box, torsos on the top. Heads all by themselves." Avery turned off the TV and ejected the memory stick.

"Do we know who . . . who is responsible for what we just saw?" Charles asked."

"Phil thinks it was the Scorpions, but in a deal that had nothing to do with the Lobos, one that predates any idea about joining the Lobos. Undoubtedly a separate contractor. They were paid to kill the twenty people who disappeared from Happy Village, obviously kidnapped and probably tortured to get them to change their wills, take funds from their stock portfolios, whatever. We don't know yet who collected the insurance or how that was done. My people are working on it. Cosmo was probably an initiation, pure and simple. It could have been anyone that day according to this theory, but he was the one who happened to show up in the middle of the afternoon. We have to run with that until Cosmo can tell us himself what he was doing at Happy Village the day he got shot."

Jack shook his head violently. "I'm not buying that, Snowden. What was Zack Meadows doing out at Happy Village at four o'clock in the morning in his own car sporting a pilfered license plate? Nah, I'm not buying your theory. I think he's up to his eyeballs in this unholy mess."

Maggie returned to the table. Espinosa handed her a stick of gum. She accepted it gratefully, then apologized and only gagged once before she headed for the coffeepot and proceeded to clean it out to make a fresh pot. It was something to do, and she wasn't ready to defend her bolt to the lavatory. She knew in her gut it would take forever to live that down, especially since she was the one who pressed and pressed to see the pictures.

"All I'm saying, Jack, is what Phil told us. That was his theory, or maybe Abner's, I'm not sure anymore. I do know they both agreed, and they are the world's best hackers, so we have to pay attention to what they say. Doesn't mean they're right. And remember this—they didn't know about Meadows's middle-of-the-night run to Happy Village when they came up with this scenario."

"So what do we do now?" Ted asked.

All eyes turned to their fearless leader, Charles.

"At this precise moment, it pains me to say that I do not have a clue."

"How about we do a snatch-and-grab on Meadows?" Jack suggested. "We sweat him till he tells us what we need to know."

"How about we call Lionel and ask him where and how we can get in touch with the Scorpions and snatch-and-grab them?" Dennis said.

"Meadows might be easy to snatch. Then again, maybe not," Fergus said, pouring fresh coffee into everyone's cup. I don't see how you could possibly take on the Scorpions and snatch them all. We're outnumbered."

"No, we're not outnumbered. We have all of Harry's friends. We help them with the pillows, they help us with the Scorpions. Sounds fair to me. Dennis, run that by Harry and see what he thinks. How'd the pillow deal go over?"

"He didn't get back to me on that yet. I'm thinking that the longer it takes is a plus for us. Means he's talking it up and hasn't yet convinced his guys it's a good deal."

"So send our query," Jack said.

"I did."

Cyrus bounded through the hall the minute the penthouse elevator came to a stop. Jack looked up at Abner, who seemed to have regained the color in his face. "It's raining out," he said inanely.

"Good for the gardens," Charles said.

"Terrible for traffic, though," Fergus said. "I'm thinking the casino owners pray for rain so that customers stay in the casinos and gamble."

Dennis reached for his phone when a zippy little tune filled the room. Everyone turned questioning eyes on him.

Dennis grinned. "It's Harry."

Chapter 11

Rap music vied with the thunder that rumbled overhead. Streaks of lightning zipped and danced across the black sky, lighting up the night like a Fourth of July fireworks display. The members of the Scorpions all huddled under a cluster of half-dead trees, watching what they considered a light show and hoping for a stray breeze or a few drops of rain. Anything to drop the temperature even a few degrees. It wasn't happening, though.

It was one-thirty in the morning, and the temperature was a mega ninety-seven degrees, making sleep impossible for the gang members. The cold beer was all gone, the ice long melted. Now there was nothing to do but listen to rap, watch the lightning, and hope for rain.

With the rap music at full throttle and the thunder booming, Alonzo Zuma Santiago was glad he'd put his cell phone on vibrate; otherwise, he never would have known he had a message coming through. He looked at his phone, saw the time, and felt a tickle of alarm. It was late to be getting a call or a text. He debated a few seconds about clicking it on. Did he really need a problem on this bitching, miserable night? No, he did not, but his thumb clicked on the right button anyway. He stared down at the image he saw on the small screen. His heart took on an extra beat. Salty sweat rolled down from his forehead and into his eyes, burning them. It didn't matter; he could still see the image he had been shown, which was not going to go away.

Miggy poked Alonzo in the arm and asked what was wrong. Alonzo didn't bother to respond. He simply showed Miggy the picture on his phone.

Miggy stared up at Alonzo and started to shake, just the way Alonzo was shaking. They both peered down at the three eyeballs glaring up at them from the small screen. "Mig, turn off the music and gather everyone close. Like right *now*."

One minute later, all eighteen members of the Scorpions were hunkered in a tight circle under the half-dead trees. The thunder continued to boom while the lightning continued to dance across the night sky. And then it started to rain, fat drops of water that splashed down, making loud *splat* sounds as they hit the upturned faces of the Scorpions. All they knew was that they weren't hunkering together to talk about the rain finally falling from the sky. And then Alonzo held up his phone and waved it around so all the members could see the image staring back at them.

A voice from the outer circle grumbled. "You said this would never happen. You swore it wouldn't happen. Now what happens to all of us?"

"We need to relocate, and we need to do it right now. We talked about this two days ago. We put a plan in motion, so now we're going to carry out that plan. Pack up. Don't leave anything behind." The rain started to fall harder, forcing Alonzo to talk louder. "This is no time to panic. We always knew this was a possibility. We talked about that, too. At least we have a plan."

"What if it doesn't work?" someone shouted.

"If it happens, we'll deal with it when it happens. If you

all do your part, we should be safe and sound before day-light. Move!"

"Where are we going?" someone else shouted.

"You'll see where we're going when we get there. Now move, and don't ever question me again," Alonzo bellowed to be heard over the rain, thunder, and the cracks of lightning. Heat lightning.

Miggy got to his feet and stared down at his friend. "I'll get the cycles ready. This is not good, Al."

"Tell me something I don't already know. The one thing we have going for us is we've done this drill already. If no one screws up, we should be okay."

"How long do you think we have before the stuff hits the fan?" Miggy asked, fear ringing in his voice.

"An hour. Maybe an hour and a half. We need to move *now*."

Ten minutes later, all ten Harleys were ready to hit the road. The sound equaled that of a 747 directly overhead. One by one, rider and machine peeled away and headed for the highway, the saddlebags loaded with everything the members could gather up.

Alonzo drove the lead Harley, Miggy clutching him around the waist, hanging on for dear life. The rain continued to fall as steam spiraled up from the highway, making it hard to see. Alonzo cursed the sudden absence of lightning. When he needed light, where was it? Even with the fog lights on, the steam continuing to spiral upward in gigantic swirls from the road almost blinded him. His guts churned.

Miggy could feel his friend's tenseness. He closed his eyes and let his thoughts travel to the magical place he hoped to live in one day, where he would sleep on silk sheets and have a refrigerator full of good, nourishing food and tons of cold beer. The magical place where the closets would be full of designer clothes and aftershave lotion that would drive women insane.

It wasn't going to happen, and he knew it. The rest of the gang believed it—even Alonzo believed it—but he didn't. He wondered if that meant he was smarter or stupider. Three eyeballs! Miggy shuddered just as Alonzo slowed down, which meant they were close to where they were going to stash the Harleys. The plan was to make the rest of the way on foot.

If ever there was something to be thankful for, it was the rain coming down like a waterfall, which meant no one would be looking out their windows at this hour of the night. Maybe Alonzo knew what he was doing after all, and they would be safe. But Miggy didn't believe it for a New York minute. Not even half a minute.

Alonzo throttled down and stopped the Harley. He cut the engine and proceeded to walk the Harley into a dense copse of trees. Under the canopy of leaves, the rain was reduced to droplets. He felt as if his body were steaming from the combination of heat and cool rain. He walked a quarter of a mile and stopped. He whistled sharply, which meant for the others to gather close and park their machines. They knew the drill. Everyone fell into line and saluted smartly, something Alonzo insisted on when a job was completed.

"Listen up. We go in in teams of two. Ten minutes apart. I'm going first and will enter through the back door. I know for a fact there's an alarm system, so I'll cut the power line as soon as I get there. For all we know, power might be out with this storm, but I don't want to take a chance. Once I'm inside, I'll go around and open the French doors. Stick to the timing, and we should all be in and secure in ninety minutes. If any of you have anything to say, now is the time to say it." The silence in the mini forest was profound. "Okay then, Miggy and I go first.

Check your watches and follow at ten-minute intervals, and for God's sake, do not get lost.

"You think this is a mistake, don't you?" Alonzo said as he sprinted off, Miggy at his side.

Miggy swiped at the rain on his face and said, "I don't think this is the best plan you ever came up with, if that's what you mean. Three eyeballs means we head for the hills and take cover. Somehow we're now on everyone's radar. It's just a matter of time before the cops come calling."

"That's not going to happen, Mig. You need to trust me. So they managed to infiltrate the site on the dark web. What? You thought that would never happen? When we signed up, that was the first thing we were told. Yes, they said it was unlikely, but they did admit that it was still possible. So they shut it all down, but the damage is done. Everyone has scattered. We're on the move. This is all tied into Cricket and the shooting and the people investigating that shooting."

"I don't see anyone coming to our aid. Everyone is running for cover. What about Mr. Hot Shot. What about our payout? We're swinging in the wind here, Al."

"Yeah, yeah, yeah. We'll figure something out. This came out of nowhere in the middle of the night. Once we're settled, even if it's just temporarily, we'll figure out a course of action. We might even have to reach out to the Rats and call a temporary truce. By now, the Lobos have gotten the three eyeballs. If we're lucky, they might take pity on us. I'm not counting on it, I'm just saying.

"Okay, there's our target dead ahead. The power is still on. At least the lights on the posts are still on. The houses are too far apart to see any others through this heavy rain. I'll look for the power box, you go to the back door, and the minute you hear my whistle, use your elbow to crack the glass on the door and get in as fast as you can. I'll be right behind you. You unlock the front door, and I'll take the back. Go!"

Alonzo slogged his way through the ankle-deep water as he made his way around to the back end of the house, where he assumed he would find the power box. Using only the light from his cell phone, he finally saw it just as a horrible thought struck him right between the eyes. What if there was an emergency generator that kicked in when the power went off? He knew diddly-squat about generators. Should he take that out first, assuming he could find a way to do it? Time was marching forward. He looked around but didn't see anything that even remotely resembled a generator. Unless he wanted a bottleneck and chaos, he had to act quickly. He opened the box, held the phone up, and hit the master switch at the top of the panel. Then he turned all the others off, one by one, to make sure the entire structure was without electricity. Seven minutes! Three minutes to spare. He raced around to the other side of the house to see if there was a generator but could see nothing.

Alonzo ran back around the corner just in time to see the back door swing open. He bolted through it, slammed the door shut, and shot the dead bolt. He looked up at the alarm's keypad. He sighed when he saw no lights, green or red. Obviously, there was no generator, else it would have kicked in by now.

Following his own instructions, he ran through the massive house till he found the family room and opened the French doors just in time for his two top lieutenants to bolt through.

Ninety minutes later, every member of the Scorpions was gathered in Cosmo Cricket's monstrous kitchen, with its one-of-a-kind, custom-made twelve-burner stove that Cosmo had specially built for Lizzie, the stove on which one

could spit-roast an entire pig while using the oven to pre-
pare the rest of the meal to feed a small army.

"Listen up! This might be our only chance in a while to
take a shower and get clean. I want each of you to shower,
wash your hair, and get some clean clothes. These people
have a kid who is ten years old, but he's a big kid, so I'm
thinking his clothes will fit most of you. Bundle up your
rags and shoes and bring everything back here to the kitchen. There are four bathrooms upstairs, and there's a
shower somewhere off this kitchen. That makes five. Get
moving, and scrub till your skin is raw. Hang up your
towels!"

Miggy could feel his jaw drop. *Hang up your towels!*

Alonzo looked at his friend. "It's a long and complicated story. Just goddamn do it, okay?"

"Sure, boss, if you say so. No problem," Miggy said
quietly.

"By the time it's our turn, all the hot water will be gone,"
Miggy complained.

"No, it won't. They have limitless hot water. I saw the
gizmo next to the power box. I saw them advertised on
TV, and even if the power goes out, which just happened,
it has its own power source or something, and the water
stays hot. The guy hawking it just called it Endless Heaven
in a Shower! Let's see if there's any good food here."

Miggy opened the refrigerator and gawked at the array
of food inside. A ham, a whole roasted chicken under plastic wrap, a bowl of spaghetti and meatballs. The bins held
fruits, vegetables, and cheese of all kinds. Bottles of imported beer and Coca-Cola filled one entire shelf.

A feast that would have to be eaten cold, but still a
feast. Both men dug in and shoveled the food into their
mouths as fast as they could and washed it down with the
imported beer.

Alonzo let loose with a loud belch that could be heard

all over the house. "*That* was better than any food at a five-star restaurant, even if it was cold. Damn, that was good!"

Miggy agreed as he let his mind wander to the beds in this fine house. He wondered if the Crickets slept on silk sheets. He might not get to sleep on them, but he could at least feel them. He could hardly wait for his turn to go upstairs to check it out.

"Al, how is it you know so much about this house and the Crickets?" Miggy asked, as Alonzo pawed through a stack of mail on the kitchen counter.

"I checked them out on the net, how do you think? I even saw the blueprints. That's how I know about the kid. Cricket applied for a permit to build a pool in his yard so the kid can train. Construction was supposed to start two weeks ago. Guess there was some kind of snafu, or the shooting set it back. The kid wants to go to the Olympics. Look! This is a postcard from the kid. He's at some swim camp for the summer. It's good to know stuff like that. Knowledge is power. How many times do I have to tell you that, Mig?"

"C'mon, be straight with me, Al. What are we doing here? Why this place?"

Alonzo cuffed Miggy on the side of the head and snarled. "Where did you think we should go, Mig? Name me one place where all of us would be safe. We had an hour, possibly an hour and a half, to make tracks. In a way, it was pure dumb luck that I had researched this place before we did the hit for Mr. Hot Shot. That killing Cricket would also earn us a place in the Lobos was a real bonus. I revisited it again afterward in more detail. There weren't any other options unless you know of some, and if you do, please share them with me. Why are you questioning me anyway?"

"Because I'm scared, that's why. I don't want to go to prison. We shoot this guy Cricket, he almost dies but doesn't, which means we're on the hook to the Lobos, then we take up residence in the guy's house. That's why I'm scared. Then there is that little matter of twenty, that's *twenty*, murders we committed for Mr. Hot Shot. If you aren't scared out of your wits, then there's something wrong with the way you're wired. Another thing, what are we going to do if the wife comes home?"

"Now that's a question I do not have the answer to as yet. If she shows up, then we'll deal with it. Right now, we have enough to worry about without adding her to the mix. What's worrying me the most is that Mr. Hot Shot isn't answering any of my texts. I wonder if he's on the run too."

Before Miggy could respond, one of the guys bellowed his name from the second floor that the shower was free. Miggy shrugged and left the kitchen, his shoulders drooping, his face a mask of concern. Maybe after his shampoo and shower, with clean clothes on his body, something would come to him. He wondered if he had the guts to cut and run. And go where? He felt like crying as he peeled off his filthy clothes in the pretty bathroom that smelled like a spring day. He grimaced when he saw the line of towels hanging from the top of the shower doors.

Miggy soaped up his body three times, then washed his hair three times before he felt clean enough to step out of the fancy shower. It took him awhile before he found a toothbrush and shaving tackle in a linen closet that was as big as some people's bedrooms. Al hadn't said anything about shaving, but who cared. He could also trim his hair. All of which he did in twenty minutes. He looked around for clothes and was about to call out when Alonzo appeared in the doorway with a bundle of clean clothes and a trash bag for his old things.

"How do you feel?"

In spite of himself, Miggy laughed. "Like a few bucks

short of a million dollars. I don't know what the smell is, but I like it."

"It's lavender and lemongrass," Alonzo said.

"And you know this how?" Miggy asked as he pulled on a T-shirt that fit him perfectly.

"It was on Mrs. Cricket's profile on the net."

"Oh," was all Miggy could think to say.

"One more thing, Miggy. The Crickets do not sleep on silk sheets. I checked just for you. The tag said the thread count was one thousand, so they are soft, but they aren't silk. And the pillows are the ones you see advertised on TV every ten seconds."

Miggy wasn't sure if he should thank his friend for the information or just move on. He mumbled something about the kid having so many clothes and shoes, and the sneakers being a size too big, to which Alonzo replied, "Suck it up, pal; no one gets it all. Go on down now and keep the boys in line. They're a little antsy for some reason."

"*For some reason*," Mig muttered as he barreled out of the room. Sometimes, and this was one of those times, he simply did not understand his childhood friend and how he thought the way he did. More important, he didn't understand himself and how he was where he was right now.

Miggy shook his head to clear away his ugly thoughts. He didn't want to think about his part in the past that had brought him to this place in time. He squeezed his eyes shut, then opened them. He looked at the mess the boys had created, then simply walked away. The carcass of the chicken was picked clean, and not a smidgen of ham remained on the bone. The bowl that had been full of spaghetti and meatballs looked like someone had licked it clean. He opened the refrigerator to see empty bins and shelves. The monster cooling unit looked as if it belonged on a showroom floor, waiting for someone to buy it.

Miggy looked around for a pantry and finally found it.

It was stocked from top to bottom with paper products, canned fruits and vegetables, and packages of pasta. Extra-large scented trash bags were on the bottom shelf. Miggy shook his head again. Rich people certainly knew how to live. Scented garbage bags. He hadn't even known there was such a thing.

Because there was nothing else to do, Miggy tidied up the kitchen, including washing and drying the spaghetti bowl and putting it away. Then he sifted through the pile of mail on the counter to see what kind of letters rich people got. Alonzo was right, there was nothing interesting in the stack except the postcard from the kid. His eyes started to burn when he remembered what he was doing when he was ten years old. There was no summer camp for him. He was running the streets, hanging with the gangs, stealing every chance he got, and fighting for his life a time or two.

Miggy squeezed his eyes shut and wished the way he wished a thousand times that a genie or a fairy godmother would appear to grant him a wish. He'd wish he could turn back the clock to his early childhood before he started running with the gangs. He'd wish to spend more time on his schoolwork, listened to his mother more, helped her more, prayed more, and attended Mass with her on Sundays. Maybe if he had done those things, he would have a better life. He'd have a job, his own apartment, maybe a girlfriend he'd take home to Sunday dinner with his mother.

Miggy snapped out of his reverie when he sensed Alonzo standing next to him. He looked up at the giant standing over him. "You wearing Cricket's clothes?" he asked inanely.

"The only thing I could find. The guy is one big dude. At least I'm clean, and the clothes are clean. That's why they make belts and suspenders. The kid's sneakers fit me. Cricket's shoes could pass as canoes, that's how big they are. What were you thinking just now, Mig? You're starting to worry me."

"That's funny, Al. You always say I'm the worrier, and yeah, I was sitting here worrying about what we're gonna do when the missus shows up. She has to come home sooner or later. We got no beef with her. Those others from Happy Village, that was on a paid contract. Cricket was also a hit for Mr. Hot Shot, as well as our initiation exercise for admission into . . . you know. I don't want any part of killing the missus. She has a kid. That's what I was thinking, so if you want to pound my ass into the ground, go for it."

Alonzo laughed, but there was no mirth in the sound. "You the one who cleaned up the kitchen? Good job."

"Nothing else to do," Miggy muttered. "Anyone responding to your calls and texts?" He knew the answer just by the ugly expression on Alonzo's face.

"No. Trust me, they're all going to pay for this. We need to talk, Mig. Serious stuff." Miggy nodded.

"We have another forty minutes or so of darkness before the sun creeps up. Let's go outside on the deck. No one can hear us out there. Uh-oh, hold on, I have a text coming in. Kirby from the Rats."

Expletives flew from Alonzo's mouth like a runaway train. Miggy thought he was going to toss his cell phone to the ground and stomp on it, but he didn't. Instead, he brushed past Miggy and threw open the kitchen door. Miggy noticed that Alonzo's face was so red, Miggy feared he was going to go up in smoke. He turned around and closed the door. Then he waited for Miggy to say something, anything.

"Guess that was a you-must-be-kidding-me text, is that it?" Miggy said lightly, hoping to calm his friend's black ire.

Alonzo leaned across the railing on the deck as he tried to calm down. He would never admit it to Miggy, but he'd been counting on the Rats' help. Now he was back to square one. He took four deep breaths, held each one for seven seconds, then exhaled. When he felt calm enough to speak, he said, "Sludge is the one who responded. He said his boss said that every member of the Scorpions is nuclear waste material, and they want no part of us now or in the future and not to contact them again."

"Did you really think they would help, Al? The truth now," Miggy asked quietly.

"I did. Because if the situation was reversed, and I knew what they were facing, I'd help and get my bucket of blood later. That's how you play this game. That's why the Rats are at the bottom of the heap and not at the top, the way the Scorpions are. It's envy, pure and simple."

"So now what?" Miggy asked, his insides starting to crumble as he strained to see his friend's face in the darkness.

Alonzo moved slightly so he was closer to Miggy. Instead of answering the question, he posed a question. "What would you like to see me do, Mig? Tell me the truth. Straight up, no bullshit, okay?"

Miggy didn't hesitate. "I'm with you a hundred percent, you know that. But if you want my honest opinion right now, right this minute, then I think we should scatter and make plans to meet up somewhere down the road and into the future or maybe never. We leave, head for Los Angeles, and plant ourselves in the first sanctuary city we find. We can get new identities and blend in. You asked me for my opinion, and for what it's worth, that's what I think we should do. The Lobos aren't going to stick their neck out for us. We screwed up the initiation test, so they owe us nothing, and that's what we'll get from them, nothing. As for Hot Shot, I bet he was gone hours ago and is probably on a plane to some foreign country, where he can hide out. There's no way to track him, and we both know it."

"We need money," Alonzo said. "Go inside and tell the boys to search this house from top to bottom. People like the Crickets are bound to have a safe. Gather up all the jewelry they can find, anything we can sell or pawn. Why are you still standing here? Go!"

Miggy entered the house and blessed himself. He whispered the only prayer he could remember from his catechism class. He then did as instructed and rejoined Alonzo on the deck. Fifteen more minutes and the sun would start its slow rise over the horizon. A new day of sun and humidity and blistering heat. And here they were, stuck in this house, waiting for God only knew what.

"I don't want it to end like this, Mig."

There was nothing to say to that remark, so Miggy remained silent.

"What do you think of the idea of you and me riding into town and going to visit Mr. Hot Shot? There is every possibility he wasn't warned. He might be at the office. Just because we got the eyeballs doesn't mean he got them. What do you think?"

"Bad idea. We need to stay under the radar. Instead of leaving one of your generic messages on his burner phone, go with a flat-out threat via his secretary and see if that produces any results. You said a while back when you researched him that you had his private e-mail and his landline phone number at that ritzy place where he lives. Do the same thing there. Shake the tree and see what falls out. Other than that, I have no other ideas," Miggy said in a resigned voice.

Alonzo looked around, seeing the deck and its contents for the first time in the early morning light. He noticed the flowerpots, the leafy trees, the lounge chairs with the padded cushions with fern patterns all over them. A nice place to sit after a hard day's work. This little oasis was for a family. He bit down on his lower lip before he said, "It's starting to get light out. We need to get inside. I'll make the calls from the kitchen." He took a long, last, lingering look at the table where he knew the family dined from time to time. The pot of bright red geraniums brought a lump to his throat. He remembered another pot of red geraniums that had belonged to his mother and how the man she had hooked up with threw them at her and cracked her skull wide open. He remembered the blood being as red as the flowers. And then he remembered how he could see nothing but red as he picked up a piece of the broken pot and slit the man's throat from ear to ear. And then he couldn't tell the blood from the flowers, so he ran and ran and ran. He was nine going on ten at the time. It was a year or so before he met Miggy.

"What's wrong?" Miggy asked.

"Nothing. Must be nice eating out here when the sun goes down and they unroll the awning, don'tcha think?"

"I suppose. C'mon, get in here. It's almost full light, and people are up and out jogging."

Alonzo closed and locked the sliding doors, then drew the draperies across the entire bank of windows.

A shout from the second floor sent everyone running to the foot of the long, spiral staircase. "We found the safe and we got a ton of swag," a young voice shouted. "It's a big safe, too!"

The staircase shook as the gang members thundered their way to the second floor to stare down at a floor safe under a round table in the dressing room off the master bedroom, a room with mirror-lined walls and bigger than most people's living rooms.

Alonzo's eyes glittered as he stared down at the floor. This was no run-of-the-mill Staples safe. This safe was a one-of-a-kind custom-built job. Getting it open was going to be the challenge. "Mig, go online and find out the birthdays of the wife and kid. And Cricket's, too. It's a place to start. Now, show me the jewelry you have."

Alonzo smiled. A nice, tidy haul. If he found a good

fence, he and his boys could live for a little while on a haul like this.

"Pete, go in the garage and look for tools that will help us open up this puppy."

Maybe things weren't so dark after all.

Maybe.

He didn't believe it for a minute.

Chapter 12

Lionel Lewis walked through the downpour as he made his nightly rounds of Happy Village. As a rule, he didn't mind the rain, and he was dressed for it, with a hat and a big yellow poncho, along with knee-high Wellington boots. It wasn't often in Vegas that it rained the way it was now, and that's why it didn't really bother him. He let his mind search for a word to define what he felt. *Refreshing.* Yep, that was it.

What was bothering him was what he *wasn't* feeling. He knew every inch of Happy Village, knew every flower bed, every pothole, every loose brick. He knew where to step and where not to step. He knew where everyone was on any given night because he took his job seriously. He saw now that the little dip at the end of Primrose Avenue could vie for lake status. He moved to the right to avoid a twisted ankle as he stared ahead at Sid Donaldson's porch light. Sid never left his porch light on past nine-thirty, and it was now one in the morning.

Lionel made his way up to the stoop that led to a three-rocker front porch and looked in the window. Sid was sprawled on the sofa, with his calico cat, Piper, sleeping on his broad chest. Lionel sucked in his breath as he automatically crossed his fingers that Sid was just sleeping. He watched, but the man didn't move. He tapped lightly on the window. The cat jumped down and ran off. Lionel waited to see if Sid would move. He did. Lionel thought he would faint in relief. He moved off to finish his patrol.

Lionel's thoughts were everywhere as he finished up his rounds. He knew the beat and the rhythm of Happy Village, and tonight it was *off*. It wasn't the rain, either. He'd felt it the moment he came on duty. And because of his feeling, he'd made sure he paid attention to every little thing, like Sid Donaldson's porch light. Nothing he could put his finger on and say, aha, so that's what it is. There was nothing out of the ordinary, no traffic, no one out walking, no loud noises. No stray animals. Absolutely nothing, and yet he was absolutely positive that something was wrong. Twice he'd walked by Gentry Lomax's quarters, but they were dark. His pickup truck was parked in its allotted spot. Nothing there to cause concern.

Lionel rounded the corner of Sycamore and Acadia. He stopped and pushed back the sleeve of his slicker to look at his watch, a gift from his granny when he graduated high school. It was an old Timex that had belonged to his beloved grandfather, a watch his granny had bought with money she said she saved by doing extra ironing for people. The leather band was worn and frayed. It felt like a second skin on Lionel's wrist. The watch kept perfect time right down to the second. Cosmo Cricket had teased him about it, asking if he'd trade it for his gold Rolex. Lionel had just shaken his head no. He'd no more give up this watch than he would part with his front teeth. Time to head for the clubhouse so Dom could take over and he could dry out or catch an hour's catnap.

Lionel turned around and stopped in the middle of the road. He looked all around him. He could see or hear nothing to set off an alarm. He couldn't hear anything other than the rain splashing in the puddles and on his slicker, yet he knew something, somewhere was wrong. He could feel it in every pore of his body. What the hell was it? What was he missing?

By the time Lionel made his way to the clubhouse, the rain had stopped its ferocious onslaught and seemed to be tapering off. He hoped it would all stop soon.

"You're up, Dom," Lionel called out just as he opened the door.

Dom was already in his slicker, boots, and fisherman's rain hat. "Anything I need to know, Lionel, before I start making my rounds?"

"Sid Donaldson's porch light is on, but that's okay. I checked on him, and he fell asleep on the sofa. Sadie Davis left her light on, but she's spending the night with her friend Ada Cummings. I read the note she left on her door, and that's how I know, so don't waste your time checking those two out."

"Okay, see you when my shift is over. Nick should be getting up soon. I heard him rustling around a little while ago. He said something that's making me nervous. Well, not really nervous. Maybe *concerned* would be a better word. He said when he took the first shift, things didn't feel right out there for some reason, and it wasn't the rain. Not that he found anything wrong, it was just that things seemed off somehow. He didn't know whether he should mention it, but he did say that. He said it was nothing he could pinpoint, just a feeling he had. Of course, that was early on in the evening. The day was winding down, that kind of thing. It would explain his feelings to a point. Did you notice anything, Lionel? Should I be looking or searching for something out of the ordinary?"

"Nick is right. The beat and the rhythm is off. That's the only way I can explain it. I know every inch of Happy Village, and something is definitely off. I can't explain it any better than Nick did. Go ahead now. I'll talk to Nick when he gets up. Then I'm going to catch a few winks. Call me if you see or hear anything out of the ordinary. Do not, I repeat, do not try to be a hero out there if you do spot something. Just call or text. We're not looking to be heroes here. The rain is letting up, so it won't be too bad for your shift. It might have stopped by now. Take care, and don't do anything stupid, you hear?"

Dom grinned. "Okay, *Dad*." It was an ongoing joke, with Lionel saying the same thing every night when he and Nick left to do their patrol. The door closed softly behind the intrepid student, then opened almost immediately. "Stopped raining!" he called out, then closed the door once again.

"Thank God!" Nick grumbled as he ambled over to the table and flopped down on one of the folding chairs. "I was hoping I wouldn't have to swim my route when we come back tonight. Everything okay, Lionel?"

"I don't know, Nick. I had this . . . this . . . weird feeling the whole time I was on patrol. Dom said you felt something strange. The rain had nothing to do with it. There's something wrong, I can sense it. And yet I double-checked everything. There's nothing I can put my finger on. The three of us know every nook and cranny of this place. I know when something is wrong. I can feel it in my steps, something lurking that you can't see but only sense. It's not a sound, it's not a thing or a place. It's just . . . just . . . I guess the air. I can't explain it for the life of me."

Nick rubbed at the stubble on his chin as he stared across the table at Lionel. "You don't have to explain it. I totally understand, and I can't explain it either, other than by saying that something doesn't feel right. We've been doing this for what seems like forever, and there has never been a real blip. This is something I've not experienced before on this job with you guys. At first I wasn't going to say anything because I thought you all would think I had gone bonkers. It will be interesting to see what Dom has to say when he finishes his shift. You want a root beer, Lionel?"

"No thanks. I'm going to pull out that cot over there and catch a few z's. If you think of anything, or if something goes down, wake me right away. And lock the door."

Root beer bottle in one hand, cell phone in the other, Nick walked over to the clubhouse door and double-locked it. He looked around, grateful that there were no windows in the clubhouse. His eyes narrowed, his shoulders trembled, and he didn't know why.

He was safe.

For now.

From what?

Knowing there wasn't going to be an answer to his silent questions, Nick reached for his laptop and opened it up. He had a paper due in two days and was behind on two other assignments. He needed to crack the books, and now was as good a time as any; it had the added benefit of taking his mind off whatever mystery was going on at Happy Village.

Two hours later, Nick turned off his laptop, satisfied he'd done a good job on his five-thousand-word essay. As an exchange student, he found American academics much easier than those in England. He sighed, rolled his head on his shoulders, then got up and did some stretches. He was about to drop to the floor to do some sit-ups when he heard an ungodly whoop from the far corner of the room, where Lionel was sleeping on the cot.

"What the bloody hell! Did you fall off the cot and break something? What's wrong?"

"Nothing is wrong! Suddenly, everything is all right. Didja hear me, Nick, I figured it out when I was sleeping. I know what I missed. You missed it, too, and so did Dom. Think, man, really think. What didn't you see and smell tonight?"

Nick ran his hands through his ginger-colored hair as he squeezed his eyes shut. Normally, he considered himself to be more observant than the others, but here was Lionel telling him that wasn't the case. "See and smell? Okay," he said, his brow furrowed in thought. "If there was anything to smell, I admit I missed it because all I could smell was the earth, the rain, and something that smelled like wet fur. I didn't see them, but I felt hundreds of those tree frogs all around me. For long stretches of time, it was almost impossible to see in front of you with the way the rain was coming down. Some of the patrol I did by pure instinct. At some points, I couldn't even see the buildings. Give me a clue."

Lionel hopped around from one foot to the other as he tried to goad Nick into remembering what he failed to see. "Think back to other patrols, your route, the things you saw every night, things you were used to seeing. Not out of the ordinary but ordinary. Just part of the patrol. We see it every night, rain, snow, or sunshine, dark or light. It's always there. Damn it, Nick, think!"

"I am! I am! Nothing is coming to me. It was the rain, it was like a tsunami at some points. Twice I had to stop and wait it out before I could go on. The rain just took over the night. Stop dragging this out and tell me what I missed."

"Think Magnolia Terrace, second house on the left! Now do you see it?"

Nick's eyes popped wide. He gave himself a slap alongside of his head. "Mr. Hershel! His cherry pipe tobacco! He didn't call out! I missed the scent of the tobacco because there was no tobacco to smell. You're right, Lionel, I missed it, and I'm sorry."

"I missed it too, and so did Dom. Open up your laptop and check the Happy Village home page. They have a log that shows which tenants sign out when they go somewhere overnight. It's a mandatory rule for the twice-a-day wellness check the Village provides. The last time Mr. Hershel was away was when he had hip surgery right before Thanksgiving. He didn't get back to his house until right before Valentine's Day. He spent almost two months in rehab."

Nick looked up at Lionel and shook his head. "He didn't sign out. No one signed out today. Everyone is in residence."

"Then why wasn't he on his porch? The porch on his house is the only one in the complex big enough for four rockers. Mr. Lomax hung a bamboo blind lined with plastic that is on rollers so that Mr. Hershel can sit out on his porch in inclement weather. Before he did that, Mr. Hershel would wrap himself in an old shower curtain so he could sit out there. He doesn't sleep nights, so he sits out there and smokes his pipe. He wasn't there tonight. The rain, no matter how hard or bad, wouldn't have bothered him. He was insulated. So why wasn't he on the porch smoking his pipe?"

"I don't know, Lionel. Maybe he's under the weather. He is up there in years," Nick said miserably.

"Mr. Hershel has never missed a night except during his rehab stint. I've been here over three years, and this is a first. I'm not liking this."

"Should we walk over there and knock on his door?" Nick asked. "Or, since Dom is already out on patrol, he could go by and check on him."

Lionel shook his head. "I think we should call Mr. Emery and see what he thinks. This might be over our paygrade. No sense getting Gentry Lomax all riled up. Suddenly, too many strange things are going on here. I'm starting to get spooked myself."

"Why is Mr. Hershel so important all of a sudden?" Nick asked.

"Routine. Mr. Hershel is a man of invariable routine. He does not deviate. Do you know his story?"

"No! Remember, I joined up with you guys only ten months ago. Tell me."

"Mr. Hershel likes it when you call him Pete. He and his wife, Donna, Mr. Hershel calls her Dolly, owned a ticky-tacky casino downtown called Dolly's Dandy Dollar Casino. Donna was a Vegas showgirl back in the day. She performed for the clientele every night, and the customers loved it. They made so much money, the big dogs started sniffing around, wanting him to invest in a big casino like the one Mr. Wynn owns. He got involved, then Dolly got sick, and a week later the whole town turned out for her funeral. She was an institution.

"The story goes on: Mr. Hershel and the other investors went to Zack Meadows to apply for a license. Something went wrong. From there on out, it is all rumor and conjecture. The investors disappeared. The up-front money disappeared. We're talking millions here. It all disappeared like magic. Mr. Hershel was a basket case, he'd just lost his wife, and he was left to battle it out on his own, and I guess he made a mess of things. I really don't know any more than that. The few times we spoke on my rounds, he just said that Mr. Cricket was helping him and maybe that skunk Zack Meadows would get what's coming to him."

"Do you think the day Mr. Cricket came here and got shot he was coming to see Mr. Hershel? Ah, I can see it in your face. You do think that. Well, it makes sense now, doesn't it?" Nick observed. "But that still doesn't tell us why Mr. Hershel wasn't smoking on the porch tonight. Why doesn't he like to be indoors, do you know?"

"Actually, I do know, because he told me. Dolly isn't in the apartment. He told me once they were never ever more than a foot apart their whole married life. When she passed away, he was lost without her. He had her cremated, and he believes her ashes are out there, and he needs to be where she is. He had them scattered, but he didn't say where. He kept some of the ashes in a little gold snuffbox. Some people might think that's ghoulish, but not him. He carries her with him twenty-four seven in his pocket. Never more than a foot apart. Closer if possible. To me, that says it all. True love. I hope I find someone someday who will love me like that," Lionel said with a catch in his voice.

Nick digested Lionel's words as he struggled to imagine the man's love and devotion to his wife. He shook his head to clear his thoughts so he could function in the present. "It's almost light out now. Dom should be back soon. What's the plan, Lionel?"

"Mr. Emery is the plan. I'm going to call him and turn it all over to him. I'll just tell him everything we've discussed and hope he can do something, or at least make sense out of what's going on."

"What if Mr. Hershel is inside and sick or . . . or . . ."

"Don't go there, Nick," Lionel said as he pulled his cell phone out of his pocket, scrolled through his directory, and punched in the numbers for Jack Emery's cell phone.

Jack picked up after the fourth ring, his voice groggy with sleep. Lionel went right into his spiel and ended up with, "We'll be leaving here in fifteen minutes. I can give you Mr. Hershel's address and his phone number, but he never answers the phone. And he doesn't know how to text and has no desire to learn. I'll be free at eleven-thirty and can come back here if you need me. Just shoot me a text." He ended the call and turned to Nick.

"I think we should meander over to Magnolia Terrace before we leave here. What do you say, Lionel? We have a few spare minutes."

"Yeah, sure. Magnolia Terrace was dark last night. No porch lights, and no lights were on in any of the houses. If he was inside earlier in the evening when I made my first patrol, I would have noticed. No lights, that's why nothing registered. That does open up another avenue, that he's sick in bed or, God forbid, dead."

At six-thirty on the dot, Dominic Petro opened the door and breezed through like a prequel to a hurricane. "Everything is okay. I'm so very ready for a long, hot shower. And boys, the good news is it stopped raining. I'm so hungry I could chew that doorknob. Do we have time to stop at the Waffle House?"

"I can drop you off, but you'll have to find your own way from there. Okay, everything looks shipshape. Let's hit it, boys," Lionel said.

"Okay, Cyrus, we're up. I'm going to call the guys and get dressed. You want to eat first or wait to grab some *real* food later?" Cyrus tilted his head before he let loose with two soft barks. *Such a silly question.* He made his way over to the door and lay down. He was ready to go. At last some *action*.

Jack hopped about the big room, punching in numbers as he held the phone with one hand and used his other hand to pull on the clothes he'd taken off the night before. "Maggie, call everyone and meet me in the lobby in fifteen minutes. I'll explain everything when we're all together. Have the van ready and running. Text the Pancake House around the corner and order for everyone. We'll buzz by and pick it up on our way. Cyrus gets two sausage patties, four scrambled eggs, and four strips of bacon. Get him two bottles of water, too. Move, girl!"

Jack moved quickly then, washing his face, brushing his teeth, and slicking back his hair. He'd take a shower later when they got back. His mind raced as he recalled Lionel's clear, concise, articulate report. The young guy had it going on. Cosmo couldn't have picked anyone better to provide security for Happy Village. It simply blew his mind how much Lionel and the Cavaliers knew about the tenants at Happy Village. He wouldn't be afraid to bet the farm that the kid knew more about the residents than Gentry Lomax did. Which was a good thing as far as he could tell.

"Okay, big guy, let's hit it!"

Cyrus stared at his owner. Couldn't he see that he'd been ready since the moment the phone rang? He didn't bother to bark. Sometimes his owner wasn't all that sharp early in the morning.

Jack blinked when he stepped out of the elevator. Vegas would never cease to amaze him. The lobby was just as full and busy as it was last night when he entered the elevator to go up to bed. He spotted Ted first because he towered over everyone else at six-four. The red hair also helped. He waved but didn't break stride. "Outside, everyone! Where's the van?"

"Dennis is getting it," Maggie said. "I called in the food order. What's going on, Jack? What happened? And where is Abner? Does anyone know?"

Charles held up his hand. "He's with Avery in the conference room where they have everything set up. I just sent him a text. His return text said to go without them. They were too busy."

Outside, the humidity slapped at them with a vengeance. Jack strained to see through the low-lying, swirling fog that seemed to be everywhere. "I'm starting to hate this place," Jack mumbled to no one in particular. "How can it be so damn hot and humid at seven o'clock in the morning? Where is this fog coming from?"

No one bothered to reply because they were all moving the moment Dennis pulled alongside them in the rental van. Everyone piled in and buckled up, even Cyrus, who knew the drill. He knew the wheels did not move until he was safely buckled in.

With little traffic leaving Babylon, Dennis pulled away just as Fergus exploded with, "All right, we've waited long enough. What's going on? What happened, and where are we going at this ungodly hour in the morning?"

Jack repeated Lionel's phone call verbatim. "So to answer your question, we are going to Happy Village. When we get there, we are going to go to Magnolia Terrace and knock on Mr. Pete Hershel's door. If no one answers, I am prepared to pick the lock. We are not going to involve Gentry Lomax in what we're about to do. Any questions?"

"Shouldn't we know a little more about Mr. Hershel before we invade his privacy?" Charles asked quietly. His tone of voice clearly indicated he did not like it when one of the group made a decision without first consulting him.

"Of course we should, and that's what Ted and I are doing right now," Maggie said. She muttered as she clicked away. "A creature of habit. Set in his ways. Rich."

"I'd like to revise that to *extremely* rich," Ted said. "He doesn't own a car. He stays close to home. If he wants to go somewhere, he calls an Uber. He pretty much lives on his front porch."

"Where are you getting all that?" Dennis called from the driver's seat as he put on his signal to turn into the Pancake House parking lot.

"The Happy Village once-a-week newsletter," Maggie shot back. "He dresses like a bum. Said clothes do not make him a man. He was a man to start with. Guess he has a bit of a sense of humor. Ah, food! I am *so* hungry." Maggie was always hungry. It didn't matter the day of the week or the hour of the day. She could always eat because of what she called her whacked-out metabolism.

Exactly eight minutes later, Dennis said, "I'll park in the back." He reached for bag after bag after bag of delicious-smelling food and handed them over his shoulder to whomever could reach them.

Thirty minutes later, their trash cleaned up, they waited for Cyrus to finish his business before Dennis put the van in gear. "Next stop, Happy Village. Our ETA is twenty minutes, possibly thirty-five if this fog doesn't lift."

The gang settled down for the short ride, each of them busy with their own thoughts.

Jack found himself dozing off just as his cell phone buzzed. He groaned out loud, shaking everyone from their thoughts. "It's Harry!"

Jack read the text and whistled. "Harry's boys are okay with going with the pillows! That's it. He didn't write another word. Now what the hell do we do? I don't know anything about the pillow business."

"This is where you call Lizzie and turn it all over to her," Maggie said. "She'll know how to proceed. I might be wrong about this, but I think Harry's boys only have four or five days left on their visas. They have to go back home. I miss Harry." All this was said as she continued to tap furiously on the tiny keyboard.

"Anything for Harry, right, guys?" Everyone ignored the comment except Cyrus, who woofed three times to show he agreed with his master as Jack sent off a text to Lizzie Fox.

Nine miles away as the crow flies, Lizzie Fox was holding her husband's hand in her left hand while her right caressed his cheek. "Joe says he is kicking me out of here and I can't come back till dinnertime, so I guess I have to go. They have plans for you now that you're in this private room. I don't know exactly what that means, and I'm not even going to ask," Lizzie said as she felt the cell phone in her pocket vibrate. Well, whoever it was would just have to wait. Saying good-bye to her husband was more important than any incoming text.

"Joe said you can get out of that snazzy gown they have you in and into your own pajamas. I'll bring them when I come back. He said I could bring you your pillow, too, if you want it. I know you must have missed that pillow. Just blink for yes." Cosmo blinked.

Lizzie looked around to see Dr. Joe Wylie standing in the corner, waiting for her to say her emotional good-bye and not wanting to intrude. He smiled from ear to ear, and in that instant Lizzie knew it really was safe to leave her husband. She leaned over and kissed Cosmo's cheek, nibbled on his ear, then planted an earthshaking kiss full on her husband's lips. "Time to go," she trilled as she literally ran from the room.

The moment Lizzie settled herself behind the wheel, she realized she felt wonderful. She was tired, but that was okay. Yes, she was sleepy, but that was okay too. Yes, she longed for a nice hot shower, and yes, she longed to slide under her thousand-thread count sheets, but at that moment nothing felt as good as it felt sitting here in her car and knowing her husband was going to be okay and the wonderful life they shared would continue. "Thank you, God!" she said over and over as she inched her way out of the parking lot and onto the highway, where she finally noticed the low-lying fog. She clicked on the special fog lights and followed the traffic.

Thirty-five minutes later, Lizzie pulled into her driveway. She debated a second as to whether she should put the car in the garage. She decided not to, since she would be going back out later. That's when she fully noticed that the fog had dissipated. She also noticed something else. She would have missed whatever it was she saw if she hadn't leaned over to pick up her cell phone, which had slipped out of the pocket of her sweatpants. Someone was inside her house. Someone who didn't belong inside her house. Her heartbeat kicked up. What to do? Did she imagine it? Was it a trick of the early morning light? Someone was watching her. What to do? What to do? She clicked on the message and saw it was from Jack. She read it, read it again, then formed a plan. She sent off a text that simply said, **Meet me at the office.**

Lizzie looked around to see if anything else was out of the ordinary. Nothing was, but it was too early in the morning for much activity. There, she saw it again—the movement behind the plantation shutters. Because the sun hit the front window early in the morning, she always kept the shutters three-quarters closed, making it impossible to see out between the slats. The shutters were now three-quarters *open*, allowing anyone inside to see the outside world, mainly her, clearly. Would whoever was inside rush out and snatch her if she got out of the car? Should she call the police? Jack? No. Not yet. She knew she needed to do something and do it quickly so that whoever was inside didn't get impatient and rush out and grab her.

Lizzie sucked in a deep breath as she threw open the driver's-side door, indicating to whoever was inside that she was going to enter the house. She hoped by opening the door they wouldn't do anything rash, like trying to grab her in full daylight in her very own driveway.

Phone in hand, she walked nonchalantly around to the back of the car just as the trunk lid popped open. She stared down at her son's baseball mitt, his bat, his tennis racket, and a pile of sweaty shirts that had been left in the trunk way too long. Her eyes grew misty at the sight. On the far side of the trunk was a cardboard carton full of library books. She picked it up, closed the trunk lid, then stopped in her tracks as she pretended her phone was ringing.

She brought the phone up to her ear and started talking to herself. She propped the box of books on her knee as she leaned into the car, still pretending to talk. She shoved the books to the passenger side, and then it was time to go into her act. She waved her free arm, forced a scowl on her face, and stomped her foot a few times to make a point to the nonexistent listener on the other end of the phone and the people watching from inside her house. All the while she was pretending to be an irate woman. She did what every mother of a ten-year-old would do—she looked everywhere, but she was really looking at her front window to see if there was still movement. There was. Finally, she let loose with a wide bellow, tossed the phone onto the passenger seat, and slid into the driver's seat with one fluid move. She slammed the powerful car into reverse.

She was safe in the car, all the doors locking automatically because the engine was still turned on, the motor purring like the salesman said it would, the sound of a contented cat.

Before she could change her mind, Lizzie buckled her seat belt, her eyes on the rearview mirror, then back to her front window. Once she was on the road, she headed back the way she'd come. The moment she hit the highway, she put the pedal to the metal and roared down the road. She knew enough law enforcement that she was confident she could talk her way out of a speeding ticket.

Nine minutes later, Lizzie Fox could have been mistaken for a race car driver as she careened around the corner at ninety miles an hour to come to a screeching halt, tires burning and smoking as she bolted from the car screaming her head off. "There's someone inside my house! I saw the shutters move. I didn't get out of the car, I just backed up and tore out of there."

The gang gathered around the shaken lawyer, mouthing all manner of reassuring words until Lizzie calmed down. Then she started to babble about clean pajamas for Cosmo and how she needed to call her son and that Cosmo wanted his favorite pillow. She would have kept it up, except Jack whistled sharply and put his hands up. "Enough already! Let's get inside and talk, not out here in public."

That was the moment Lizzie sagged, and Ted caught her and slung her over his shoulder in a fireman's carry. "It would help if someone opened the door!" he yelled.

"It would also help if we had a key to open the door," Espinosa yelled in return.

"Check her key ring," Maggie said. "Ah, this must be it!" she said, waving an oversized key ring that jingled and jangled as Maggie tried to pry it from Lizzie's clenched fist.

"Got it!" she said triumphantly. She slid the key in the lock and turned the tumbler.

Espinosa was the last one through the door. And he made sure he locked the door behind him.

Strange things were going on. Better to be safe than sorry later.

Chapter 13

Lizzie sat up straight in the melon-colored club chair in her office and looked around. She homed in on Jack and waved her hands in the air. "It's been a while since I had my first and only meltdown years ago. If my memory serves me correctly, you were there for me that time, too. I'm sorry, everyone. Believe me when I tell you I am okay. I really am. It was seeing someone in my house. *My house.* Touching my things, touching Cosmo's things and Little Jack's stuff. My house is my castle. It's sacrosanct. I feel violated. I don't know if I'll be able to go back there. Okay, that's all I have to say on that. Now that we have that out of the way, let's get down to business and do what we came here to do.

"I guess my first question is, where are my clients?"

"They just pulled into the parking lot. I'll go back and let them in," Ted said.

Lizzie bounced up and out of the melon-colored chair and walked around to take her place behind her massive desk. She reached for a yellow legal pad and centered it in front of her, her signal that she was ready for business.

Suddenly, the spacious office where Lizzie toiled six hours every day was filled to capacity with Harry and his entourage. Introductions were made, hands shaken, and Cyrus barking.

"We can adjourn to one of our conference rooms, or if some of you don't mind standing, we can work here. I'm sorry about the seating, but I don't usually have this many clients in my office at one time." The gang opted to stand. Harry took the floor and went into his spiel. Lizzie let her jaw drop and her eyes pop wide. "Nine point two million dollars! You all won nine point two million!" Harry dug around in the pocket where he kept his sprouts and pulled out a sheaf of chits. He laid them on top of the yellow legal pad. They all watched as Lizzie riffled through them and did a mental count. "It appears your number is correct, Harry."

The five men stood at attention, grinning from ear to ear as they waited to hear what was going to happen next.

"I'm going to need quite a bit of help on this. Virtually my entire staff. What that means to you is that the bill is going to be astronomical. You need to know that going in. I feel confident in saying that the rousing total on these chits will be depleted by at least one million dollars when all is said and done. I'll leave you all here to talk about it and make your decision. If you change your mind, that's fine. I just want you all to know what you're getting into."

More smiles as Lizzie left the office, the gang behind her as they headed for the kitchen and coffee. The kitchen was fragrant with the scent of freshly brewed coffee and the heavenly smell of cinnamon buns and donuts thanks to one of Lizzie's partners. "Help yourself. I need to find my partners and get them on this ASAP." A second later, Lizzie was gone and Charles was pouring coffee for everyone. Everyone started to jabber at once as they made bets among themselves as to what the men would do.

"A no-brainer!" Maggie snorted before she chomped down on a jelly-filled donut dusted with sugar and cinnamon.

"Has anyone given any thought to calling the pillow

company to see if he wants the job to begin with? They might not be equipped to handle eight million dollars' worth of pillows. I've seen the commercials, but that doesn't mean anything," Fergus said.

"I'm sure Lizzie has someone on that as we speak. I'm just as sure the orders would be staggered and not all the pillows would be made at one time. Even I know that's impossible," Dennis said. "I need to research the export business. Don't forget taxes. That eight million might seriously dwindle to a more believable number. It's possible everyone in China won't be getting a pillow after all," Dennis observed.

Jack snorted. "Buy one and get two more free. I'd say they can make a healthy dent in the population. I'd like to remind all of you we're just helping out here. This is not our *mission*. Right now we should be trying to decide what to do about visiting Happy Village and seeing if Mr. Pete Hershel is okay, and doing something about the unwelcome visitors who have taken up residence at Lizzie's home. Plus, now that Harry's friends are getting a dose of reality where all that money is concerned, they are on the way back to the casinos to try to win some more money."

"Maybe we should split up and see what happens. I want to talk to Avery and Abner. I was sure they'd be in touch by now. They must be onto something. Ferg and I can go back to Babylon and find out what's going on. I'll get a suite for Lizzie. We do not want her going back to her house," Charles said, quietly but firmly.

"We have to decide which takes precedence, Lizzie's unwelcome guests or Mr. Hershel. Talk it up, people, and tell me what you want to do," Charles said.

Maggie reached for her third donut, this one loaded with chocolate frosting and colored sprinkles. "We split up. We concoct some kind of story that allows us to go right up to the front door and knock. Whatever reaction we get will let us know what we have to do, like fall back and regroup, call the local authorities, the feds, whomever we can get to investigate. Sounds pretty simple to me. But I would like to know what Abner and Avery have going on before we make a move."

The intercom in the kitchen squawked to life, with Lizzie inviting everyone back to her office. The gang trooped out, but not before Maggie snatched her fourth donut, this one filled with lemon pudding with an inch of vanilla frosting on top. She rolled her eyes in delight as Ted admonished her that she was going to be on a sugar high and no good to anyone. Maggie just shrugged. She did love her sweets. The bare-bottom truth was that, when it came to food, there wasn't a single thing Maggie Spritzer didn't love.

"Listen up, everyone!" Lizzie said as she took her place behind her desk. "My people are on this. We're going to do our very best to expedite the proceedings in a timely manner. Be aware this is not an easy thing to do timewise. It's going to take as long as it takes, and you all might not like it, but there is no way to cut to the chase. You have to follow the rules, like it or not. Having said that, everyone on my staff is prepared to work around the clock if that becomes necessary.

"Harry says his friends are okay with everything we discussed while you all were having your coffee. They're okay leaving their business in our hands, with Harry sending them the reports I give him, probably every other day. Harry has their power of attorney, so that will help things a lot. A small team of gentlemen from the IRS are on their way here, so we have that covered. The pillow man said he had to call an emergency meeting of his board, his family, and his staff, and would get back to me momentarily. I think I rendered him speechless. I have three of my best paralegals on the export end of things, container ships, schedules, and so on. For now, we have that part of it covered. But here it is in a nutshell. To export to most of Asia, including China, you sometimes need an export license from here and almost always an import license there.

"The *here* part is pretty easy—as long as you aren't exporting anything that has or can be adapted for military use, they give them out quite freely, and you don't even need them for most commodities. Pillows would probably not need anything on this end.

"The *there* part is going to be much harder. Realistically speaking, money needs to change hands not only to get the permit but for each shipment that comes in. That money needs to be factored in for the boys so they understand. Do not confuse that amount of money with the legal fees. That is totally separate. I suppose you could refer to it as a *gift* in polite circles, but let's call a spade a spade. The word is *bribe*. It can be any amount, from piddling to outrageous. Whatever it turns out to be, you either pay or end up sucking your thumb.

"Goods have to clear customs over there and need to be accompanied by a commercial invoice, payment terms, and other paperwork. More bribes. Don't go getting bent out of shape here. It's how they do business. You either accept it and pay up or walk away. Also, most organic material, like pillows, might need a quarantine period. You know, if there are feathers.

"Then there is the matter of import duties that apply. Having said all that, you must realize I can't make all this happen overnight. It's going to take some time. Like I said, we'll work at it nonstop, and even though I'm going to be at the hospital a lot, I can still stay on top of it." Lizzie leaned back and waited to see what the reaction would be to all she'd just said.

The men conferred among themselves, then spoke with Harry, who nodded and then translated for them. "They understand and thank you, but now they want to go back to the casino to see if they can win even more money. They have a good grasp on money going in and money going out, and the word *bribe* is something they are all familiar with. In other words, they're good with everything. They want to leave now, so I said it was okay. They're up on the use of Ubers, so no problem there. I'm staying here with you guys. Uh-oh, wait a minute. They want to know about free shipping. Seems the commercials they saw said the pillows come with free shipping."

"Free shipping is only for the continental United States." Lizzie stood up and walked around to the front of her desk, where she shook hands with her five new clients. There were lots of smiles and double bows that she acknowledged with a smile and bow of her own.

Fergus and Charles were the next to leave, saying they would be in touch. Fergus patted Lizzie on the back, told her not to worry, and he would engage a suite for her at Babylon. Lizzie nodded. She knew she'd have to go on a mini shopping spree the minute she reached Babylon, but that was okay; it had been ages since she'd gone shopping. Maybe the simplest thing, like picking out new clothes, would calm her down. She knew when she was wired, she was *wired*, and right now she felt like she could fly.

"Okay, boys and one girl, talk to me. I need to know everything, and I need to know it now before I leave here. What is going on? I can handle whatever it is, so do not leave anything out. I want to help if I can. I can actually concentrate now that I know Cosmo is definitely out of the woods and on the mend. Like I said, talk to me." Lizzie drew a deep breath as she returned to what she called her safe zone, the law.

Maggie and Jack both took turns explaining what was going on, what had already gone down, and what they suspected. "We would have kept you in the loop, Lizzie, but you were in no condition to do anything other than what you've been doing, taking care of your husband and being at his side. Now you know as much as we know. We're hoping to find out more when Charles talks to Abner and Avery," Maggie said.

"So who is going where now?" Lizzie asked.

"To be decided. You should leave now, Lizzie, you look beat. We know where to find you if we need you. If you don't mind, we need to sit here a bit and figure out our next move. Is that okay with you?"

"No problem. Stay as long as you like. If it's okay with you, then I am outta here," Lizzie said. "Call me if you need me. My plan is to head back to the hospital around five."

Kisses, hugs, and hard squeezes followed; then Lizzie was gone.

"You guys waiting for a bus or what?" Maggie growled. "What are we doing, and who is doing what? What's the plan here? Why are we wasting time?"

"Why don't you go first, Maggie, since you always have the best ideas," Jack said, sarcasm ringing in his voice.

The sarcasm did not go unnoticed by Maggie. "You're just saying that because you know it's true and you're jealous that none of you ever comes up with a workable, doable plan. I said a *plan*. But that goes for *ideas*, too."

"Let's hear it," Ted barked.

"Well, for starters, we need to know what we as a group are prepared to do once we knock on doors, meaning Lizzie's front door and Mr. Hershel's front door. Do we go in like gangbusters, or do we say hello when and if the door opens, wanna buy a subscription to *People* magazine? What?" Maggie sputtered irritably.

"We need to get the lay of the land, see which way the wind is blowing. That kind of thing," Jack said. "When we walk away with our opinions, that's when we make a plan. So let's decide now who is going where."

"How about if Ted, Espinosa, and I take Mr. Hershel.

Our cover story can be we're going to do a write-up on his wife, Donna, also known as Dolly Dandy. A nostalgia piece. Just the mention of the wife he loved and adored might help Mr. Hershel make a decision to give us some sort of subtle clue, if he can. Assuming he's being held hostage. It's an idea, a thought, but if you can come up with something better, I'm all for it. In the meantime, Dennis, Harry, and Jack head for Lizzie's house. I don't know how you want to play that. There could be one person in there or there could be a dozen. There are only three of you. Bear that in mind," Maggie said.

"Now, having said that, Jack, you are more familiar with Happy Village than my little group. We can switch up if you prefer to go there. Dennis went with you the first time, and while it's going to be new to Harry, you might need Harry. I can concoct some kind of story when we knock on Lizzie's door. So what's it gonna be?"

Cyrus reared up and let loose with a sharp bark.

"Sorry, big guy," Maggie said, as she ruffled the fur on Cyrus's head, "*four* of you!"

"Okay, let's go with what Maggie just suggested. We take on Happy Village and Mr. Hershel. But we'll need another vehicle, so we'll get out at Babylon and rent a vehicle from there. Dennis, can you do that now? Ask for something fairly conservative for a visit to Mr. Hershel's."

"I'm on it," Dennis said as he brought all his fingers into play on the mini keyboard.

Jack tapped Harry on the arm the minute they were seated in back of the van. "You okay, Harry? You're looking a little frazzled."

"A *little!*" Harry hissed, outrage ringing in his voice. "Those guys do not eat or sleep. All they do is gamble. *AND WIN.* I'm afraid to go to sleep for fear of what they might do. Do you have any idea what it's like to have six security guys standing behind you all day and all night

watching every move you make? Even though I wasn't gambling, I was with *them*. I was their host. To be perfectly
honest, I think they think I'm a shill of some kind for the
guys. I know security thinks they have some secret magic,
something or other that lets them win, win, win! The truth
is, they're just dumb lucky. Plus, they are oblivious to
everyone and everything except the cards or the machines.
When they got on that gold-buying gig, I wanted nothing
more than to shoot myself."

Jack patted Harry's arm to show his sympathy. Cyrus
nuzzled his leg in a show of support. "Don't beat yourself
up over this, Harry. Chalk it up to beginner's luck. We just
turned it all over to Lizzie, so you're off the hook. Look, if
you want to go back to the hotel and grab some sleep,
Dennis, Cyrus, and I can handle this. We'll come get you
when we get back. You're not going to be any good to us
if your timing is off and your head is with your friends.
Get some sleep and a take a nice long shower. You'll feel
like your old self in no time."

"I'm never going to feel like myself until those guys are
on the plane and cruising at thirty thousand feet."

"That bad, huh?" Jack grinned.

Harry laughed, a sickly sound. "Yes and no. Don't get
me wrong. They're all great guys. This is the first time
they've been to the States, and they love it. They love all
this Vegas claptrap, and they absolutely love the money.
They are having the time of their lives. They really got off
on the pillow thing. I don't know how you came up with
that, but I'm glad you did. But, yeah, I'll stay at the hotel
and grab some sleep.

"The truth, Jack. What the hell is going on here?" Harry
whispered.

Jack shook his head. "The truth is, we do not have a
clue. We're all just waiting to see what Abner and Avery
come up with. All we know is that it involves the dark

web. When I say dark web, I'm not talking about identity theft, credit card theft, and stuff like that. I'm talking sicko stuff, depravity, murder, blood, all kinds of killings just for sport. God, I can't even go there. You are getting my point, right?"

"Yes, sorry to say," Harry said.

"We're here!" Dennis chortled happily. He handed the van key to Ted and hopped out of the van. "I'll sign out our new rental and meet you right here." He looked at Harry and winced. "You don't look so good, Harry. You coming down with something, or are you just exhausted?"

"You writing a book or something?" Harry muttered as he waved to Jack and headed for the lobby and the elevator that would take him to his room for some much-needed sleep.

"No," Dennis called out, "I just care about you, and I worry when I see something that concerns me. Right now, you concern me, and I want to know if there's anything I can do for you."

Harry stopped in midstride and turned around. "I'm a little short of being okay, Dennis. A shower and some sleep will have me up and back to my old self. I appreciate your concern." With that, Harry turned on his heel and headed for the elevator.

"I knew it! I knew it! He is sick. We need to do something for him. Harry is like our rock. When Harry is nice like that, then you know something is wrong. What should we do?" Dennis said, bouncing from one foot to the other. He was so agitated, his face was beet red.

Jack clapped Dennis on the back. "Harry is fine, but he is exhausted. Trust me on that. Do you think I'd leave him even for a minute if I thought there was something wrong?" Cyrus backed up his master's statement with two short barks.

"Well then, okay, if you say so. I'll get the car and meet you out here. Stay put and don't wander off."

"Okay, Dad." Jack laughed. "Go already!"

Ted slid behind the wheel. Maggie and Espinosa piled in and sat down behind Ted in the plush seats.

"Call in every twenty minutes," Jack called as Ted slipped the van into gear and drove off.

Jack looked down at Cyrus, who was staring up at him expectantly. "For now until Dennis shows up with our new ride, it's just you and me, big guy." Cyrus didn't bother to bark. It was so obvious. One human plus one dog made two. He sat back on his haunches and waited more patiently than his master.

Ten minutes into the wait, Jack looked down at his phone to see an incoming text. He read it once, then again, before he shoved the phone back into his pocket. "Change of plans. We're headed up to the penthouse for a briefing with Avery and Abner. Let's just hope they have some good news."

In less than twenty minutes, all the guys and Maggie were seated at Annie's dining-room table. Coffee was perking, and everyone was chattering a mile a minute until Charles blew the whistle that he was never without. The room went silent instantly. Fergus handed out cups of coffee while Avery and Abner shuffled papers and folders in preparation for their brand of show-and-tell.

"You have the floor, Avery," Charles said the moment Fergus sat down.

Avery didn't bother clearing his throat the way he usually did before giving one of his reports. Nor did he rotate his neck to ease the tension he was under. He looked over at Abner, who nodded, and dived right in. "None of this is good. That's for starters. I think, and Abner agrees with me, as does Philonias Needlemeyer, that we have every piece of information there is on the dark web. I also want to say we would not have what we have without Phil's help. So kudos to Phil.

"Let's start with Mr. Zack Meadows. He loves money.

Actually, I think it's safe to say he worships money. He's also a high-stakes gambler. We can throw all kinds of shade at him, and it would fit. He takes bribes. *Big* bribes. He has two sets of friends. Normal people he associates with on a daily basis, personal as well as professional. None of those people have a bad word to say about him. Then he has a dark set of friends, the kind you don't invite to Sunday dinner. In other words, he lives two separate lives, with the dark, black side the more prominent one. It seems to be where he *thrives*.

"As near as we can tell, somehow, in some way, Cosmo Cricket must have seen or heard something that caused him to be concerned about Zack Meadows as far back as a year ago. We were not able to find out what it was or even if we're right. But he had many meetings with Meadows, which was unusual, given that they were not even serving on the same regulatory outfit. The meetings took place off the beaten track, so to speak—a diner here, the park, a pub, all public places. This is where we think Meadows got spooked. Cricket was closing in on him. One possibility is that he somehow lured Cricket to Happy Village that day with the intent of having him killed.

"Meadows's contacts on the dark web put him in touch with the Devil's own. The Lobos. He made contact with them and suggested that they recruit the Scorpions, with whom he had an ongoing relationship. He promised the gang some big bucks to take out Cricket. At the same time, he introduced their leader to several members of the Lobos. Meadows is on a first-name basis with those bastards. They also thrive on the dark, black web. Hell, I think they own it."

Abner held up his hand. "Stop right there—go back to how Meadows got into this in the first place. The tenants at Happy Village, the ones who disappeared. Meadows had access to all the tenants' applications right down to how much money they had in the bank. The guy is a pretty good hacker himself. He found out that they all had massive insurance policies. All of them were older. He cherry-picked the ones he wanted, hacked into the insurance companies, and raised the amount of their policies by several million each. He routed the billing statements through a dummy address at Happy Village, collected the mail late at night, and paid the premiums out of some offshore secret fund. He used a different Happy Village address for the payments.

"Phil told us that Meadows has collected fifty-one million dollars to date on those policies."

"Who . . . what . . . that . . . that . . ." Maggie started to stammer and couldn't get her question out.

"I don't think there is anyone here who wants to hear or could handle the gory details. The missing tenants are deceased. By the worst means possible. For sport as well as for money," Avery said. "We need to move along here."

"Meadows hired the Scorpions to abduct and kill the Happy Village tenants and paid them half at the outset. They were to get the final payment on that contract next week, we think, and the same sort of arrangement was agreed to for killing Mr. Cricket, but then Mr. Cricket was shot but not killed, and things ground to a halt. Since Mr. Cricket survived the shooting, we think Meadows refused to pay the second half of the money due on that contract.

"At the same time all this was going on, the Scorpions were trying to become members of Lobos and decided to kill two birds with one stone, so to speak, and use killing Mr. Cricket as their initiation exercise. It appears they were stalking him, just waiting for the right time to take him out.

"And now we have the second possibility. If Mr. Cricket was not at Happy Village because Meadows arranged for him to be there for the express purpose of having the Scorpions kill him, they may have gotten ahead of themselves and shot Mr. Cricket ahead of schedule just because he was where he was at the time. As I said, we're pretty sure Meadows refused to pay them for the hit on Mr. Cricket since he was still alive. So when the Scorpions were not paid the rest of the money due them for the hit on Mr. Cricket, they threatened Meadows. We are almost certain that Zack Meadows is hiding out at Peter Hershel's house on Magnolia Terrace. That's why we sent you the text. We didn't want you going there and upsetting the apple cart.

"We realize this is a lot of conjecture on our part, but you have to remember who and what we're dealing with here. While it's conjecture on our part, that idea—or something very much like it—is the only thing that makes sense."

"This is crazy," Ted said.

"Yeah, you think so?" Abner drawled. "We didn't even get to the really absurd part yet. We think the Scorpions are holed up in Lizzie's house. We think it's a standoff between Meadows and the Scorpions. Thank God Lizzie didn't go into the house. They would have killed her for sure. Here's the thing—killing Cosmo, or anyone for that matter, was to be the Scorpions entrance exercise for membership in the Lobos. What they did to the Happy Village tenants didn't count in the Lobos's eyes because it came before they sought membership. Fortunately for Cosmo, they flubbed the shooting. This is when it all turned into a three-ring circus. Everyone is after everyone else, and with the Scorpions having flunked their entrance exam for membership in the Lobos, they can expect no help from that quarter," Abner added.

"Where does that leave us? Where do we go from here?" Jack asked.

"I guess this is where we have to decide what to do,"

Charles said. "Time to run it up the flagpole to see if anyone salutes."

"Why Mr. Hershel?" Maggie asked.

"Did you miss the part about Meadows buying Mr. Hershel's casino in town? Then shafting him and the people he was going to invest with for a brand-new casino? Meadows was to approve the license. The investors disappeared and left Mr. Hershel holding the bag. God alone knows what happened to them, and I don't even want to guess. Meadows knows Hershel, has had dealings with him. He's elderly, and Meadows is in his prime. He could take out the old man with one hand," Charles said.

"Okay, yes, I get it. I just got confused given all the different characters we're dealing with," Maggie said. "I'm not sensing any urgency here with any of you, or am I wrong?"

"Yes and no," Charles said. "I don't think there's any immediate danger to Mr. Hershel. I'm sure Meadows is trying to figure out his next move, assuming he hasn't made it already, and I'd hazard a guess that he's been in touch with the Scorpions for two reasons. First, he owes them money for the killing of the tenants, if not just for the hit on Cosmo, and he knows they'll go after him if he doesn't pay up. He knows what they are capable of, so he might want to offer to pay off his debt to them. Second, he wants to entice them to help him, and the way he'd do that, we assume, is to promise to go to the Lobos and ask them to give the Scorpions a second chance to join their devilish gang. The Scorpions want that more than anything. Will they bite? I'm thinking they will."

"I'm not getting any of this," Espinosa grumbled. "What is Meadows getting out of this? What's his end game? If the Scorpions get inducted into the Lobos, that means they could then take out Meadows. What am I missing here?"

Everyone in the room looked as perplexed as Espinosa sounded. They all turned to look at Charles for an answer.

Charles threw his hands in the air.

"His safety! Nothing else makes sense," Dennis said. "Think about it. Gangs don't squeal on anyone. That's a given. The only person who stands in Meadows's way is Cosmo Cricket, who is going to live to fight another day, and by that I mean he'll start talking to the authorities once he's well enough to do so. He will tell them all about what he suspects, what he can prove and not prove. Meadows has to take it on the lam and get away clean, so he can spend all that insurance money plus the money he got for the sale of Hershel's casino. He's looking for safe passage."

"But he could have left at any time. Right now, in fact," Jack said. "Why hasn't he gone to ground already? Why is he still messing around with the gangs and the dark web?"

"Because he needs the Lobos to take out the Scorpions. Once they're gone, there are no witnesses to what he's done. He needs that to happen before he can even think about leaving. I'm sure he's got something all set up, a plan of action, and he just walks out one day and never returns. It's just my opinion." Dennis defended his statement when he saw the dubious expressions on everyone else's face.

"Makes sense in a cockamamy kind of way. Actually it's better than anything the rest of us came up with," Jack said, clapping Dennis on the back. Dennis beamed his pleasure.

Maggie raised her hand. Everyone groaned, knowing she was going to shoot down Dennis's idea. "Whoa! Whoa! Stop looking at me like that. I was just going to say that maybe we need to beat the Lobos to it and take out the Scorpions ourselves. We aren't the JV team here." Maggie held up her hand, which meant she had another thought.

"It would only work if we are one hundred percent sure that all the Scorpions are in Lizzie's house. And . . . and we get Harry's friends to help us. Those guys won't have a prayer of getting away."

"So you're saying that we, as in all of us here in this room plus Harry's friends, raid Lizzie's house while Avery and his people take out Meadows at Mr. Hershel's house. Do I have that right, Maggie?" Charles asked.

"You absolutely have that right, Charles," Maggie said with a whoop of joy. "And man, do I ever have the perfect punishment for that gang of cruds!"

Chapter 14

Alonzo Zuma Santiago cursed first in Spanish, then in English as he watched Lizzie Fox climb back into her car. He continued to curse, making up new words, each one filthier than the one before. He stopped his vitriolic tirade to glare at Miggy. "You spooked her. She must have seen you at the window! Now she's going to call the cops, and here we sit. Say something, damn it!"

"I wasn't standing in the window, and she did not see me. The missus wasn't spooked either. I could see her clearly. She got a box out of the trunk and was going to bring it into the house. I saw her balance it on her knee when her cell phone rang. Whoever called her gave her some news she didn't like. I thought she was going to cry. I think it was something bad she was hearing. She tossed the box onto the passenger seat, got behind the wheel, and peeled out. It was probably the hospital calling her back. Maybe her husband died. I don't know. What I do know is that she did not see me, so knock it off, Al. I'm getting sick and tired of your blaming me for everything. You want me gone, just say so, and I'm outta here."

"You know what, Mig. Sometimes you act like a prissy little girl. If you say you didn't spook her, then that's good enough for me. Know this, pal. If the police show up, I *will* kill you. We can't stay here forever. The next time she shows up, she will come into the house."

"I thought you had a plan," one of the members shouted.

"I said I was working on a plan. No one is cooperating. What that means is no one is calling me back. I have four calls in to Mr. Hot Shot and four calls in to the leader of the Lobos. If we don't hear back from one or the other in the next few hours, we're going to have to leave here and split up. We'll have to take the jewelry and pawn it."

"Where do you think Mr. Hot Shot is, Al?" Mig asked quietly.

"My best guess would be he's holed up in one of the empty apartments at Happy Village. Since he's a part owner, he must have a master key. He said he was going to call, said he had our money and that he had one more job for us, along with the cash to pay for that job, too, whatever it is. That was hours ago. I don't trust him any more than he trusts me. I should have plugged him the day we met him."

"I wish you had. We wouldn't be in this mess now if you'd put him down like a rabid dog. That's what he is," Mig said. "He turned us into serial killers for a pittance, and he walks free with millions of dollars. What's fair about that?"

"The promise to get us into the Lobos. Once we're accepted, we rule. That's the fair part. I think he's lying about convincing the Lobos to give us another chance. If he were telling us the truth, then the Lobos would have returned my calls. Hot Shot is doing what he always does. He's using us. Think, Mig, he said he had another job for us. At this stage, what could that job be? Unless I'm having a stupid day today, and considering the current circumstances, I have no idea what kind of job he would or could offer us. You got any ideas?"

"He's out there on his own, and he's swinging in the

wind, so it has to be he's looking for us to protect him or he's waiting for the Lobos to take us out. And then *they* protect him. I hate to mention this, Al, but we're the only ones who know who Hot Shot really is. I'm not even sure he knows we know. He could still be thinking he's a mystery man who hires us to kill people and pays us. To him, that would be enough. He thinks he's covered his tracks. Sometimes smart people are pretty damn stupid, Al."

"Damn it to hell, he should have called by now," Alonzo said.

"So call him. Tell him we're leaving or make up something, but let's get this show on the road. We can't hang here forever. If he has a job for us, then let's get to it so we can put all this behind us. The longer we hang around here, the more danger we're in. Surely, you can see that. Make the damn call already."

His hands shaking, Alonzo rooted through his pockets for his phone. Miggy wondered if he was the only one who could see how Al's hands trembled. Miggy was stunned to realize that his leader was scared out of his wits. He looked away, feeling disloyal somehow, yet grateful to know that his friend wasn't going to do something stupid that would land them all in jail. At least for the moment.

Miggy's heart fluttered when he heard the ugly bravado in Alonzo's voice as he started the conversation. "Me and my crew are sick and tired of your bullshit, Mr. Hot Shot. We're preparing to move out in the next hour, so if you want to avail yourself of our services, you need to be here before that happens. Do we understand each other? I know it's broad daylight. I'm not blind. The Cricket woman is going to be back before it gets dark, so get that idea out of your head. I have my boys, and I need to take care of them. I'm going to give you an hour to think about this, and if I don't hear from you, we're coming to get you and, yes, we know you're in Happy Village. Short of a flesh-and-blood visit, we can call the police, and the Village will be surrounded in a New York minute. Think hard, Mr. Hot Shot. And don't forget to bring the money you owe us, for both the hit on Cosmo Cricket and all the tenants you had us abduct and kill."

Miggy and the others stared at Alonzo, waiting to hear what he had to say. "Hot Shot wants to wait for darkness. He has a point, I have to give him that. The same thing goes for us if we decide to peel out of here now. Darkness is ideal for both sides. I say we take a vote."

While Alonzo and his gang were voting on what to do, Pete Hershel was eyeing the man with a gun in his hand holding him prisoner. How, he wondered, had his life gotten to this point? He chewed on the stem of his pipe, wondering what if anything he could do to the evil man standing over him. He was too old to fight, his bones too brittle. The surgery on his rotator cuff wouldn't allow him to pick up something and throw it at the man's head. Pure and simple, he was stuck. He turned away and stared out his front window, wishing he was sitting on his front porch. He hated being cooped up indoors with canned air. He'd rather sit outside and sweat.

What would Dolly do if she were here with him? He felt a pang in his heart at the thought of his deceased wife. Dolly was never that physical, but she was a whizbang with words. In the end, she'd probably whisper in his ear to just wait it out. Like he had any other choice.

Zack Meadows ended his call, a scowl on his face. "Looks like we're going to be together for a while longer. Make us some food."

Hershel looked at the man standing over him like some wicked giant and snorted. "You want something to eat, you're on your own. I don't cook, never did, and don't plan to start now. I eat out or order in. You said you were leaving. I want you out of here."

"Like I give a good rat's behind what you want, old

man. I can't walk out of here in broad daylight. I'm waiting for an escort once it gets dark. I'm just waiting for confirmation. Call someone and order a pizza with the works on it. Everything from soup to nuts, and don't tell me you don't eat pizza or you don't have a number to call. It's right here on the refrigerator, so do it, old man. Order two large pies."

Hershel knew he had no choice, so he did Meadows's bidding. But first he said, "I only ever order a small cheese pizza. They're going to wonder why I just ordered two large ones. Someone somewhere is going to put two and two together. If you care to step up to the window, you can see all manner of strangers milling about this place. They're looking for someone or something. Your name comes to mind, Mr. Meadows."

"Just call and order the damn pizzas already, will you? I'm hungry." Hershel shrugged and called Tony's Pizza Parlor and gave his order. "You have my credit card on file. Add a ten-dollar tip and we're good. How long? Twenty minutes is good. Thanks."

Zack Meadows hugged the wall as he made his way to the front window. He craned his neck to see what Hershel was talking about. He blinked. There were indeed many people out and about on Magnolia Terrace. It was impossible to tell if they were law-enforcement people or tenants.

"I've been watching for a while now. I think they're going door to door. I guess they're looking for you. What's your plan when they knock on my door?" Hershel asked.

"How stupid can you be, Hershel. No wonder you couldn't make that casino work. You're just too damn stupid. You ignore it. Most people do not open their doors to strangers, especially elderly people. Just be quiet and stay away from the window."

"I think you must have forgotten what kind of place

this is. Management does wellness checks on us twice a day, and we get one personal visit, sometimes two, depending on the staff. They know our patterns. Whoever the door checker is, he or she will go back to Gentry Lomax if I don't open the door, and he'll show up with his master key and open the door. For someone who owns half this place, you certainly do not know the inner workings of Happy Village. Like I said, we all have patterns. They'll also notice I have not been on the front porch." Hershel craned his neck to see better what was going on outside. "There are three guys out there, and they're two doors away. I don't think they are on the Happy Village payroll, so I'm guessing they're some form of law enforcement."

Zack Meadows digested Hershel's words and knew the old man was probably right. All this wellness crap had been a big bone of contention between him and Cosmo Cricket. Cricket said it was necessary, and he'd countered with it was an unnecessary, exorbitant expense when all the tenants had to do was press the button on the mandatory emergency necklaces they all wore. Cricket was adamant, and the wellness checks continued.

"Okay, okay. When they ring the bell, you open the door. I'll be right behind you on the left, so don't think you can outfox me, you old buzzard. You breathe wrong, and I swear I will shoot you and take my chances on getting out of here. I might make it and I might not, but you'll be dead. Do you understand what I just said?"

Hershel just nodded as he let his brain race all over the map as he tried to figure out what he could do or say to whoever knocked on his door. If only the pizza delivery was sooner, he might have a prayer. Someone with a brain would put it together, why he would be buying two *large* pies when he normally only ordered one small one. Then again, maybe not. He waited.

Pete Hershel knew the knock was coming, expected it, but he still almost jumped out of his wrinkled old skin when it happened. He looked over his shoulder at Zack Meadows and saw the maniacal look in the evil man's eyes. There was no doubt in his mind, not even a little one, that the man would shoot him if he didn't do what he had been told to do. He realized then he wasn't ready to die to go be with Dolly. Not yet anyway. He still had things to do, like getting a dog or a cat, and there were still places to go on his bucket list. Which of them to go to first would be determined at some future point.

Hershel opened the door to see Jack, Harry, and Dennis. "Well, hello there, young fellas. What can I do for you today?"

"We're checking on all the tenants, Mr. Hershel," Dennis said. "Are you doing okay? You weren't on the porch yesterday. That's what it says on your wellness chart."

"Is that why you're here!" Hershel said, putting as much surprise into his tone as he could. "It was the rain. Sometimes it gets my lumbago and lays me low, and other times it doesn't bother me. Yesterday was one of those days, so I just stayed in with a heating pad on my back." And then a brilliant idea hit him smack between the eyes. "Add my lumbago to maybe some food poisoning from some sushi, and here I am."

"What's lumbago?" Harry asked, his brow furrowed at the strange word.

Anything to stall. "Well, it's like this, young fella. Old-timers like me say we got lumbago. The ladies of a certain age refer to it as rheumatism and you young'uns today probably say arthritis. Lower back pain, hip joint pain, it's not a good thing no matter what you call it." Hershel made his voice sound as jovial as he could.

"Oh," was all Harry could think of to say.

Not so Jack. For some reason, the old codger's words

weren't ringing true to his ears. "So, you're feeling better today, then? You should be sitting on your porch enjoying the birds singing and the warm sunshine if you are. My wife would say just eat toast and drink hot tea, and rest."

"Yes, yes, my wife used to say the same thing. I might give that a try. Is there anything else?" Hershel asked hopefully. He rolled his eyes, hoping that would clue the young man into asking more questions.

"You sure you're all right, Mr. Hershel?" Dennis asked. He gave Jack a look that said I'm picking up on the same thing you are.

Tired of the conversation and wanting to move things along, Cyrus reared up and let loose with an unholy bark that literally shook the ground. He moved from Jack's side and nosed Hershel's leg. The old man leaned over and ruffled the dog's ears. "Now this is one mighty fine handsome animal you have here. I've been thinking about getting a dog to keep me company on the porch. Sometimes it gets lonely out there. Is there anything else, young fella? I hate letting all that hot air in here." Then he winked at Jack and screwed his face into a tight grimace. Cyrus threw back his head and howled as he pawed at Jack's leg. To Jack, it was a clear sign Cyrus wasn't buying the man's story either.

Jack winked in return to show he got it. "Nope, it works for me, and you're right, no sense letting all this hot air inside. Take it easy, Mr. Hershel. We'll check on you when we do our second round for the wellness check."

"Nice meeting you," Hershel said before slamming the door shut with what Jack thought was a little too much force.

"Someone is in there," Harry said.

Jack's eyes narrowed. "What was your first clue?" he asked just as his cell phone rang. A moment later, Harry's phone rang. Both men looked down at the numbers for the incoming calls.

"Little Jack. I'll take it later. We need to move *like now*," Jack said.

"It's Ted," Harry said, mouthing the reporter's name. As they moved away, with Cyrus in the lead, they could all hear Harry's end of the conversation, which was, "Stay the hell away from Lizzie's house then. Nine or ten Harleys translates to nineteen or twenty gang members. Make your way back to the boulevard and park in the Chinese restaurant's parking lot. We'll meet you there. We're wrapping it up here."

"What?" Jack demanded as he tried to think about why Little Jack was calling him so early in the day.

"Ted did a Google Earth check and said he saw nine, possibly ten, Harley Davidson motorcycles hidden in some brush a mile or so from Lizzie's house. You don't need to be a rocket scientist to know what that means. To me, it means the Scorpions are holed up in Lizzie's house. Either nineteen or twenty of them. Possibly more. What do you want to do, Jack?"

Jack was saved from a reply when Dennis broke ranks, turned around, and ran hell-bent for leather to skid to a stop when a small white van with the name TONY'S PIZZA painted on the side pulled to the curb. Cyrus barked but stayed next to Jack. All eyes were on Dennis as he peeled bills out of his pocket, snatched the Tony's Pizza ball cap from the delivery driver, plopped it on his head, and grabbed the two large pizza boxes.

"Son of a bitch!" Jack seethed. "Hershel said he had an upset stomach from some iffy sushi, and here he is ordering two large pizzas. That kid is on the ball. C'mon, Harry, we need to move before something happens to that kid, who is just too damn smart for his own good. I totally missed that. Looks like you did too. Cyrus, slow and easy here.

Quick now, we go up on the side so we're out of range of the window. When Hershel opens the door to take the pies, that's when we bust through. Cyrus, go in low but not on your belly. The guy probably has a gun, but he'll be holding it waist high and not expecting you to go for his ankles, and yes sireee, you have my permission to go for the jewels if you can." Cyrus started to shake with anticipation as he crept up the steps to stand behind Dennis. Jack swore later that the big dog was laughing at how easy this was turning out to be.

It all happened in slow motion and yet at the speed of light, was the way Jack later explained it to Ted, Maggie, and Espinosa.

Dennis held out the two large pizza boxes, shoving them against Hershel's chest and driving him backward, then darting to the right as Jack took the left, with Cyrus snaking through Hershel's wobbly legs. Hershel then fell to the floor and rolled out of the line of action. Harry took a flying leap upward and came down solidly on top of Meadows's shoulders as Cyrus clamped his pearly whites on Meadows's ankles. The gun, which was equipped with a sound suppresser, bounced across the room. Jack quickly picked it up and shoved it into the back of his cargo shorts. He looked around at the situation to see Dennis trying to scoop up the pizza from the foyer floor while Harry did some stretching exercises. Cyrus had all four legs planted on Meadows's long, lean body, his teeth digging into his ankle.

"It's okay, pal, you did good. Treat yourself, and don't go easy on this bastard. Go for it!" Jack yelled. Cyrus released Meadows's bloody ankle, his big head moving higher and higher, and then the only sound to be heard was Meadows's shrill mewling howl of pain. No one cared enough to help the man or to call off Cyrus, who was in his glory.

Jack looked over at Dennis and instructed, "Help Mr. Hershel and clean this up. Harry, call Snowden and tell him we need an extraction like now. Not when it gets dark. Don't worry about Meadows. Cyrus can stay in that position for hours. He's loving every minute of this. I gotta call Little Jack back now."

One minute into the conversation with his one and only godchild told Jack he had nothing to worry about and no dire crisis was invading LJ's summer camp experience.

"Slow down, slow down. Let me make sure I have this right. The swim meet for tomorrow has been canceled till next week, and I do not have to make the trip." *Thank God,* Jack thought, *because I completely forgot about it.*

"Because the girls, with Emily as the ringleader, made you guys some brownies laced with ex-lax. Even the counselors are . . . *indisposed.* What do you mean this means the girls win the meet by default? Well, that's not fair. Okay, okay, I'll talk to the boys and see if we can come up with something to score a win for you guys next week. Yeah, yeah, I promise, LJ. I know how hard it is to lie in bed, then have to get up to run to the latrine. I'm sure you *are* exhausted. You'll get over it. Okay, okay, if you gotta *go again*, then go! Call me tomorrow to let me know how it's going. Love ya, kid."

Dennis was laughing so hard, Harry had to clap him on the back. "I can't believe kids still do that at camp. Boy, do I ever remember when that happened to me. And it's all because of the swim meet with the boys versus the girls." Then he sobered and said, "Damn, hearing all that makes me feel old."

Grinning from ear to ear, Jack called off Cyrus, who immediately trotted over to the elderly Hershel to be praised and petted.

"You just convinced me, big fella. I am definitely gonna get me a dog. I know he or she won't be anything like you, but maybe close." Cyrus woofed twice. *Anything is possible, just not probable,* the big dog thought before he lay down, crossed his paws, and went to sleep.

"We need to get this guy tied up in a nice tight bundle. Do you have any rope or twine, anything to hogtie him with, Mr. Hershel?"

"Got some fishing line, but that's about it."

"That will work," Jack said, as Hershel rummaged under the kitchen sink and came up with a ball of fishing line. He tossed it to Jack, who had Meadows trussed up like a Thanksgiving turkey in mere minutes.

"You wanna talk to us now or wait till later, when we have all your pals corralled in one spot?"

Meadows sneered. "I don't have anything to say to you. I didn't do anything, and I am going to sue all your asses for kidnapping me and holding me as a hostage. Whatever plan you have up your sleeve is not going to work, I can tell you that right now."

"Yeah, right, and my name is Robin Hood," Jack said, sneering in return. "We know all about you and the Scorpions. We saw that bag of money by the front door. You're planning on paying off the Scorpions for whatever you hired them to do. Knowing what I know about you, I'm thinking you were trying to get out of paying the second half of the money to those animals. Then they came down on you, and here you are, holed up in a senior citizen's house rather than daring to live in your own multimillion-dollar condo."

Jack turned to Dennis. "Call Abner and tell him to freeze all of Meadows's money or move it to a safer place. Every penny. Hold on a minute here. We need this guy's records. The insurance he collected, and so on. I don't care how smart he claims to be, he can't keep everything straight, especially when it comes to killing people. I'm going to send Dennis back to Happy Village with his laptop and phone. We're meeting up with Maggie, Ted, and Espinosa after Snowden shows up. How long, Abner?"

Jack ended the call and said to Harry, "He said a couple of hours, so we should have everything by the time we meet up with the others and make it back to Babylon. Unless we're needed here."

Dennis was halfway to the door with Meadows's laptop under his arm and his phone in his hand. His hand was on the doorknob when he turned and asked if Jack was going to need Meadows's phone log. "Never mind, I'll send them to your phone the minute I get in the Uber. You need me, call."

"I like that youngster. Dolly would have loved him," Hershel said with a catch in his voice.

"Yeah, the kid is okay. He's got heart," Harry said quietly. Cyrus woofed softly in agreement.

Jack swung around and gave Meadows's prone body a none-too-gentle kick. "You want to talk yet? Makes me no never mind if you want to go the alternate route and have one of our friends pull it out of you one way or the other. I'm thinking we would enjoy having her do that very much. Yup, the friend in question is a woman, and you would not believe how much she would like to get hold of you after she saw Ellie Harper's head. Right now, I'd say we're the lesser of two evils."

"Screw you and the horse you rode in on. I didn't do anything, and you can't prove I did. I want a lawyer," Meadows snarled.

"You hear that, Harry? This piece of garbage thinks he's entitled to a lawyer! How funny is that?"

"Pretty darned funny from where I'm standing. He'll be singing a different tune, begging is more like it, when Maggie gets a piece of him. I heard she has something spectacular planned for all those guys in the Scorpions."

Pete Hershel looked from Jack to Harry and back to

Jack. "Are you fellas some kind of . . . you know . . . special forces working out of uniform? Not that I care, I'm just curious," he hastened to add.

"In a manner of speaking." Jack grinned.

Hershel cackled in glee at Jack's response. "I kind of figured something like that when I met this here dog, who I know is the only one of its kind. That means he's had some real special training."

Harry laughed out loud. "Oh yeah," he drawled. "He understands Greek. He can make his own bed, answer the phone, and his specialty is folding towels. That's just a few of the things he's really good at. The list is endless. He has so many medals and commendations, we can't keep track of them all."

"You don't say! I could tell just by looking at him that he was special. Greek, eh?"

Cyrus rolled over and covered his eyes with one massive paw. Sometimes, and this was one of those times, his own accomplishments overwhelmed him.

Harry moved closer to the window and laughed. "Mr. Meadows's ride is here! A big, beautiful ambulance. Snowden is backing it up the driveway. Mr. Hershel, you have to open the garage door for him. We don't want your neighbors seeing any of this."

Hershel hobbled as fast as his arthritic legs would allow. "I think I'll go out on the porch in case some of my neighbors come by thinking something happened to me. I'll just tell them I had a guest who collapsed. What we do not need right now is Mr. Gentry Lomax sticking his snoot into what is going on here."

"Good thinking," Jack said, as he walked over to where Meadows was lying. "Last chance to fess up, Meadows."

"Screw you!" the trussed-up man bellowed.

"Can't say I didn't try." Jack laughed.

"Well, well, well!" Snowden said boisterously. "What do we have here?"

"This is Mr. Zack Meadows. He owns half of Happy Village along with Cosmo Cricket. You and Abner have all his creds, so you know who he is and what he's done. This is him in the flesh. I'm not sure what we should do with him right now. Stash him somewhere at least until it gets dark out. Maybe the parking garage at Babylon. Unless you can come up with something better. When you leave, Harry and I are going to meet up with Ted, Maggie, and Espinosa out on the boulevard in the Chinese restaurant's parking lot. We nixed their going to Lizzie's house when we heard about a bunch of motorcycles stashed nearby, then found this piece of garbage here. Dennis is on his way back to Babylon as we speak. Anything you want to say, Snowden?"

"Not at the moment. But I do have a question. Mr. Hershel, do you have any duct tape? We don't want this piece of human trash caterwauling at the top of his lungs when I take him out of here and wherever it is we end up."

Pete Hershel returned to paw through the contents of the bottom of his sink. He triumphantly held up a roll of bright purple duct tape. "My wife loved the color purple," he said, explaining the flamboyant color.

"Works for me," Snowden grunted as he ripped off a long strip of tape and slapped it against Meadows's mouth.

Snowden bent down and hefted Meadows to his shoulder in a fireman's carry. The three men watched as he unceremoniously dumped Meadows on the floor of the ambulance, then gave him a shove so he would slide deeper into the lifesaving vehicle. He slammed the door shut and snapped the lock.

"Guess I'll be seeing you when I see you. Call or text if you get a brainstorm. I can't be riding around too long with that guy in the back. Nice to meet you, Mr. Hershel," Avery added as an afterthought.

"Uh-huh," was Hershel's response.

Jack looked around at the pizza mess on the floor. "I'm sorry to be leaving you with this mess, but we have to get going. Take my card, and if you need me, no matter the time of day or night, you call, and we'll be here. I'm going to text Lionel and have him put extra eyes on your place for a while. Are you okay with that?"

"I am. Don't worry about this mess. It will give me something to do. After that, I think I might take myself over to the SPCA and take a look around. Thanks for your help, and you, too, big guy," he said, addressing Cyrus, who just nuzzled Hershel's gnarly old hand.

"Guess our work here is done," Harry said, disappointment ringing in his voice.

Jack grinned. "For the minute, Harry, just for the minute. I'm thinking the best is yet to come. What do you say, Cyrus?"

Two sharp barks were Jack's answer.

Chapter 15

Everyone except Avery Snowden was seated at the dining-room table in Annie's penthouse, with Charles presiding over the meeting. The room was silent, a rarity. Phones and laptops were on the table but not in use. Another rarity. It was Dennis who finally broke the silence. First, he pointed to Zack Meadows's silver phone, and said, "The Scorpions are waiting for him to get back to them. We need to think about sending them a text. They'll never know it didn't come from Meadows."

Before anyone could respond, the phone next to Charles pinged that a text message was coming through. Charles read the message aloud, word for word. "Change of plans. Am in parking garage. Send private elevator down with guys to help transfer Meadows from ambulance. Will back right up to elevator. Garage very busy right now."

Jack, Harry, and Ted, along with Cyrus, were headed for the door before Charles could respond to the text.

Fifteen minutes passed before a trussed-up Zack Meadows was unceremoniously dumped in front of the kitchen sink in the penthouse. Jack stooped down and ripped the purple duct tape off his mouth. Meadows cursed long and loud. Too long and too loud for Cyrus's liking. He waltzed over and bit down on the man's ear. Meadows howled his outrage. No one cared, least of all Cyrus, who settled himself a foot away and kept his eyes glued to the man tied up in fishing line.

The private elevator sounded its zippy little three-note tune, and Avery stepped into the foyer. "Sorry I'm late, but I had to secure the ambulance. What's the plan now?"

"This might seem a little droll to you, Mr. Snowden, but when you said there was a change of plans, we thought *you* had a better plan," Maggie said, her tone as sour as the words she spoke. "Sorry to say *we* have no plan."

"The man is not cooperating," Ted said.

Snowden waved his hands in the air. "He really doesn't have to cooperate. We know what his plans are. I'm not sure if he believes we intend to thwart his plans, which we are going to do. Text messages are a wonderful thing. No voice giveaways. That sort of thing."

"Listen, before we get into all of that, I think we should have the Scorpions' Harleys disposed of. Can your people take care of that like now? Just in case their supreme leader decides to take it on the lam without waiting for darkness," Jack said.

"I already gave the order. One of my people is picking up the ambulance I left in Annie's parking spot, and they'll fit as many of the Harleys as they can in the back. It's just a shell vehicle, so there's plenty of room, but it will still require two trips. Possibly three. That's why I said there was a change in plans. And before you can ask, yes, I have operatives watching the Cricket house in case the Scorpions opt to skedaddle before dark. This is just a wild guess on my part, but I don't think the Scorpions trust Mr. Meadows any more than he trusts them."

"I think you're right, Avery," Charles said. "What do we need from him that we aren't getting from his laptop and cell phone?"

"The names of the Scorpion members as well as the

names of the Lobos members he's in contact with," Jack said as he drew a deep breath. "And we need the records of . . . of tenants he had killed and dismembered, and where we can find their remains."

"I don't know what you're talking about, and I don't know any members of the Lobos. You have this all wrong," Meadows bellowed.

"Really! Do you seriously think we believe that?" Maggie snapped. "You need to get it through your head—it's over. You lost. We won. We caught you. By tonight, we'll have all of the Scorpions and those Lobos members under lock and key. Mr. Cricket is talking. If you help us, maybe we can help you. Or not."

Meadows tried to inch his way farther from Cyrus to avoid the dog's hot breath on his neck. In his whole life, he'd never been this scared. These people were crazy, and the damn dog seemed like a human robot more vicious than Alonzo Santiago and the Lobos members. Was it really over? He perked up a bit when he thought these people still needed him. Maybe he could negotiate. Such wishful thinking. These people would not negotiate. Not now. Not ever. And yet here he was, alive and more or less unharmed, which was the proof they still needed him. His mind raced. What to say, what to give them? He squeezed his eyes shut so he wouldn't have to look at the killer dog fixated on him.

Meadows wondered if their computer expert with the straggly hair had found *all* of his stashed funds. If he could get away safely, there was still a chance he could live out his days in relative comfort, providing they hadn't found his nest egg. If. Right now, that little two-letter word was the most powerful word in the English language.

"I just sent off a text to the Scorpions' supreme leader, telling him that Meadows would be at the house no later than nine o'clock tonight and they all needed to be ready to go. Then I added a P.S. saying he was bringing the money he owed them and the money for the new job he had for them. Then I added a P.P.S. telling them to make sure that Javier Vincente Rodriguez, the leader of the local chapter of the Lobos, was there too."

Meadows's eyes popped wide. How the hell did that smart-ass kid get all that information? If his hands were free, he would have smacked himself upside his head. His cell phone, of course. He fought the urge to vomit as his mind continued to race.

With people like the Scorpions and the Lobos gang, there was no such thing as honoring a promise. All they cared about was money, killing, maiming, raping, and dismembering anyone who got in their way. How stupid he was to ever think he could control those devils. Now he was going to pay the price. He closed his eyes, wishing he could go to sleep and wake up someplace like Trinidad, where he could live like a king.

"Okay, we're getting a response," Dennis shouted ten minutes later.

The room went tomb silent as they all waited for Dennis to read off the incoming response to his text.

"Okay, here we go," Dennis said gleefully. "Nine tonight. Come alone. Carry nothing but bag of money. Rodriguez transports you to private airfield you requested. Chartered plane and private pilot will be fired up and ready to go."

The gang looked at one another, then down at Zack Meadows, ugly expressions on their faces. Meadows once again squeezed his eyes shut.

Maggie broke the silence. "What do you suppose would happen if this piece of human garbage fails to show up tonight at nine o'clock?"

No one had an answer to Maggie's question. Once again, all eyes turned to Meadows for the answer.

"I don't know. All I know is you can't trust any of them," Meadows said through clenched teeth. He did know that the minute he walked through Cosmo Cricket's front door, he was a dead man. He corrected the thought—two minutes, maybe three, because Santiago would have to take the bag and count the money in it. Yeah, yeah, three minutes and he was a dead man. There wasn't going to be any trip to a private airport, not if Javier Vincente Rodriguez was calling the shots. The man was the most evil, repulsive deviant walking the planet. With that thought in mind, Meadows decided his fate was better left in the hands of the people staring at him than the Scorpions and Javier Vincente Rodriguez.

"All right. I'll do whatever you want. Just tell me what you want me to do."

"Hold on, everybody. There's another text coming in on Meadows's phone," Dennis said. "Uh-oh! He wants to know what the other job is and how much you'll be paying. If they accept whatever job it is, they want the money up front. Do you have that much with you?"

"Well of course he does." Maggie giggled.

"What's the job?" Charles demanded in a voice none of them had ever heard before. Even Cyrus tilted his head and looked up at the big man towering over all of them.

"Kill Javier Vincente Rodriguez. Then Santiago can take control of the local Lobos chapter and bring his members into the fold. That's been his goal from the beginning. He just couldn't make it happen. A cool million. It's all in the bag," Meadows said.

"Someone google Javier Vincente Rodriguez," Fergus said.

"On it," Ted responded.

Dennis flexed his fingers as he itched to fire off a response as soon as Charles gave the okay. When he nodded,

Dennis's fingers flew over the keys. "Done!" he said triumphantly.

Zack Meadows's eyes misted over. Then he closed them. Might as well practice what it felt like to be dead. His thoughts took him through his life as he wondered how he had gotten to this place in time. Once he'd been a decent, upstanding guy like Cosmo Cricket. Once. And then the glitz and the glamour of Vegas took hold, and he embraced it along with all that money could buy. He let his mind roll call all the people he'd cheated and stolen from and the lives he'd ruined before he stepped down into the bowels of hell. This was Vegas. If you lived and worked here, you knew the rules. If you played, you ended up paying. It was that simple. Before he allowed himself to fall asleep, he wondered what it would be like, living in hell.

"Now what?" Jack asked.

"Now we plan," Charles said. "Gather round, boys and one girl. We need to talk."

The hours dragged by as the group schemed, talked, planned, then broke for lunch and, later on, an early dinner.

At one point, Espinosa untied the fishing line that bound Zack Meadows. The man didn't so much as twitch, nor did he wake. Cyrus never took his eyes off the sleeping form except to eat and when he went out to do what he had to do.

At seven-thirty, the elevator pinged and Harry's friends arrived. Charles briefed them and then asked if they had any questions.

Kee, one of Harry's friends, looked at him and grinned. "You telling me you can't take those guys on yourself?"

"Yeah, that's what I'm telling you." Harry grinned in return. "Plus, I wanted to give you guys a royal send-off so you'll have something to remember us by besides pillows."

One by one, the men lined up against the wall and dropped

to the lotus position, where they remained until Charles gave the signal that it was time to leave for Lizzie's.

"Shall we run through this one more time?" Charles asked.

"*NO!*" Maggie bellowed. "But if you insist, and it will reassure you, then I guess we can do it." The others agreed.

Zack Meadows, who had been awakened by Cyrus nipping him on the rear end, groaned. "I go in alone. I just walk up the driveway and knock on the door, the money bag in my hand. I'm going to be fifteen minutes late because we need full darkness, and the rest of you are going to surround the house from the back and enter through the basement door, which is next to the air-conditioning unit. You have a key that will let you in. How'm I doing so far?"

"Keep going," Jack said.

Meadows muttered something obscene under his breath, but when Cyrus moved, he hastened to say, "We sent a text to Rodriguez telling him not to show up till nine-thirty, which will place all of us inside and in place when he arrives. You said one of your people is monitoring Santiago's phone in case a call goes through to him from Rodriguez. If that should happen, then your guy will somehow divert the call, so we're all in the clear till he shows up. Then it's a crapshoot as to what happens. You happy now?"

"Didn't you leave something out?" Jack barked.

"Yeah, guess so, the two . . . um . . . portly gentlemen who seem to be running this gig will be out front in the shrubbery in case anyone tries to make a run for it. The one who hogtied me will be a little farther down the road in case one or two of them slip past the two in the bushes. Don't go telling me I left anything else out, because that's it in a nutshell."

Jack nodded. "Okay, he's got it down pat. I think we're

good to go. I am a little surprised that Santiago hasn't been in touch. Anyone have any thoughts on that?"

"Not on that, but I do have a question. What happens to all my money?" Meadows asked.

That's when Maggie Spritzer lost it. She was like a wild woman as she attacked Zack Meadows before the men could figure out what happened. "What happens to your money? What happens to your money? Is that what you asked?" she screamed at the top of her lungs. She started swinging wildly, popping Meadows on the nose, the chin, and the side of his head. Then, just to be even more ornery, she brought her knee up and made contact with the family jewels. Meadows doubled over, tears rolling down his cheeks. For good measure, Maggie kicked him and continued kicking him till Ted pulled her away, still screaming about where all his money was going to go.

Charles decided it was time to intervene. He blew his whistle, and everyone froze. "Enough already. It's time to leave. You all know what you have to do. Do not, I repeat, do not make me blow this whistle again. On your feet, Meadows, and no one is going to help you. Crawl if you have to, but *move now*."

When they arrived at Lizzie's, Jack looked down at his watch—8:50. Everyone was in place behind him in single file. The key was in the basement lock and turned. All he had to do was turn the knob and the door would open. Charles and Fergus were deep in the shrubbery on the right side of Lizzie's front door. Zack Meadows, according to Charles's last text, was at the end of the driveway, standing behind a thick wooden post that was as dark as the night around him. He was bent over in pain, the money bag at his feet. He waited for the birdcall from the bushes, his signal to walk up the driveway to ring the bell. At that same moment, Jack would open the basement door, and he and his posse would enter the house and make their way up the back steps leading to the kitchen.

Cyrus inched closer to Jack, his massive body quivering with excitement. This was what he lived for, what he'd been trained to do. He felt his master's hand on his head and rubbed against it to show he was in control. If he could talk, he would have shouted to the housetops.

"Now!" Jack hissed, as the word went down the line. They were inside and lined up on the stairs leading to the kitchen, where he could hear all hell breaking loose, with Meadows talking the loudest to be heard over the snarling voices demanding that the money be counted.

"Then turn on the damn light so everyone can see I'm not cheating you. No one is coming here, especially Mrs. Cricket. She rented a suite at Babylon so she could be closer to the clinic where her husband is recovering. So count already and be done with it. Where the hell is Javier Vincente Rodriguez? We had a deal, Santiago. Where is he?"

"On his way. Traffic. Who knows," he said, never taking his eyes off Miggy, who was counting the money into neat, tidy piles.

"Okay, it's all here," Miggy announced.

"So when are you going to pop him?" Meadows asked.

"When he gets here if he gets here."

The doorbell rang. In the bright light of Lizzie's kitchen, everyone looked at everyone else. The decision had not been made as to who was to open the door for Rodriguez. Miggy took it upon himself to do it.

Under the fluorescent lights of the kitchen, Javier Vincente Rodriguez was a sight to behold. Never having seen him before, Miggy was in awe, as were the others who were gaping at him. His wild, rainbow-colored hair stuck up six inches over his head. He was tatted from his forehead to the toes sticking out of his run-down sandals. A swastika sat in the middle of his forehead. Tattoos of snakes, vermin, and other reptiles adorned his ears, his nose, his cheeks, and his neck. Alligators and pythons ran up and down his arms, with tats on each finger, along with a silver ring. Two round, gold circles were embedded in his oversized front teeth so that his lips couldn't close together. A nose ring with a tiny bell tinkled when he moved or spoke.

"Well?"

Meadows stepped forward, obviously in pain. "I'm ready when you are," he said through clenched teeth.

The door leading to the basement swung open, and Jack and the gang blew into the kitchen like a tsunami. Taken off guard, the Scorpions raced and scrambled for their weapons, but they were no match for Harry, his friends from China, Jack, and Cyrus, who was a black streak flying through the air when one of the Scorpions was about to swing a chain around Harry's neck. Cyrus brought him to the ground, sat on his head, and waited for the order to release. Harry's fist shot in the air in Cyrus's direction as he leaped and twirled, dodging a machete that he snatched and threw into one of Lizzie's kitchen cabinets.

Cyrus eyeballed Javier Vincente Rodriguez, who whipped out a gun and pointed it at his beloved master. He ignored the wait-to-release order and streaked across the room to body slam the tattooed man to the ground, sink his teeth into the wild mane of hair, and toss the man from one side to the other like a rag doll. When he was done with him, he body slammed him again up against the Sub-Zero refrigerator and left him lying there, out cold.

"I saw it go down," Harry said. "That dog saved your life, Jack. Big time."

Jack buried his head in Cyrus's neck and held on to the big dog for dear life. "I love you, you big *galoop*. You get two rib eyes the next time we eat." Cyrus barked and licked Jack from the top of his head to his neck and any place in between he could find.

When the front door opened, Fergus, Charles, and Avery made their way to the kitchen to observe the carnage the boys had wrought. There was blood everywhere. Tough gang members were crying into their arms, sniveling and mewling like beaten animals wondering what had happened to them. Miggy bit down on his lower lip, knowing this was barely half the payback they all deserved for what they'd done. He, too, cried as his tongue sought to find his teeth, which were no longer attached to his gums. He looked over at Alonzo, who was a bloody, pulpy mess, and something in him secretly cheered at his friend's condition.

"Oh my," was all Fergus could think to say.

"Lizzie isn't going to like this," Charles said.

"No, she isn't," Avery said.

"She won't care," Dennis said.

"Now what?" Harry asked.

"Now we turn it over to Avery."

"Whoa! Whoa! No! No! No! I have the punishment for these cruds all picked out. I want them punished for what they did to the tenants and Cosmo," Maggie bellowed. "And we still need to find the remains of the people they butchered over the last seven months."

"Well then, okay, dear. What do you need us to do?" Charles asked.

"Strip that guy Santiago down to the buff, and Meadows, too, along with that Rodriguez guy, the walking advertisement for all that's evil in the world. Find me three broom handles and some duct tape. See that twelve-burner, one-of-a-kind, custom-built stove. We're going to turn it into one big rotisserie and roast these guys. C'mon, chop chop, don't make me do it all here!"

Jack swallowed hard. "Are you serious?"

"Do dogs have fleas, Jack? Damn straight, I'm serious.

These devils cut off Frances Gossett's best friend's head. Frances doesn't have anyone to play bingo with anymore or anyone to take the jitney with her to the dollar store. Hurry up, I want to see these guys roasting."

Cyrus ran to the front door, Fergus right behind him.

"Turn on the burners so all twelve are the same temperature. That range is so big, we can line up all three guys and flip them at the same time. What's the holdup, guys?"

Harry's friends watched what was going on until one of them finally whispered to Harry to explain what it all meant. Harry patiently explained, a wicked gleam in his eye. "You want to watch or leave?"

"You're one crazy, wild sum of a bitch, Harry Wong," Kee whispered as he ushered his friends to the front door.

"Okay, Maggie, as you can see, all three are out cold. The rest of this gang is so traumatized right now, I don't know if they know their own names," Ted said.

"Good! Good! Now they know how it feels. Even this is too good for what they did to those people from Happy Village. I can't wait to go back and tell all of this to Frances Gossett and her cat, Sawdust. After I pretty it up, of course. I don't want her having a heart attack or anything like that.

"We need to move this right along here. Throw some cold water on them so they sizzle when they hit the burners. It's gonna stink in here because they're so hairy and greasy. Yuk! Okay, let's do it! Keep it up with the water or they're going to black out again. Meadows, you go first since you started all this. Have at it, boys!" Maggie yelled happily. "This one is for Lady Justice!"

"Santiago, you're up next!" Maggie singsonged. "One minute on each side, boys. Okay, Mr. Rodriguez, you're up. Give him two minutes! After that, Avery, they are all yours."

Maggie walked over to the range and looked down at

the three roasting forms on Lizzie's stove. Their tortured screams were music to her ears. "You all deserve worse than this, but we're in Vegas now, so you work with the hand you're dealt. Bye!" she trilled.

"Wait a minute, where are you going?" Ted bellowed.

"When I get there, I'll let you know. Carry on, boys. Make me proud of you!"

Epilogue

Three days later

Maggie Spritzer fanned herself with the summer camp program as she took her seat with what Jack called the Little Cricket contingent. It was noon, and the blazing sun had finished burning off the early morning fog and dew, leaving it blistering hot. Sweat rolled down her back and arms. "How long is this meet, Jack? I don't know how long I can handle this heat." She pointed to the various swim team members, mostly kids Little Jack's age, as they scampered about screaming and yelling, poking and prodding each other, sometimes shoving an opponent into the crystal-blue water.

"Five minutes once his race is under way. I haven't even set eyes on LJ yet."

Espinosa stood up, focused his camera, and moved about, trying to get the best angle to record the swim race so he could send it to Lizzie as promised. Cosmo was making such a rapid recovery, Lizzie said, that watching his son swim in the meet would put him over the top. That all meant that Cosmo Cricket was definitely out of the woods and on his way to a full recovery. Regardless, Lizzie still refused to leave his side.

Charles looked up from the long incoming text he was receiving. He smiled from ear to ear as he motioned for the group to gather close. He lowered his voice to a harsh whisper. "As we all know, the rule here is that 'what happens in Vegas stays in Vegas,' and since we're no longer in Vegas, we can talk about it. Annie's casino manager took it upon himself to go to the owners of the casinos and explain what happened to Cosmo Cricket's home and the condition it was in when the Scorpions, Zack Meadows, and Javier Vincente Rodriguez were incapacitated from an attack by an *unnamed vigilante* group. Just the mention of Zack Meadows and what he'd done brought all the owners front and center and willing to do anything that would help the Cricket family.

"Twenty-four hours after being informed, a magnificent house owned by a high roller who went belly up became available in the desert only two miles from where the Crickets lived. It only took an hour to complete the paperwork and another hour to take pictures of Cosmo's oversized furniture to complete the deal. Four hours after that, every single item in the house was gone, all donated to several different charities. Assurances that all the new furniture would be custom-made and delivered in thirty days sealed the deal."

Charles continued to read from the overlong text. "It's unclear who will tell the Crickets at this point, but it's done, and the Crickets will not be homeless. Vegas takes care of its own, as we've come to find out."

"That's great. Lizzie said she was never, ever going to enter that house again. I hope they take it apart, board by board, and burn it," Jack said. "She told me to sell off all the jewelry and stuff that was in the pillowcase and donate it to Happy Village. That's being taken care of as we speak. The money in Zack Meadows's money bag is going to be used for upkeep, to finish work on the grounds, and increase the size of the park. We used a portion of it to divide among Lionel and his boys for all their hard work and dedication. There was more than enough to buy them mopeds so they can get around a little easier without having to depend on Lionel all the time.

"A portion of the money is being used to identify the remains of the twenty people the Scorpions had killed and dismembered after that guy Miggs, threatened with the same fate as the three who Maggie had roasted, revealed the location. Once the remains are identified, there will be funerals for all of them so that the residents of Happy Village can get some closure. The rest of the money that Abner found stashed away will be turned over to someone who will know what to do with it. I'm sure there are many long-lost relatives of the deceased tenants from Happy Village.

"Charles and Fergus, along with Avery, had a heart-to-heart talk with Gentry Lomax, soldier to soldier, that sort of thing, and he managed to soften up, according to Charles. I think it was win-win all the way around."

"Who is going to tell the tenants about the fate of their missing friends?" Maggie asked.

"Gentry Lomax said he would do it," Charles said.

"Well, I wrote a personal note to Frances Gossett and told her about her friend Ellie. I promised to return the key, so I thought I would write the personal note. I included a second note for Porter Flannery about his friend Will. I just said they were . . . deceased. I saw no reason to give them nightmares with . . . what really happened. The desk clerk at Babylon said she would messenger it to Happy Village."

Abner leaned into the group. "I'm staying on through next week. Isabelle's birthday is Sunday, and she's flying in, so she'll drive home with me. I'm gonna miss you, Cyrus. You're a good wingman."

"So what are you giving Isabelle for her birthday?" Dennis asked.

Abner started to laugh and couldn't stop. In between gasps of pure merriment, he managed to choke out the words, "Four new pillows from Harry's new best friend, the pillow guy! Specially made for her and scented with lavender. And I got them wholesale." Abner continued to laugh.

"The only thing I can add to any and all of this is wheels up at three sharp. We're going home, chums," Dennis shouted.

From somewhere behind them, a whistle blew, then came another sound, like a foghorn. Kids of all shapes and sizes appeared from nowhere to take their places in different lines. Girls to the right, boys to the left.

Jack looked around, surprised to see how few parents had come to see their children swim. Then he let his gaze search for LJ, who wasn't hard to find, since he was the tallest kid in any line. He wished he knew the kid's game plan, since they hadn't had a chance to talk since the tearful ex-lax debacle.

LJ's event was listed as the fourth on the program. Jack let his gaze roam to the ten-year-old girls' line opposite LJ's, wondering which girl was Emily, but his main focus was in keeping his eyes on LJ, thinking he'd at least look her way at some point. But the kid never did. He was focused. That was a good thing.

The pool area suddenly went quiet at some unseen, unheard signal. Whatever it was, Cyrus understood and got up from his sleeping position under the bench Jack was sitting on. Jack poured water into his special bowl, and Cyrus lapped it up before he hopped up on the bench to wedge himself between his master and Harry Wong.

The first three races went off as scheduled to a lot of shouting, arm waving, and foot stomping by all the kids and the spectators.

And then it was time for LJ's race. The boys lined up, followed by the girls. No one looked at anyone else. The boys' swim coach walked down the line, whispering in each swimmer's ear. The girls' coach did the same thing. Cyrus leaned forward to see Little Jack better. He knew all about races and how they worked. If you won, Dr. Pappas handed out a special treat. He made sure he always won. He waited for the pop of the air gun for the start of the race. The minute he heard it, he was off the bench and streaking toward the pool, where he waited at the finish line of lane 4, where LJ would climb from the pool.

"What the hell!" Harry muttered.

"Oh crap, I should have remembered, but hey, this is on me. Cyrus likes to participate. He knows how to win. He was trained to do stuff like that. Damn, I hope they don't disqualify LJ for this."

"Look at that kid go," Dennis yelled as he stood up on the bench to see better. "That kid can really swim!"

Cyrus started to bark at the turnaround and kept it up until LJ's fingers touched the edge of the pool, the clear winner in Jack's eyes. He about choked up when he saw LJ reach up for the big dog and pull him into the water. If there was a rule against it, no one knew what it was. The spectators watched as LJ dove deep and struck out for the opposite end of the pool. When he surfaced and saw Cyrus a length ahead of him, he did a somersault and floated the rest of the way to the edge. Boy and dog leaped out to a rousing round of applause from everyone in the pool area.

"Damn!" was all Jack could think of to say, other than, "Espinosa, if you missed even a second of any of that, I'm going to personally strangle you."

"Got it all! Man, that was something. What's the prize?"

"A basket of junk food," Maggie said.

The gang was gathering their gear together before saying good-bye to LJ and heading for the airport when conditions by the pool became tense for a few moments. The male counselors were arguing with the female counselors about Cyrus. Cyrus pranced around, allowing himself to be petted and scratched, mostly by the girls, and Emily in particular. He loved every minute of it. The counselors looked at one another and just shrugged. No two-legged winner here. They walked away, smiling.

"We gotta go, Jack," Dennis said, pointing to his watch.

"Just give me a minute, okay?" He ran down the bleachers, hugged his godson, and congratulated Cyrus and Emily, who looked like she was going to cry. He watched as his godson picked up the basket of goodies and handed them to her. "You and the girls deserve this. I couldn't have won if I hadn't eaten all those brownies you made for us guys. I lost five pounds this week and picked up two seconds. See ya next year!"

Jack stared at LJ. *God, I love this kid.*

"Gotta run, kid. Stay in touch, okay?"

"You bet." LJ leaned up to whisper. "So, Uncle Jack, whatcha think about Emily?"

Jack whispered back. "You know what I think? I think next year that girl is going to blow your socks off." Cyrus barked to show he agreed.

"I'm thinking the same thing, Uncle Jack." LJ giggled.

"Come on, guys, time to go home! Our work here is done!"

"Amen!" Maggie said.